Acclaim for ELINOR LIPMAN'*s*

The Ladies' Man

"Exquisitely funny. . . . A wicked little comedy with a superbly obtuse and self-absorbed fellow at large in its pages."
—Katherine Powers, *The Boston Sunday Globe*

"Elinor Lipman is so good, *so good,* and with perfect pitch, to boot. *The Ladies' Man* is not just flawless, word by word, and delicious and hilarious—the Ladies' Man and all his Ladies are sublime."
—Jane Hamilton

"Lipman describes human beings in all their funny, quirky, glorious individuality. . . . [She] possess a gift for creating memorable characters."
—*USA Today*

"Delicious. . . . Poisonous asides, wicked observations, and great style."
—*Salem Daily News*

"Dialogue that actually snaps, crackles and pops. . . . [A] breezy wit that entertains intelligently."
—*The Hartford Courant*

"Nobody is better at distilling motives and first impressions in narrative shorthand. . . . You won't find better reporting from the front lines of the battle between the sexes."
—*The Seattle Times*

"Witty, romantic . . . rich in character development and rife with familial discord."
—*St. Louis Post-Dispatch*

"Smart, darkly comic . . . Lipman's sharp satiric sense recalls that of Alison Lurie."
—*Chicago Tribune*

"Lipman perfectly evokes a world in which the dance of love looks suspiciously like a game of musical chairs."
—*Self*

ELINOR LIPMAN

The Ladies' Man

Elinor Lipman is the author of the novels *The Inn at Lake Devine*, *Isabel's Bed*, *The Way Men Act*, and *Then She Found Me*, and a collection of stories, *Into Love and Out Again*. Her work has appeared in *The New York Times*, *Salon*, *The Boston Globe*, *Cosmopolitan*, *Self*, *Ladies' Home Journal*, *Gourmet*, *Yankee*, and *Playgirl*. She has taught writing at Simmons, Hampshire, and Smith colleges, and lives in western Massachusetts with her husband and son.

Also by Elinor Lipman

The Inn at Lake Devine

Isabel's Bed

The Way Men Act

Then She Found Me

Into Love and Out Again

The Ladies' Man

The Ladies' Man

A Novel

Elinor Lipman

Vintage Contemporaries
Vintage Books
A Division of Random House, Inc.
New York

FIRST VINTAGE CONTEMPORARIES EDITION, MAY 2000

Copyright © 1999 by Elinor Lipman

All rights reserved under International and Pan-American Copyright Conventions. Published in the United States of America by Vintage Books, a division of Random House, Inc., New York, and simultaneously in Canada by Random House of Canada Limited, Toronto. Originally published by Random House, Inc., New York, in 1999.

Vintage is a registered trademark and Vintage Contemporaries and colophon are trademarks of Random House, Inc.

Grateful acknowledgment is made to Steve Karmen for permission to reprint brief quotes from *Through the Jingle Jungle* by Steve Karmen (New York: Billboard Books, 1989). Copyright © 1989 by Billboard Books/New York. Reprinted by permission of Steve Karmen.

The Library of Congress has cataloged the Random House edition as follows:
Lipman, Elinor.
The ladies' man : a novel / Elinor Lipman.
p. cm.
ISBN 0-679-45694-5
I. Title.
PS3562.I577L34 1999
813'.54—dc21   98-56450

Vintage ISBN: 0-375-70731-X

Author photograph © Hing/Norton
Book design by Mercedes Everett

www.vintagebooks.com

Printed in the United States of America
10 9 8 7 6 5 4 3 2 1

For Bob,
with love
and thanks
from your lucky wife

The Ladies' Man

One

In the months before Albert DeSalvo confessed to being the Boston Strangler, the three Dobbin sisters established their custom of arranging empty glass bottles like bowling pins inside their apartment door. They adopted the idea from *Life*, from a spread illustrating how women living alone near the crime scenes were petrified and taking precautions. The practice continues decades after the Boston Strangler confessed and died in prison, because the Dobbin sisters are cautious and intelligent women who expect the worst. The last sister to turn in checks the locks, latches the chain, and sets the booby trap of ten near-antique bottles that once held ginger ale, sarsaparilla, and root beer brewed by a defunct soft-drink company.

And what's the harm? It allows three women to sleep peacefully without sedatives, without surprises, and without expensive motion detectors. If Richard Dobbin, their brother, occasionally trips a false alarm, it is viewed as his own fault, his own stubborn resistance to calling ahead. He claims to forget between drop-in visits that they still arrange the bottles nightly. He has a key; he thinks he will slip in, sleep on the couch, leave a note on the kitchen table for the earliest riser, and be welcomed enthusiastically. The chain stops him, but, as designed, the door opens enough to trigger the pandemonium his sisters count on.

"It's me," he yells. "What's going on? It's me."

"Richard," says one, then each of the other sisters, hurrying into their bathrobes. "Let him in. Undo the chain. It's Richard."

"There've been some copycat murders on the north shore," explains Adele, the oldest, turning knobs and unhooking chains. "We've started setting our burglar alarm again."

"Jesus," says Richard, knocking over the last row of standing bottles. "I guess it works."

Adele asks him not to swear in the hallway.

"Can you stay?" asks Lois, the middle sister.

"Think I was popping in for a visit at ten forty-five?" Richard answers.

"Where's Leslie?" asks Kathleen.

"Home," he says, in a way that suggests home was not peaceful when he left.

"Is everything okay?" Kathleen asks.

"Fine."

Always good hostesses, they choose masculine striped sheets and brown towels from the linen closet; one sister disappears down the long central hall in search of a guest pillow and blanket. Kathleen offers to take the daybed and give their taller, bigger brother privacy and a real bed.

They range in age from Adele, fifty-three, to Richard, who is forty-four. No one is currently married or spoken for. Social lives vary from moribund (Adele's) to overactive (Richard's); in his sisters' opinion, he flirts too easily and cohabitates prematurely. Without evaluating their brother's capacity for monogamy, they assume he'd be happier if he settled down.

As for the sisters, it could have been different: There were many beaus in any given year, and a distribution of graces that made no one redheaded sister the most in demand. Adele had brains and the most classically pretty face. Lois had height and good bones, while Kathleen had—still has—wavy hair and the greenest eyes. Outside the immediate family, the unstudied explanation for their shared spinsterhood is what happened to Adele decades ago at age twenty-three: an engagement broken, unceremoniously and unilaterally, by an unsuitable boy.

Today they consider themselves career women, with nice clothes and with jobs that provide either satisfaction or high seniority: Adele raises money for public television, Lois works for the Commonwealth, and Kathleen sells lingerie in her own shop downtown. Richard is the family underachiever, which is not acknowledged or even thought, because he is tall and charming, quite good-looking, adds new friends without dropping his old ones from high school or college, owns his own tuxedo, and has been an usher at no fewer than ten buddies' weddings. He delivers subpoenas for a living, and cultivates the understanding that it is a career that straddles law and law enforcement.

So picture the household: three adult sisters and a displaced brother on an unseasonably cold April night with a dusting of snow deposited by a passing squall. Richard will have settled into the den on the daybed, where the sisters usually watch their programs. He's made himself a cheese sandwich with relish on dill-cheese bread, which he doesn't like but eats cheerfully after fixing the TV's tint, which the women never adjust, even if the actors' faces are orange.

The downstairs buzzer rings after the sisters have returned to their rooms. They wait, assuming it is Richard-related, or the buzz of a careless visitor who has hit the wrong bell. In any event, they don't panic or even get out of bed, because Richard, an expert on getting into places where he's not welcome, is there in case of danger. The buzzer rings again, more insistently.

"Richard?" Adele calls from her room.

He is watching television, so Adele tries again, louder.

"What?"

"The door. See who it is."

"Want me to buzz 'em in?"

"You don't buzz anyone in unless you know who it is," says Adele.

"It's probably one of his friends," says Kathleen. "They have a sixth sense about when Richard is visiting."

"It's probably Leslie," Richard says. "I better go down."

Richard puts his shoes on without socks, and takes the elevator to the lobby in his trousers and undershirt. On the other side of the glass door, squinting in from the vestibule, is a man, a stranger, tall, with a high forehead and wavy gray-brown hair. He is tanned, and his shoes are beautifully shined. It seems to Richard that this man with a Burberry raincoat over his arm is both rich and benign, that Richard can open the door and ask if there's been some mistake at this hour; that this is not a copycat murderer.

"Yes?" says Richard.

The man says, "Good evening."

"You rang Three-G?"

"The Dobbins."

"That's us," said Richard. "And you are . . . ?"

"I was hoping to see Adele. If she's in."

"It's late," says Richard. "So why don't you come back in the morning? No, they work in the morning. Give 'em a call after work."

"Richie," says the man, putting out his right hand as if peacemaking were in order. "It's Nash Harvey. I went with Adele a long time ago."

Richard peers into the man's gray eyes, and sees that it is true. "Harvey? Jesus Christ—what, like twenty-five years ago? The guy who disappeared?"

"Nineteen sixty-seven."

Richard is famously good-natured and optimistic, so he feels only curiosity and mild delight. "Some brothers might punch you in the nose right now. Or worse," he says.

Nash releases Richard's hand.

"Nah," says Richard. "I don't mean me. I was speaking hypothetically."

"Do you think she'll see me?"

"You're a brave man, Harv," says Richard.

"I've been on the West Coast."

"I know," says Richard. "Lois spotted your name on a box in a video store."

The intercom squawks, "Richard?"

"It's okay," he answers.

"Who is it?" asks the voice—Adele's.

"An old friend of mine. Didn't realize the time. He's going to a hotel."

She hesitates then says, "The Holiday Inn on Beacon Street probably has rooms available. Tell him we'd offer him a bed but we're full up."

Nash opens his mouth, presumably to acknowledge the suggestion of hospitality, but Richard releases the button as if it had pricked his flesh.

"Wasn't that her?" asks Nash.

"They all sound alike over the phone."

Nash asks if they all live together, but Richard ignores the question. "Go back up to Beacon," he says, "then right, toward Kenmore, not even a half mile on your left. It's nothing fancy, but it's clean."

Nash asks if they could talk, man to man, tomorrow. Is Richard free for lunch?

Richard says, "My schedule's my own."

"One o'clock. Is Jack and Marion's still open?"

"Gone. Closed at least a dozen years. Maybe more."

Again, "Richard?" squawks from the intercom.

"I'll call you at the hotel," Richard confirms before reassuring Adele that he is on his way up.

⌒ On the other side of the country, it is 73 degrees Fahrenheit and still light. Dina Dorsey-Harvey walks her Yorkies on a sidewalk that borders both highway and Pacific Ocean. Nash has gone home to Boston, where the Weather Channel map shows the dark green radar that means snow. Serves him right: Boston. Ridiculous. She hopes he'll have to circle Logan. Or crash. She could accept that, hating him for today's announcement. She'd be a young widow. Technically, a young roommate/lover/relatively longtime companion compared to the fits and starts that were Nash's previous liaisons.

The dogs are sniffing everything with greater interest than usual, and she is letting them. People on walks used to smile at the puppies, but it seems that no one does anymore. Women pushing strollers want Dina to smile at their human babies, whom they consider more compelling, and more of an achievement than owning animals. Runners and in-line skaters are too intent, too self-important with their golden retrievers and Labradors to see Daisy and Tatiana as anything but moving obstacles to be sidestepped.

The separation is less than twelve hours old. Nash had said, upon waking up, "I'm leaving for Boston this morning."

"Good," she had said, still annoyed from a disagreement the night before over her inviting two clients and their husbands, none of whom Nash had met, for dinner.

"It's too late now," Dina had argued. "I can't *uninvite* them."

"Yes, you can," he said. "Tell them you invited them before you checked with me and I was making my own unilateral plans." He repeated disdainfully, "Clients."

She'd slept in the guest room to make the point that she did not like his taking such a tone with her. Now she realizes that while she slept and worked on an adequate excuse—Nash had come home with tickets for the South Coast Repertory, which regrettably took precedence over a small, impromptu supper, easily rescheduled—he was packing and calling airlines.

Dina hasn't told anyone yet, nor will she call it a breakup when she does. For a week, maybe two, she can say, "In Boston," and "No, I couldn't get away." She believes it is a mistake, a whim, a vacation. Relationships have dry spots, and you have to crawl along on your belly through the desert until you come to a lush, green, cool valley. She'd read that somewhere. She'd sit this out and let him miss her. Because he would. He wasn't looking for a fling; men looking for flings went to New York or Vegas or Cancún, not Boston. He'd said it was something more complicated than sex with a thrilling new body; something about breaking the heart of a girl a long time ago who sounded to Dina as if she'd been no fun at all. Maybe an apology in person would fix whatever was wrong with him. He said grouchily that he'd call her when he had a room and a phone, and when he knew himself what he was hoping to find.

Dina walks across the bridge to Balboa Island for a low-fat latte. Inside the narrow coffee bar, she takes her pulse with regard to the blond counterboy's physical attractiveness, and calculates his age as early twenties—too old to be steaming milk for a living; too young for a serious affair, though not out of the question for a one-time vengeful lapse—then commends herself for feeling no twinges, except of loyalty to Nash. She sits on a bench outside the shop and smiles for the first time this day at Daisy and Tatiana, who are begging in tandem for what they must think is frozen yogurt in her paper cup. She doesn't really hate Nash, she concedes after the first sip; maybe she isn't even angry anymore. The blond boy walks outside to tell her she forgot the change from her five, and she says from behind her sunglasses, with her beautiful capped smile and her silver-pink lips, that she meant for him to keep it. She appraises him, as she does all handsome and fit men, as a sperm donor, for the baby Nash refuses to father. This one would give her a baby with platinum-blond hair and skin that tanned, and he wouldn't try to be a father. On the other hand, she'd like a college graduate. She shakes off the thought as fantasy and nonsense, as she always does: Respectable women don't find their sperm donors behind counters on Balboa Island. The doom she has felt since breakfast shifts slightly into what she thinks may be forgiveness. Nash will hear it in my voice when he calls tonight, she thinks. He loves that about me—my inability to hold a grudge.

But nothing is simple: Flying to Boston in business class, Nash meets a woman.

Two

Across the aisle from Nash sits a big-boned woman whose olive skin is smooth, and whose upswept hair is shiny black. Arranged over Cynthia's high, old-fashioned bosom is a fringed stole of burnt-orange wool that Nash takes, at first glance, for an airline blanket. Her high heels are off, and her feet, under frosted stockings, look daintier than expected, and pampered. He had noticed her, her height, chest, and black felt gaucho hat at the gate and had thought, "Italian or Greek. Forty."

Nash is terrible at estimating age. Cynthia has recently turned fifty, and doesn't lie about her age because announcing the truth draws gasps and compliments about her complexion. She is five feet, ten inches tall, of a Lebanese father and French-Canadian mother, born and raised in New Jersey. Nash evaluates her when he thinks she won't notice, and makes the overture as soon as the plane takes off and the glasses of business-class beverages are poured. She is reading. "Business or pleasure?" he asks.

"Business," she says, and returns to the book.

He finds her answer chilly, but at the same time he admires the rebuff. It is in the style of a woman who isn't hungry for attention. He likes her for it, for being content with her lot.

"Forgive me," Nash murmurs, opening his own briefcase. "I won't interrupt again."

The woman lowers her book and pronounces it deadly dull.

"Why bother, then?" offers Nash. "Life is too short."

"The author's a client," says the woman. "I've put it off as long as I could, but I'm meeting him first thing in the morning."

The word *client* doesn't move him; he hears it too often to be impressed because it is what Dina calls the housewives who pay her to rub their feet. He asks this woman what the book is about, and she says, "Interstates."

"In what respect?"

"Roads. Who built them, why, and where." Cynthia, yet to introduce herself by name, makes a disparaging face.

Nash asks if she is in the book trade.

"The investment trade." She takes a sip from her mimosa, so he takes a sip from his, holding the glass so as to display his ringless left hand.

"You're based on what coast?" he asks.

"East."

"New York?"

"Boston."

"Me, too," says Nash. "At least, I may be."

Like all women traveling in business class, she brings forth a palm-sized leather case designed especially to hold her cards. Nash takes one as if it were exactly the delicious tidbit he'd been hoping to taste. "Cynthia M. John, M.B.A." it reads, "Registered Investment Adviser Representative, Investment Management Consultant," in dark blue script on a salmon stock.

"And you?" she asks.

"Composer," he says lightly.

Cynthia asks if he is famous.

He shrugs and says his name. She repeats "Nash Harvey" without inflection.

"Actually, what I do now is sound design, mostly for the television medium." He smiles modestly as if he knows the mention of television will elicit some degree of awe.

"What does that mean?"

"I write music and lyrics for product enhancement."

"TV commercials?"

"That's one way of saying it."

Cynthia waits.

"Saturn," he offers. "Mitsubishi. Maytag."

"Would I know any that you wrote?"

He hesitates because it is both instantly recognizable and painful—no residuals, a one-time composing fee—but he hears it everywhere. "Legacy Insurance." He hums the famous, thankless seven notes.

"That's yours? Are you incorporated?"

Nash tells her he has, more or less, a consultant's status. He doesn't have to pound the pavement. The phone rings: Detroit or Japan one day, a fast-food chain the next. Sometimes arranging instead of composing.

"What exactly does an arranger do in a commercial?" she asks.

"Oh, God, tons: takes a melody and stylizes it to whatever mood the commercial requires: rock 'n' roll, disco, Latin. Really, what I like to say is we create the bed on which the song is sung. You don't just take a cut from your favorite record and give it to your favorite singer."

"I would think that would be interesting work," she says politely, "and something that requires a very specific set of skills."

Nash concedes that this is very true.

She asks if the work is, well, for lack of a better term—steady?

Nash smiles and says, "Steady. Too steady. I can work twenty-hour days for a week straight out."

Cynthia, pleased with this answer, says, "How awful—no time for family and friends."

"I chose it—the life, the craziness."

"As opposed to what?"

Nash assumes a thoughtful, philosophical posture. He peers into his plastic glass like a man with artistic regrets. "Composing in another idiom, performing . . . teaching."

"Starving," she adds.

Nash laughs. "A pragmatist. That's good. Obviously you're in the right field."

She picks up her client homework again with an exaggerated sigh.

"That's what I need," Nash adds after a short silence, as if musing to himself. "Someone to look over my portfolio."

~~~ She has her car, and asks about his destination.

"I'm not sure," he begins. "I'm on a mission. There's someone I need to apologize to."

"You flew all the way cross-country just to apologize to someone?"

"If I get up the nerve," he says. "I won't know until we're face to face."

They are on a down escalator. Cynthia's carry-on bag is between them. "Is this 'making amends'—that A.A. thing where you go back to apologize to everyone you ever treated badly?"

He says, "I know what you mean—Twelve Steps. It's an epidemic in California. But this is something much more . . ." He makes a fist and raps his shirt where he thinks his heart is beating. "An old wrong I have to right."

"A woman?" asks Cynthia.

Nash nods; manages to look both chagrined and blameless.

They have reached the bottom of the escalator. Cynthia, wheeling her carry-on expertly, returns to the original question: Can she drop him somewhere?

Nash admits that he doesn't know the exact whereabouts of the former Adele Dobbin, the wronged party, or her married name, but has reason to think she never left Brookline.

"How long ago?"

"We were kids," he says.

Cynthia says she knows a web site that can find virtually anyone's phone number, and she owns a CD-ROM that draws maps of any block in the United States. Would that be useful?

"I couldn't trouble you," says Nash.

"Not at all," says Cynthia. "I'm not going into work at five-thirty. What else are you going to do? Call Directory Assistance?"

She drives a 3-Series Bimmer convertible, automatic transmission, with a tissue dispenser and miniature wastebasket suspended from the dashboard. At what seems to be a luxury high-rise, an attendant waves her enthusiastically into an underground garage as if genuinely glad to greet her, as if Cynthia John tipped well at Christmas. The building is on what she calls "the waterfront," which she explains was rat-infested warehouses in his day. When did he leave Boston?

" 'Sixty-seven," he says.

"Before Quincy Market," she says. "Maybe even before Government Center." She asks if he remembers Scollay Square—the old red-light district? Nash says, "Vaguely. From newspaper headlines."

"They tore it down to put up Government Center."

"Did it work?" asks Nash, and Cynthia understands what he is asking.

"Of course not. The hookers moved a few trolley stops to the Combat Zone."

"Human nature," says Nash as clinically as he can.

⟶ Her computer is in her white bedroom in a dramatic condo with skylights, blue neon tubes as artwork, a wall of windows that look out to the harbor islands, and a gorgeous, gleaming, ebonized mahogany Steinway grand. Nash circles it as Cynthia chats about the creative financing that led to her outright ownership of the condo in five years. She is not flirtatious because she views Nash and his Hollywood earnings as a potential trophy client. But questions that reveal one's financial obligations at the same time sound personal. Own or rent? Married or single? Ex-wives? Children?

Nash is sipping seltzer with twists of both lemon and lime, and eating Gorgonzola on pear slices, which have been fanned out on a granite slab next to cocktail napkins bearing the seal of Harvard. All told, an impressive hostess offering, he thinks, for someone who wasn't expecting a guest. Cynthia is graceful on her stockinged feet, moving between refrigerator and cutlery drawer. There is evidence all around the kitchen of advanced culinary skills—a food processor, an espresso machine, copper pans, wooden spoons and wire whisks.

"Do you like to cook?" he asks.

"Love it," she says. "Wish I had time to throw dinner parties every weekend."

"But your work doesn't give you that much free time?"

"I travel too much."

He runs his fingertips across the spines of her cookbooks.

"Thai," he reads. "Indian. Chinese. Italian. French. New Orleans. Lebanese. Mexican. Wow."

"I do more takeout than I should," she says, agitating their martinis in a silver shaker. "Cooking for one is not that rewarding."

It appears to Nash that Cynthia is making the first move, which is normal for him, even expected. He is used to being admired and approached by women of all ages. It's why he never married—this social, often sexual, goodwill that his combination of handsome features, expensive clothes, and good manners invites. He believes in pheromones; he thinks he may give something off, and wears a touch of musk to enhance his natural chemicals. Having left Dina behind in Newport Beach, knowing the utter West Coastness of her blond, ex-actress (a Zest commercial), skinny-bodied (large, implanted breasts notwithstanding) identity, which has turned to the submedical field of reflexology, he is charmed by the idea of an ethnic, olive-complected, nonstarlet with an M.B.A., and how it reflects on his own maturity and his symbolic flight eastward.

Cynthia slaps her forehead in a way Nash finds authentically . . . something, and announces that she left her client's unreadable book in the seat pocket! What would Freud say about *that* rather blatant act? But she'd pull it off; she'd buy another copy on her way to her meeting, and skim enough to make the client think she'd read every boring word. "On the bright side," she says, "I won't have to cram tonight."

It is only right, he states, to repay this hospitality, this gorgeous view, and her invaluable computer assistance. Dinner?

"Now?"

"Sure," says Nash. "You must have a favorite neighborhood bistro."

She allows—not yet a commitment—"Down the elevator, across Atlantic Ave., two blocks west."

"In the North End?"

"Or we can do that," says Cynthia. She gets their coats from her bedroom, along with the computer printout of Adele Dobbin's block. "What about your date with destiny?" she asks wryly, waving the grid.

Nash feels a pinch of duty and guilt, but it passes. "First things first," he says.

⎯⎯⎯⎯⎯◯ She takes his arm against the snow that seems to be blowing up from the sidewalks and off the renovated granite warehouses. He says he is delighted—unseasonably bad weather custom-made for a Boston boy returning from a sun-baked, spoiled life.

"Ugh," Cynthia responds. "You can have it. I need a vacation."

Nash conjures Cynthia on a white beach under a coconut palm. A shelf circles the tree trunk and holds their suntan oil and their tropical drinks. She's wearing a smart sarong over her bathing suit, and her visible flesh is the same smooth olive as her face. The scene changes suddenly to a Caribbean island of French ownership, to a topless beach, to the unveiling of Cynthia's God-given breasts leaping like baby mammals off her five-foot-ten-inch frame. It's been ages, he thinks wistfully (and not without stirrings), since he's kneaded a real breast.

"Closer might be better," says Cynthia. "Mind if we go down a notch, foodwise, to get in out of the cold?"

"I'm completely open," says Nash.

She crosses the street and leads him to a diner that looks both brand-new and authentically retro. They slide into a booth, laughing as if they have outwitted or outdistanced someone. The banquette is upholstered in swirly, cobalt blue; the waitress—young and adorable in peach and white (an actress looking to break into pictures, Nash assumes in his West Coast way)—brings menus shaped like the State House.

Cynthia orders without making excuses: the meatloaf with the horseradish mashed potatoes, Roquefort-creamed spinach, and spiced apple rings.

"The same for me," says Nash, who hasn't eaten chopped meat in any form since *E. coli* made the news.

"They also make the best hamburgers in the financial district," she tells him after the waitress has yelled their orders in diner lingo that is part of the show. "They use real cheddar and both raw and grilled onions."

Nash grins until Cynthia is compelled to ask why.

"What am I smiling at? You. Your enthusiasm. Your lack of self-consciousness. It's very refreshing."

"It's fattening," she answers dryly. "Not that I spend ten seconds worrying about that anymore. I've accepted the hand I've been dealt, which is no size six."

Nash chuckles again, as if he hasn't noticed and agrees completely.

Cynthia continues. "It was my fiftieth-birthday present to myself: Enjoy life. Experience life. Which means, on some days, order what you want."

Nash is thrown by the "fifty" but doesn't show it. Almost immediately, the number charms him for unexpected reasons. He is, after all, older than that. He is not looking for a wife or a mother for his unborn children. Adele Dobbin, when he sees her, will be fifty-three. This Cynthia is a good transitional experience, particularly if he ends up in bed with Adele. And California has taught him that aging is not as unalterable as it once was.

"You're not shocked, are you?" she asks.

"Not me," he says.

Cynthia says, "Tell me what you did to this Adele that's made you feel guilty since you were a kid. How old *are* you, by the way?"

"Fifty-five."

"What did you do—love her and leave her?"

"Worse."

"Love her, *impregnate* her, and leave her?"

"Not that bad."

She lifts her hands from her lap and folds them on her paper place mat. "You tell me."

"I disappeared," he says, looking straight into her eyes as if he were a man accustomed to facing consequences.

Cynthia does not flinch. "At what point?"

It's not the first time he's confided to a woman about his romantic history, so he knows how to shade his answer. "Just as we were about to announce our engagement."

"Define 'just about'?"

"Her parents were throwing a party—"

"*A* party or *the* party?" asks Cynthia.

"I don't know what you mean."

"Was it an engagement party for you and Adele?"

"Look," says Nash. "I was a brash kid. Insensitive and selfish. I admit it. If I could undo what I did that night, I would."

"Meaning you wish you had gone through with the marriage?"

"No. That's not what I'm saying. What I'm saying is, I wish I hadn't been such a heel."

Cynthia is not a soft touch, but Nash is exceptional at sincerity and contrition.

"A heel," he repeats. "I don't blame anyone for agreeing with that."

"I'm not blaming you," she says. "I don't know the facts. Besides, I wouldn't want to be held accountable for anything *I* did when I was still a kid."

Nash smiles gratefully. He is quite beautiful at fifty-five, especially around the eyes.

Cynthia taps his hand. "I've been told I interrogate people as a form of conversation. It's left over from the case-study method in business school. At least that's my excuse."

"It's charming."

Cynthia laughs with her head thrown back, revealing molars free of fillings.

"I'm having a wonderful time," Nash tells her. "Third degree or no third degree." He fixes her with another stare, this one boyish and hopeful.

"Wine?" she asks. "They have a surprisingly good list."

"I like an assertive Bordeaux with my meatloaf," he says. Cynthia laughs again; she points out the window to a man chasing his wife's runaway umbrella.

"Is this what they call a nor'easter?" Nash asks.

"This is nothing," says Cynthia. "This'll pass before we get our coffee."

"I'm not so sure," says Nash.

She thinks he is interested in seeing her again, in pairing up with her, in forgoing a fiduciary relationship for a personal one.

He thinks: I wonder how long it's been, if she's overdue, and if gratitude makes her a little wild. "Hungry?" he asks.

She tips his wrist toward her. "We're still on Pacific time. Early for dinner."

"Damn right," says Nash. "The night is young."

⟵◡　　They argue over the two slips of paper that constitute the check. Nash prevails after saying, "What kind of men invite you to dinner and let you pay?"

"Clients," she says dryly. "Cousins on my father's side."

Even with a bottle of wine, the checks total less than forty dollars. Nash leaves a fifty-dollar bill on the table. As he exits behind Cynthia, the waitress mouths, "Thank you," and Nash blows a clandestine kiss.

The squall has ended, as Cynthia predicted. They walk the few blocks back to her high-rise so Nash can collect his suitcase. Inside her apartment, in her black-and-white marble foyer, she thanks him for a lovely time.

"Am I being kicked out?" he asks, then begs her indulgence to say what is on his mind.

Hanging up her coat, Cynthia listens over her shoulder.

"I am not in the habit of forcing my company on women," Nash begins. He pauses, then shifts his suitcase to the other hand as if he were a gentleman caller making his first adult declaration. "I know you must be tired after your trip—and I am too—but I have reached a point in my life where I find it harder and harder to walk away from something when every note playing in my head is telling me not to."

As designed, the reference to "note" reminds her that he is a musician, an artist.

"I'm not a kid," he continues. "I should be less impetuous, not more. But I'm also less patient. Also, I've been around. I know when something clicks."

Cynthia waits; does not liquefy; in fact, appears to be unmoved.

"Feel free to jump in at any time," says Nash. "Second the motion that I'm not the only one who feels something."

Cynthia reminds him of his mission across town, the woman he flew cross-country for.

"I'm jet-lagged," he protests. "I think I should wait until tomorrow."

"You're a big boy," she says. "Get it over with."

"I *am* a big boy," says Nash—but solemnly and without eye contact so that Cynthia will imagine that his double entendre is a figment of her own growing hope.

"What are you thinking?" he asks.

"Men," she says. She uses her fingers to tick off the guidelines: "The no-no's are: Men I meet on airplanes. Men in town for a week. Men far from home who can make up any stories they want. Men who were never married. Men who have unfinished business with their first loves."

Nash takes Cynthia's hand in camp-counselor fashion and leads her to a living room love seat. "Let's say, for the sake of argument, you're right to be suspicious. I am, in fact, a man. I did meet you on an airplane. I was never married—which I understand is supposed to mean I have trouble with commitment, or the sex act, or both. Yes, I came to Boston, in part, to apologize face to face with a girl I used to date." Nash pauses. "Have I misstated anything?"

"I have no way of knowing," says Cynthia.

"My return ticket is for May twenty-third. One month from now. Would you like to see it?"

"I believe you."

"Do you think all men are alike?"

"Of course not—"

"Do you think a man who meets you on an airplane, who's never been married, can be sincere? Can have genuine feelings? Or are we all cardboard cutouts?"

"No," says Cynthia.

"Have *you* been married?" he asks kindly, then shakes his head along with her in woeful tandem.

"Do men make assumptions about women who haven't married?" he asks.

"I know they do."

"Is that fair?"

"No."

"But it's acceptable to make assumptions about my character?"

"Consider the alternative," says Cynthia.

He smiles a kind, pedagogical smile. "Go on; say what's on your mind."

"I meant, falling for the lines and jumping into things with both feet," she says.

"What things?"

"Bed," says Cynthia.

"Bed!" he scoffs.

"Look," says Cynthia. "We're both grown-ups. We don't have to use euphemisms. 'Things clicking' and 'notes playing' generally refer to physical attraction. Am I wrong?"

"No," Nash says sadly. "You're not wrong."

"In other words—to sleeping together."

"Is that bad?" he asks. "Is it a terrible prospect?"

Cynthia protests that she is not talking about the prospect, but the timetable, the pace.

"I see," says Nash. He slouches until his misunderstood head rests on the back of the love seat, then stares at the recessed light above him. After a minute he says, "I wouldn't have opened my big mouth if I didn't think I was picking up on something that both of us were feeling." He closes his eyes, exhausted.

At last she emits a "Nash"—part question, part declaration.

He raises himself as if in slow motion to a sitting position, and kisses Cynthia. It is a sweet, lingering, but still chaste kiss, as if it's meant to be all the ecstasy he requires in this lifetime. She raises her chin an inch so that her neck is that much more hospitable, and finds his hand.

"My darling," says Nash.

Three

*R*ichard, rummaging through his sisters' refrigerator, asks, "Got any milk that isn't skim?"

"There should be a half-gallon of two percent," says Adele. "Check the date."

"What did he want?" asks Lois.

Richard takes his time: shakes some cereal into a bowl, reaches for a banana, and says, "Nothing."

"What took you so long if he didn't want anything?" Adele asks.

"He needed directions."

"Why didn't he go to a gas station?"

"I didn't ask."

"What did he need directions to?"

"A hotel."

"He was looking for a hotel on a residential side street in Brookline?"

"He was lost," says Richard, as big chunks of banana fall into his bowl.

"What did he look like?" asks Lois. "Could you identify him if you had to?"

"In a lineup, you mean?" Richard smiles, and shakes his head: You girls.

"Not every criminal looks suspicious," says Adele.

"You don't think I can spot someone trying to burglarize an apartment or rape my sisters?"

"He could be a con man," she insists. "They come in three-piece suits with briefcases."

"It wasn't a con man," he states calmly. "It was someone we used to know."

Adele and Lois, in identical motions, tighten their respective bathrobe sashes and wait.

Richard chews and swallows a mouthful of Grape-Nuts Flakes. "It was Harvey Nash."

Lois gasps and appears to sag slightly, but Adele just stares at him.

"Where?" says Lois, taking a step toward the front door. "Is he here now?"

"He wanted to speak to Adele, and I told him it was late—you don't just show up at someone's apartment in the middle of the night without warning—and he should call tomorrow."

"Who the hell made you the dorm mother?" scolds the red-faced Lois.

Richard says, "Yeah, right: 'Come on up, Harv. The girls are in their bathrobes, but I'm sure they'd love the company. That's Adele over there in curlers.'"

"Did he ask about Adele?"

"He asked *for* Adele."

"Is he married?" asks Lois.

"We didn't get into things, especially with Adele interrogating me over the intercom. I'm meeting him for lunch tomorrow."

"Was he wearing a wedding ring?" asks Lois.

"Look," says Richard. "It took a few minutes before I even realized who he was. I didn't recognize him—"

"How long is he here for?" asks Lois, sharply enough so that Adele looks away from Richard to examine her sister's feverish expression.

"I don't know. I'll find out tomorrow."

"What if he doesn't show up for this lunch?"

"He'll show," says Richard. "It was his idea."

"Why didn't you find out what happened?" Lois cries.

Richard looks at Adele, whose face is white. "I'll find out to-morrow," he says quietly.

Adele finally speaks. "I'm going with you," she says.

⌒ Nash takes one look at the modest motel on Beacon Street and decides it won't do for someone trying to impress the Dobbin family or Cynthia John. He asks the taxi driver for something more . . . "a notch up," is the phrase he chooses, rejecting the adjectives "upscale" and "deluxe" before speaking them aloud.

"The Ritz or the Four Seasons," says the driver, "but they can run you three hundred bucks a night."

"Where else?"

The cabby rattles off the names of a half dozen hotels, all of which Nash recognizes as chains, and one that sounds familiar for reasons he can't name.

"The Copley Plaza?" Nash repeats.

"Old," says the cabby, "but fixed up. Takes up a whole block. Five, six minutes from here at this time of night."

"Think they have a room?"

"If they don't, it's across from the Westin. The doormen will know if they're full up, and I can swing around the block. Have you been to Copley Square ever? Because that's where I'd wanna be—Copley Square or the waterfront."

"Fine, Copley Square." The cabby pulls away from the unsatisfactory motel. Nash looks around the interior of the cab with interest (he rarely takes cabs at home), and sees a little girl's school picture hanging from the rearview mirror along with a Saint Christopher's medal. After a minute he adds that he's been to the waterfront already, for an early supper and . . . other diversions. Smiling in the back seat, his hand steadying his suitcase, he notes the sound of "waterfront," its manly, risky, cinematic ring, and right behind it, again, a ticklish unease he associates with the Copley Plaza.

⌒ Between seven and seven-thirty P.M. on the night of March 11, 1967, Harvey Nash was considered nothing worse than unforgivably late for his own engagement party. "Always was unreliable," Mr. Dobbin complained. "Typical wise-guy behavior."

"Selfish," said Mrs. Dobbin. "So thoughtless to arrive after the guests."

Adele's sisters and mother took turns at three posts: at the revolving door of the Copley Plaza, where one could spot the breathless arrival of a bleeding and remorseful Harvey; on the dance floor, smiling gaily as if nothing were amiss; and by Adele's side upstairs, reassuring her that Harvey was merely irresponsible and untrustworthy. Not dead, not hurt, not trying to hurt her. Adele herself called the tailor to ask if Harvey had picked up his tux the day before. He had not. "He's not coming," she told them. Mr. Dobbin and Kathleen took her home.

Lois, on ballroom duty, walked up to the mike. The drummer hit a wholly inappropriate drumroll at the sight of such a pretty girl, in yellow chiffon, offering what was sure to be the family welcome. Fighting back tears, Lois managed, "Due to circumstances we hope are not serious, Harvey Nash has been detained. We can't say for sure when . . . if . . . Harvey . . ." She looked to the bandleader for help. He mouthed something to the orchestra, which struck up a lugubrious version of "Lara's Theme." Lois stood, stricken, at the mike, until a male cousin offered her his hand and she stepped down.

⟶ For the record, Harvey had called the Dobbin house with a minute to spare before he ran for his platform. Naturally no one was home and no one answered. What would he have said, anyway, that couldn't be said more effectively after Adele had calmed down? Look, kid, have the party without me. Have a ball. Bet you look like a million bucks. Tell everyone I had to go to California for a job opportunity, something that was too hot to put on ice. Smile when you tell them, because it's not that far from the truth. You can't make any inroads from three thousand miles away. They don't want mama's boys who can't leave their families and their music teachers. The guests will understand—most of them anyway. Even your parents will if they know it's for a good reason. They never thought much of me, but now I'll have a chance. Maybe you'll come out when I get a job and a decent place.

Because he had this conversation with himself, the problem seemed disposed of and etiquette appeared to have been served.

He meant no harm. Things had snowballed. He was too young to marry. And he'd been honest—inside his own head, at least—because there was never a day in his romancing of Adele or her planning of this party that he didn't have faith in things going his way, which is to say, he'd never have to rent a tux, dance in a spotlight, or walk down the aisle.

Harvey's mother sent an unapologetic letter to the Dobbins, barely acknowledging the disgrace, claiming that Harvey didn't feel up to the responsibility of marrying the oldest Dobbin daughter. If only he had felt freer to discuss his dreams with her, she added. If only she were more like Harvey, more adventurous, less attached to her family, perhaps he wouldn't have panicked.

Just before Christmas, Adele gave her modest engagement ring to the mildly retarded man who ran errands for her father's law firm, who wanted to propose marriage to the mildly retarded woman who cleaned the building after hours. The stone had belonged to Mrs. Nash's late shop-girl mother, and was said to have—in lieu of clarity or size—great sentimental value.

⌐⌐⌐ Since Dina will not interrupt a reflexology session to answer the phone, she has canceled her evening appointments. Several hours have passed since Nash's plane was to have landed, five-fifteen Boston time, plenty of time to check into a hotel. She's heard nothing. At seven-thirty P.M. Pacific Time she decides that a healthy woman would not wait by the phone. She calls her sister, an actress-turned-paralegal, who also hasn't eaten yet, but they can't agree on where to go. Maureen, her sister, loses interest; decides to stay home and work on her already-late taxes. She urges Dina to go out, to try the new Japanese restaurant in Corona del Mar and sit at the sushi bar, where guys eating alone sit.

Dina changes into a beige linen tunic over matching pants, chosen along with jade beads for their Chinese influence. At her jewelry box, she considers a large black pearl ring that Nash never liked because it was a gift from an old boyfriend who traveled to Hong Kong on business. She puts it on her right hand, and slips her wedding-like diamond band off her left. She rerecords her answering machine's outgoing message, changing "we" to "I," then backs her little red Miata out of the garage, angrily and too fast into the big Mercedes parked squarely opposite her driveway.

Its owner is remarkably gracious, almost unconcerned by the damage to his driver-side doors. He calls the Newport Beach police from his car phone, while Dina cries as if her life is ruined.

"Are you insured?" asks the Mercedes owner, searching for the source of such anguish.

"Of course I'm insured," she wails.

"Does this happen frequently?"

"Never! I never do this. I'm a great driver!"

"Accidents happen," he says.

Dina stops crying and reflects on this odd absence of anger. "I'd go nuts if you did this to me."

"Do you have a car-rental provision?" he asks.

Dina says she doesn't know. Does that matter?

"It would give you transportation while your Miata is being repaired."

"We have more cars," she says, then corrects herself: "I have a car I can drive in the meantime."

"It's not so terrible," he says. "It might only be cosmetic. And no one was hurt."

Dina says she is sorry. If only she had looked. It's her fault. Today has been a horrible day, and this proves she is in much worse shape than even she herself realized.

"Do you want me to call your husband?" he asks.

Dina says, "He's in Boston." After a pause she adds, testing the feel of the words, "He's not a husband."

"Literally?" asks the man. "Or did you mean that figuratively?"

"We're not married."

"But . . . ?"

"He went back to Boston today. He's from there." She displays her left hand, where a circle of untanned skin tells the tale.

"What's your name?"

"Dina."

"Maybe you'll want to get checked out by a doctor, Dina."

Dina says weakly, "Maybe, if I can use your car phone, I'll call my sister. She's doing her taxes. She'll come get me."

The man says, "If it's a matter of escorting you home . . ." He points across the street to the white stucco house and host garage. Dina's embarrassed laugh sounds like the bleat of new crying.

"It's only a car," he says. "Well . . . only two cars."

She evaluates his appearance for the first time. He is tall and balding, somewhere in his forties, with an egg-shaped, freckled head, and eyelashes the color of an apricot poodle's fur. He is wearing tennis shorts, a Yankees warm-up jacket, and boat shoes of butterscotch leather. His pale blue eyes are red-rimmed, as if his contact lenses hurt. She guesses that when he wears his glasses, they are flesh-toned and professorial.

"If you're this calm, you must be either a shrink or the owner of a body shop," says Dina, squinting left, then right, in search of the summoned police.

"I like to think I have a sense of proportion: No one was hurt. We're two civilized people with insurance."

"But, still—" She points to his bashed-in doors and their streaks of scarlet Miata paint.

"And I have a feel for the dramatic," he continues. "If you and I were to fall in love, and people asked how we met, I could say, 'Car crash. She shot like a rocket out of her driveway across a four-lane highway into my new Mercedes.' "

Dina, charmed but ignoring the bid for now, winces and says, "*How* new?"

"Doesn't matter. It's a rental." He extends his right hand and says, "Byron Sprock."

⟋⟍ Adele, at fifty-three, considers that it is too late for everything: for getting married, for getting another graduate degree, for adopting children, for learning to figure skate. After the night of March 11, 1967, everyone said, in more or less these words, "Someone will come along, you'll see, and make you forget that Harvey Nash ever existed." When Adele said, "No, they won't," people thought she meant, No, no one can ever replace Harvey. All she meant was, I see no one on the horizon and I'm a pragmatist.

She is not studying her hair in the mirror now, nor rummaging through her closet for smart outfits, nor plucking her eyebrows for tomorrow's lunch, because Adele—unlike Lois—despises Harvey Nash.

⎯⎯⎯⎯⎯ Byron Sprock is a playwright. "Remind me of what you've done," Dina prompts, offering him a swig from her water bottle, which she's rescued from her back seat.

"*Rhyme or Reason? Dog at a Dance?*"

Dina shrugs: Sorry.

"*First Night?*"

"I've heard of that," she says.

"Probably the phrase rather than my play. Most big cities have a First Night celebration."

Dina asks what it's about.

"Renaissance Weekend—New Year's Eve with the Clintons on Hilton Head."

"Comedy?"

"I hope so."

"Still running?"

He shakes his head, then looks as if he would like to add something, but is holding back.

"What?"

"You may have heard of it because it won an Obie."

Dina realizes now that Byron Sprock is successful, at least on the East Coast, where writers can be celebrities, and fame can result from endeavors other than feature films and television. "Wow," she says. "That's fantastic!"

They are standing on the sidewalk, watching the Miata being hooked up for towing. She asks what brings him to the West Coast, but then adds, "Let me guess. They're making a movie out of one of your plays?"

"Close enough."

"Which play?"

"*First Night*—but it won't happen."

"But you came all this way."

"They flew me out first class, and leased me a car."

Dina says, "I used to act."

"I'm not shocked to hear that."

"Just commercials."

The tow-truck driver offers Dina a clipboard and a pen. She scribbles her name in three places. Byron suggests she read what she has signed.

"It says you pay if the insurance doesn't," says the man.

"Fine," says Dina.

"I'll walk you home," says Byron, and leads her to the crosswalk a block north, which makes Dina think he is both chivalrous and safe.

⟋⟍⟍⟶ Nash watches TV in his gray-green bedroom at the Copley Plaza, king of his remote control. At home he has picture-in-picture, allowing him to monitor two sporting events at once, but here he is limited to a solo view of the Celtics at Vancouver. He orders room service at midnight—a turkey club and a decaf—and calls Newport Beach. Dina doesn't pick up. He leaves a message that says, neutrally and erroneously, "I made it. I'm staying at a hotel called the Plaza," with no number offered, and no clue to his state of mind. "Take care, Deenie," he adds after a pause. When she plays it back at one A.M., Pacific time, she knows he won't be back.

Four

Cynthia, despite her birthday vow to love, honor, and accept herself, wakes up Friday morning thinking about a diet. She stays in bed past the strictly observed seven A.M. rising, and clicks on the *Today* show. Usually the sight of Matt Lauer creates a mild yearning for the male warmth he lavishes on his costars, but this morning Cynthia says to the screen, "I met someone yesterday."

A few sentences into the news, Cynthia speaks again. "I actually had sex with him." She thinks of whom she could try these rehearsed sentences out on; considers her mother, who in her widowhood has begun to date a restaurateur and confide embarrassing personal details to Cynthia; one sister in Tenafly and the other in West Orange, and two best girlfriends, all of whom will still be asleep at five after seven. She gets out of bed, takes a shower, then rubs her Persian-lilac-scented oil onto her skin with more motivation and appreciation than usual. She vows to get a pedicure the next free hour she carves out of her life, and to apply the Dead Sea mud pack that her friend Suzanne brought her back from the Holy Land.

Cynthia walks between bath and bedroom without a robe and stands brazenly before a grinning Matt Lauer. A slight chill reminds her that she is naked, and of Nash's gusto the night before. He'd been rather intent on undressing her, especially on releasing her breasts and nuzzling them noisily, almost comically, as if he'd seen it done that way, but in an impersonal manner that left Cynthia somewhat alone and above the commotion. If she were being perfectly honest with herself, she would acknowledge that Nash's seduction talents were principally in his salesmanship. Their love-making seemed to be between Nash and her physical equipment, but she is willing to excuse his shortcomings as shyness and as an orientation. It was she who interrupted his pleasure to coax him off the couch and into the bedroom, away from the picture window and the imagined binoculars of passing sailors. He barely undressed, only freeing that of his which was necessary. He had a condom handy, in his shaving kit, in his carry-on. Intercourse seemed to be the goal, with ejaculation the signal that they were finished. Afterward, he lay next to her, checking his watch, less grave and attentive than he'd been while campaigning for the privilege.

"Do you need to leave?" she asked.

Nash said, "That matter I told you about."

"Adele."

"Right."

"At this hour?"

"She's a night owl," he said.

"How would you know that?" asked Cynthia, then immediately regretted her wifely tone.

"I'll go by her place, and if the lights are on, I'll knock."

Cynthia slipped out of bed and took from her bottom drawer a flimsy black peignoir that she'd never worn, a joke floozy gift at her fiftieth that still had its tags. Nash sat up, seeming to revive as she fastened the one satin rosebud at the neck, and the peignoir covered nothing.

"Wow," he said. "Now *that's* my idea of a bathrobe."

Cynthia looked down. "I think it's supposed to be worn over something."

Without any thought to the promise it held, Nash said, "I hope you wear it every time I come over."

Cynthia seized this as testimony to his good intentions. "Do you want to stay here tonight? I mean, after you square things with Adele? You could come back here instead of a hotel."

"Thanks. But I couldn't impose."

"I leave before eight," she said. "You'd have the whole apartment to yourself."

"Thanks just the same. But I'd hate to be the kind of guy who'd take you up on that."

Cynthia stood still, posing, pretending that the peignoir was not a costume and not ridiculous. "Is there any such thing as a hotel room with a piano?" she asked.

Nash answered by lowering the blanket to expose himself, proud and unself-conscious, showing Cynthia that ten minutes after intercourse his penis could do tricks.

She murmured, "I find that remarkable."

Nash stroked himself with one hand and reached out for Cynthia with the other. His eyes went soft and his face grew solemn— the old, sweetly anxious appeal he had kicked off at dinner and clinched on the couch.

"Really?" said Cynthia. "So soon?"

Nash hesitated, appeared to rethink the impulse, then pulled the blanket back over himself. "Times like this I forget I'm not a teenager," he said sweetly.

What he was actually remembering was Adele—at twenty-three, her cap of dark red hair and lips that were painted brighter than the fashion, the kind of debutante good looks that he thinks may have aged well. It wasn't loyalty or guilt that changed his course, but pragmatism: Should Adele be home, unmarried, and receptive, he'd need something in reserve.

⟜ If Lois seems overly interested in Harvey Nash's return, and agitated, she is. At the time of his disappearance, Lois was twenty-one, and believed from phone flirtations and compliments, and from stares that lasted a few seconds longer than was polite, that something reciprocal was going on in Harvey's capacious heart. Feelings for her, she thinks, contributed to his flight—a theory that gave Harvey unearned credit for being an honorable young man who would deprive himself of love altogether rather than betray and disappoint Adele. In fact, Harvey did engage Lois whenever she intercepted him in the front foyer or answered the phone, but Lois didn't know that his flirtations were automatic and meaningless.

For a year or two, Lois secretly expected that Harvey would send for her, or send a signal, and they'd hatch a plot where she would visit a college friend in California, and then she'd announce to the family that she'd bumped into Harvey Nash on a neutral site, completely by accident and coincidence. She would say that they had agreed to meet so she could interrogate him and satisfy the family's curiosity once and for all, and now, inexplicably, the most astonishing thing had happened: She and the enemy had fallen in love.

Harvey, of course, made no attempt to contact Lois, overtly or surreptitiously. She wrote to him once, just after her divorce, after seeing his credit on a box in a video store. Her note did not mention Adele; it was in fact lighthearted and friendly, and said she might be traveling to California. She wrote a short paragraph about her marriage and divorce—a coded sexual message: I'm the Dobbin who's slept with a man and might like to again. She mailed it to the reinvented Nash Harvey in care of Paramount Pictures, but never heard back. She assumes it never reached him.

The old theory about Lois, pre–Unspeakable Act, is that she could have had any number of boyfriends and marriage proposals, but she wouldn't march down the aisle ahead of Adele. Her sisters and her brother still call her "Lovely Lois" whenever they are in the mood—prompted by a particularly unglamorous, late-sleeping dishevelment at the breakfast table—because of a caption that ran more than thirty years before in the Brookline *Chronicle*, showing Lois modeling a wedding gown in the grand finale of a charity fashion show. "Lovely Lois Dobbin, a daughter of Mr. and Mrs. George Dobbin, is resplendent in tulle over crepe de chine from R. H. Stearns." Lois has a disdainful, superior, ironic expression that some longtime friends from high school still haven't mastered.

Now Lois wants to sit on Adele's bed and discuss the possible reasons for Harvey Nash's return, but Adele has closed her eyes, feigning exhaustion, and has sent her sister away. In fact, Adele is wide awake. She hears the elated Lois invade Kathleen's room, wake her with a hushed outburst, deliver the astounding news: Harvey Nash is back.

Adele knows Kathleen, the famous softie, and hears her gasp, a room away, with shock and foolish optimism. She is the family romantic and mother. She meal-plans and files coupons, and even though the other sisters help, Kathleen is the acknowledged head of the kitchen. She has sponges for washing dishes (pink or yellow) and others for wiping counters (blue or green), which are sterilized nightly in the dishwasher, a system her sisters are supposed to follow but can't get right. Recent press attention to salmonella and other illness-causing bacteria has proved that she is not germ crazy, merely careful. Soon, Kathleen will knock gently on Adele's door and ask if she's okay, and if she'd like to talk. Adele will pretend she's answering from a deep sleep, not because she doesn't want to relieve Kathleen of some anxiety, but because she doesn't want to see eager Lois at her elbow, trying to look sympathetic while she is actually thrilled.

When the talk stops, and both sisters have gone back to bed, Adele gets up. She joins Richard in the den, where he's watching the Celtics on the West Coast with their mother's last afghan, sewn together and fringed by Kathleen, pulled up to his chin. "What's the plan?" she asks.

Richard says he thinks—how did they leave it?—that he'd pick Harvey up at his motel.

"Did you propose lunch or did he?"

"He did."

"Richard," says Adele, and her tone draws his full attention. "What did he say exactly?"

"Nothing concrete. He wanted to talk to you. I said, 'Forget it. You don't just show up on someone's doorstep after thirty years.' So he asked if he could talk to me, man to man, tomorrow."

"Does he look the same? I mean, an older version of Harvey Nash or completely different?"

Richard says, "Wasn't he a little stocky? Or am I thinking of someone else?"

It is astonishing to Adele that her brother might be so careless or cavalier as to let the image of Harvey Nash, Jr., fade. She says faintly, "It depends what you mean by stocky. He was never skinny but he had a nice build."

"He's gotten better-looking," says Richard. "More distinguished. More polished."

"What did he ask you about me?"

"I didn't give him a chance. I wasn't going to invite him up, and I wasn't going to stand there in my undershirt getting grilled."

"What was he wearing?"

"Trousers, jacket, a raincoat. He had a suitcase."

"So he must have come directly from the airport."

"He didn't say when he got in."

"How odd—just showing up without knowing anything first. It makes me think there's something wrong with him."

"I don't know about that," says Richard. "He was awfully polite."

"Had he been drinking?"

Richard says, "Not so I noticed." He grins. "Know where he wanted to go for lunch? Jack and Marion's. I told him it closed, like, twenty years ago."

"We used to go there after a movie," says Adele. "He could eat a huge corned-beef sandwich at ten o'clock at night."

"I miss that place," says Richard. "Remember the Number One Club?"

"People don't eat like that anymore."

"It's coming back," said her brother. "In fact I could go for a corned-beef-Swiss-and-cole-slaw right now."

"With Russian dressing?"

Richard smiles and rearranges the afghan so it reaches Adele's lap. "What will you say to him?" he asks.

Adele says she hasn't decided yet.

"How about 'Harvey, what the fuck happened that night? And what have you been doing for thirty years that's so fucking important that you couldn't make a phone call?'"

"Or write. Not that I would have answered."

"The point I'm trying to make is, I'm not letting him off the hook. I'm asking him why he left and why he came back."

"And then what? You punch him in the nose? Serve him a subpoena?"

"It depends what he says."

"It really doesn't," says Adele. "Nothing he says will change anything."

"Honestly?"

Adele nods.

"There's a hundred possibilities: 'I'm moving back here.' 'I have a month to live.' 'I'm deeply, deeply sorry. Will you ever forgive me?' "

"No, I will not."

"Or 'Just came back to see my folks—' "

"They're dead."

Richard asks her what she thinks the reason is.

After a silence, Adele answers. "It doesn't really matter why he came back."

"Because . . . ?"

"It's too late. It was too late an hour after he ran away."

"So why go with me tomorrow?"

Adele hasn't put words to her conviction, nor would she say the reason aloud if she were admitting it: People seem to think she is still beautiful. She hopes Harvey Nash is unattractive, alone, lonely, filled with regret, and has returned in some kind of pain to beg her forgiveness. She has even conjured, fleetingly and for her own amusement, a scene where she brandishes a small gun, and the speech she'll deliver before cocking it.

"I want to see what he turned out to be," she says.

Richard shrugs. "Then why not let me take a Polaroid?"

"Maybe I want him to see me."

Richard points the remote control at the TV and raises the volume. Adele asks, "Are you staying here because you and Leslie had a fight?"

"I'm here, clearly, because the gods wanted someone other than you to answer the door when Harvey Nash showed up."

"That's not an answer."

"Kathleen asked me the same question."

"And what did you say?"

"I said, 'Sometimes I need a night away.' "

Adele touches his knee lightly before rising to her feet. "So I shouldn't worry?"

"Not about me," he says.

⟶ Kathleen's lingerie shop is located in the lobby of a luxury apartment building with a conscientious doorman who is close to asking Kathleen out on a date. His name is Lorenz, and since

January he has been taking his coffee breaks inside her shop, and refusing to let her reimburse him for the cappuccinos he brings. Though shy, he is dignified and professionally gallant; he leaves immediately when a customer arrives, understanding that a male presence among the undergarments would make a woman self-conscious. He opens the door for her customers, sometimes stays if the customer is male; leaves if the man looks embarrassed to be there, touching his visor in an unofficial salute. His day off is Tuesday, and Kathleen has noticed how long Tuesdays feel, and how she looks forward to Wednesdays. She also notices he doesn't wear a wedding ring, and has never mentioned a wife, an ex-wife, or children. Last Christmas he returned her Hallmark billfold with a note saying, "I don't feel right taking this from you."

Tonight, after she learns that Harvey Nash is back, she dreams about Lorenz. He is walking around the store fingering camisoles on her silver half-mannequins, checking their price tags, just as if he were a customer. She wakes up, and resolves to make the first move, jobs and stations aside. If she lived alone, or even had the kitchen to herself one night a week, she could pick up a baguette at lunch, stop by his alcove, where he sits reading and keeping his charts between visitors, and say, "If you're not busy tonight, I could make a beef stew"—the main dish changes in each rehearsal: "a chowder," "a big pot of chili"—"and you could join me." Kathleen talks about her sisters, so Lorenz knows they share an apartment, and she knows he lives in the North End and walks to work. He's also heard Lois's story: that she is the middle and most difficult sister, that she was for a short time the second wife of a lawyer in Mr. Dobbin's firm. That Lois moved back in with her sisters because the prenuptial agreement gave her a lump-sum settlement and no alimony; that something went wrong that the sisters, who were fond of their onetime brother-in-law, wish they didn't know.

Kathleen decides as she emerges from the T station at Haymarket and as she walks toward the waterfront that she will tell Lorenz about last night's shock in order to guide them, conversationally, into the arena of personal affairs.

She doesn't even wait for his coffee break, but stops just inside the door to announce breathlessly, "We had quite an evening at our place last night."

Lorenz smiles and says, "And what would that be?"

Kathleen tells him the short version, beginning with a capsule history: the 1967 engagement party for Adele and Harvey Nash, Jr., who ran away, never to be heard from again until last night.

Lorenz reacts with just the open-mouthed, bug-eyed astonishment Kathleen was hoping for.

"Can you imagine?" she continues. "The nerve? Not a word in thirty-odd years and he rings our doorbell at midnight?"

"Seriously?" he asks. "Midnight?"

"We have no doorman," she explains. "Richard was staying over and he answered the door, and sent him packing."

Lorenz winces.

"Not forever. They're supposed to have lunch today."

"Is he back? I mean, is he looking to start things up again with your sister?"

"No one knows! Richard sent him away before he could say anything."

"But they're having lunch?"

"Today. Adele's going."

"Whoa."

"She's determined. She'll make him sorry he ever . . ." Her voice drops off, unsure of what verb applies.

"Lived?" Lorenz supplies.

"Not quite."

"Came back?"

"I don't know. I'll find out tonight. And I'll tell you tomorrow."

Lorenz smiles and says—having heard the formidable-Lois stories—"I think I know what *Lois* would do to any guy who left her at the altar." He lifts his brow, but doesn't speak the name of the indecent surgical act of aggression. Kathleen laughs knowingly.

"Forgive me," says Lorenz. "That was crude."

"Don't apologize," said Kathleen. "I don't know where you got the idea that I'm such a delicate flower."

She fishes her key out of her purse, and says, "Come by on your break?"

"You can count on it," he says.

There, she thinks. The line has been crossed, thanks to the legend of Lois. Now she and Lorenz have alluded to that most private of things—that which drives the sale of intimate apparel, after all—and it is a relief.

⌒ Cynthia, in no-nonsense teal-blue sweats, picks up a quart of skim milk in the lobby convenience store. Fredo's has become increasingly gourmetlike, with recent additions of goat cheese, coffee in sleek decanters, baguettes from a bakery in Quincy Market, and a biscotti section. She says no to a bag for her milk, and adds a copy of *Self* that offers "New exercises that melt pounds away." Not that she is going to go crazy, she tells herself. Diets are for foolish optimists and women with low opinions of themselves. It is clear that Nash is that one guy in a million who is comfortable—more than comfortable, excited by—her generous proportions. Why fix what's not broken? The ridiculous black peignoir was an unexpected hit, and an easy way to please, even if it panders to a stage of arrested male development that Cynthia doesn't like to think about.

The association is prompted by a breathtaking bed jacket of cream-and-peach-striped silk displayed in The Other Woman's window. Cynthia has admired their wares—"rich-looking," her mother would say; even the foundation garments are chic and European, provocative yet tasteful. She hasn't needed anything like that lately; hasn't even walked across its threshold or met the pleasant woman she sees locking up the shop at six.

Maybe now, as the guarded, sensible side of her goes soft, she will.

Five

Just after ten A.M. Richard calls the Holiday Inn on Beacon Street, and finds no Harvey Nash or Nash Harvey registered. He is barely disturbed by the news, because cornering slippery people is his occupation. He begins an alphabetical pursuit through the Yellow Pages, hesitates at "Copley Plaza," but not for long.

The call wakes Nash. They don't chat, but agree to meet at Maison Robert in the Old City Hall at one. Richard will make the reservation under Dobbin. Nash asks, propping himself on one elbow, "Did you tell Adele I came by?"

"Of course I did."

"Was she thrown for a loop?"

"You did a pretty goddamn unforgivable thing," says Richard, "so this attitude—'Was she thrown for a loop?'—doesn't make me think you grasp the big picture."

Nash wasn't expecting this unpleasantness. He is fully awake now, and distracted by the fact that he is naked under the covers while two women are conversing in Spanish directly outside his door. "I take it Adele never married," he says.

"No, she didn't—"

"Did Lois?"

"Did *you*?"

Nash says, "I've come close." He hears the maid letting herself in, but doesn't warn her. At the sight of him in bed, the young woman cries, "I come back." Nash says in Spanish, "It's okay. Close your eyes. I'll put something on."

The maid retreats, and from the safety of the hallway repeats, "No, is okay. I come back."

Nash confides to Richard, "I'm stark naked, and the maid just let herself in."

"You speak Spanish?"

"Enough. Maid-speak."

"Don't scare her," says Richard. "They put up with enough shit without having to deal with naked guests."

Nash laughs. "I'm a big tipper."

Richard says, "Go get dressed. I'll see you in a couple of hours."

⟜ Adele wears charcoal gray, a stunning wool jersey sheath that Lois brought back from her honeymoon in Paris. It is dressier than what she generally wears to the station, especially accessorized by her black suede high heels and her late mother's double strand of pearls. Her coworkers have been paying her compliments since nine A.M., and asking why she's all dolled up.

"Meeting my brother for lunch," she tells them. "Maison Robert."

"Not your birthday?" someone asks.

"Not a job interview?" asks the new station manager with a smile.

Later they will agree she seemed different that morning. Nothing specific, but definitely not herself.

⟜ Richard points out that Harvey could hardly be guilty of standing her up if he didn't know she was joining them.

"Regardless," says Adele. "If he's not here in five minutes, we leave."

"Fine."

"The maître d' can say, 'Your party didn't want to wait.' "

"Fine."

"I don't want to begin this lunch with his stupid apology for keeping us waiting, at which point we'll feel compelled to say, 'Don't worry about it. These things happen.' "

Richard says, "If you stay and have lunch with me, I'll ask your advice. I know how much you like that."

"About what?"

"Me and Leslie."

Adele says, "You told me there was nothing wrong."

He raises his index finger to his lips. "On the condition that we have lunch together. Until then, I'm a closed book."

"What time do you have?" she asks.

"Seven past one."

"That's long enough."

"Fifteen minutes is the usual grace period."

"Not in this case," she says.

"By the way, you look great," he says after another minute.

Adele smiles briefly; checks her watch.

"Haven't I seen that dress on Lois?"

"It used to be hers. She gave it to me after the divorce."

"That's nice—that you two can wear the same clothes."

Adele says, "You don't have to make small talk."

At exactly one-fifteen, she walks to the maître d's podium to say they'd like to be seated at a table for two instead of what they had reserved.

"Of course," says the man, as he scans his seating chart and plucks two menus from a box.

"If a gentleman asks for us, could you say 'The Dobbin party left'?"

The man looks as if such a statement would cause him pain. Richard, at her side, says, "You can't ask him to police the restaurant, Dell."

When they are seated at a small table in a line with other small tables, and have ordered drinks, Richard says, "He could be stuck in the subway. It might not be his fault."

Adele opens her menu and says, "It's always his fault."

Richard smiles the good-natured smile of the habitually dressed-down baby brother.

Adele says, "Now can I ask you about Leslie?"

Richard repeats, "Ahh, yes: Me and Leslie," as if it were the title of an often-requested and tiresome song.

The waiter brings Adele's glass of Chardonnay and Richard's beer. The party at the next table gets their salmon and their striped ravioli, which bring Adele and Richard back to the menus. "What do you feel like?" he asks.

Adele closes her menu and says, "I'm going to surprise you."

"How?"

"Steak with garlic mashed potatoes on a bed of bitter greens. I'll skip dinner."

"I'm having . . ." Richard's eyes travel down the page before he announces, ". . . the lobster B.L.T. with watercress mayonnaise."

"I saw that."

"Want to share an appetizer?"

"You go ahead," she says. "I'm taking you to lunch."

"Maybe I'll have the smoked mussel chowder."

"Good."

Adele asks if he's spoken to Leslie since he left the night before.

"Actually, I didn't leave last night. I left Wednesday morning and stayed at Nora's Wednesday night."

"Who's Nora?"

"Nora from Newton." He smiles at his own alliterative cleverness, but Adele does not.

"You've taken up with someone else?"

"Absolutely not," says Richard. "This is a friend with a couch."

"From where?"

"From the office."

"You don't have any male friends with couches?"

"You'll be happy to know Nora's a lesbian most of the time."

Adele's face, which has been registering disapproval, freezes. "I don't believe it," she says. Richard swivels around to see Harvey Nash, unescorted and unapologetic, advancing.

Richard rises and blocks Nash, who doesn't seem to interpret the stance as anything but a warm reception. "Good to see you," Nash is saying to Richard, but his eyes are on Adele, and his smile is easy, even smug, as if he's pleased with the first glimpse of his blind date. "Sorry I'm late," he says. "I got a little lost. Went to City Hall." He is wearing a sports jacket in a black-and-white pinpoint check over a black T-shirt, and looks both more elegant and more casual than any man in the room.

Richard says tersely, "I told you, the *Old* City Hall."

"Whatever. It's practically around the corner." He extends his hand toward Adele, whose right hand tightens around her water glass instead.

"The maître d' wasn't supposed to let you in," she says.

Nash, undeterred, cocks his head and asks, "Is this a private club?"

"You know what she's saying—"

Nash says calmly, psychiatrically, to Adele, "You're furious. Of course you are. Who wouldn't be?"

"That's right."

"You've never forgiven me. And I had to show up late, which was the only test I had to pass. Christ. What a jerk."

"You can say that again," says Richard.

"I had no idea you'd be here," Nash says to her. "Believe me, if I had known, I'd have been here a half hour ago."

Richard lowers himself back down into his chair, and Nash kneads Richard's shoulders from behind. "I figured this guy wouldn't be here on the dot and wasn't going to be watching the clock."

The maître d' jogs to Nash's side. "Monsieur—" he begins.

"Could you get me a chair?" asks Nash.

The maître d' says, "I believe that's up to Madame."

"We've ordered," says Richard.

"I don't mind," says Nash. "I'm not that hungry."

"Madame?"

Adele, not wanting to attract attention, and aware that her face is familiar to viewers of public television who tune in to Pledge Week, says pleasantly enough, "I don't think there's room."

The maître d' offers to relocate them—with profound apologies for the misunderstanding—to a suitable table: Leave everything. Just take your personal effects.

Nash leads and choreographs: Richard next to Adele; Adele opposite Nash, where he stares at Adele, doing his best to flash messages of wordless admiration. The waiter transfers their wine and beer. Nash says, "Coffee, please," and adds that he's just in from the West Coast, and his body clock is set at breakfast.

Adele asks, "Why did you want to have lunch with my brother? Richard doesn't speak for me."

Nash repositions pieces of silverware as if deep in thoughtful contemplation. He sighs, looks squarely into her face, and says, "I was afraid to talk to you without some sort of clearance—"

Richard said, "You rang the doorbell in the middle of the night. It was just by coincidence that I was there."

"All of a sudden?" says Adele. "After all this time you decided you had to see me?"

"You look wonderful," Nash blurts out, as if nothing else can be expressed until that obvious truth is proclaimed.

Adele harrumphs.

Nash leans in and cajoles, "And I do, too, don't you think? For a guy old enough to be our father?" He throws back his head and laughs.

Against her will, Adele smiles wanly.

"See, I'm not so bad."

"We have to disagree," says Richard.

"Are any of us married?" asks Nash.

"Are you?" asks Adele.

"Regrettably not," says Nash. "I mean, 'regrettably' in the sense that I missed out on having children."

"It's not too late for you," says Adele. "You can father a child today. You're at a distinct advantage."

Nash closes his eyes and shakes his head sorrowfully.

"You can't?" asks Richard.

"Technically," says Nash. "Am I physically capable of impregnating a woman today or tonight? Yes. Emotionally? Is that what I want to do? Am I desperate to father a child?" He shakes his head again and looks aggrieved.

Adele leans closer and says, "But you did father a child, Harv. He was born nine months after you left—Harvey Junior."

"Adele!" says Richard.

Nash says, "That's not possible."

Adele says to her brother, "He's alluding to the fact that we never had sexual congress."

"Maybe I should leave," says Richard.

"I deserved that," says Nash.

The waiter arrives with Richard's chowder. Nash asks if the chef could scramble him some egg whites.

The waiter places a menu in front of Nash, as if to say, Perhaps you didn't realize that *we* decide what the chef makes.

"French, I see," says Nash.

"*Oui,*" says the waiter.

"A salad," says Nash. He points to one. "Could you make this artichoke and shaved parmesan as an entrée?"

"I'll ask."

"And a large Pellegrino."

Adele says to the waiter, "Don't hold up our entrées while you're making his." And to Nash: "I have to get back to work."

He smiles and asks what she does.

"Development."

"For whom?"

"For public television."

"How wonderful. I'm a supporter of your sister station in Los Angeles."

Adele stares with a near scowl.

"You're in L.A. proper?" asks Richard.

"An hour south, Newport Beach."

"Bad commute?" asks Richard.

"Painless," says Nash.

He expresses keen interest in their meals. Adele answers in a monotone—No, she usually has a light lunch, but today she felt like red meat.

"Please start," Nash says.

Richard removes the toothpicks from his sandwich, and uses both hands to manage the triple-decker half.

"Your steak is just the way I like it," Nash tells Adele.

Richard says, "Mine's delicious."

Nash says, "What's yours again?"

"The lobster B.L.T."

Nash asks if a lobster B.L.T. is a new regional dish, all the rage in Boston, because he saw it on the room-service menu at his hotel and had been tempted.

"Where are you staying?" Adele asks. She lifts the fork to her mouth, English-style, tines downward, elbows perfectly poised.

Nash replies cheerfully, "The Copley Plaza."

Adele gasps. With a sharp intake of breath she inhales her first bite of steak, and it is gone—there, but not there. She cannot chew or swallow or talk. In an instant she recognizes what is happening, the excruciating embarrassment of choking in public, and the knowledge that she could die. She tries again to swallow and to find air before she must signal wildly that something is wrong.

"Adele?" says Richard, putting his napkin on the table, then his hand on her back. "What's wrong?" He stands up. "Are you *choking?*"

She tries again to make it go away. Her eyes are pleading for civilized behavior, for putting a discreet end to this potential public scene. But the piece of steak is unswallowable, lodged in a place that has no muscle and no traction.

"She's choking," Nash says, and he is behind her, ripping off his jacket. "Stand up," he commands. His arms encircle her, and his fingertips probe below her rib cage. He pulls a fist into her stomach, but futilely. Again, harder. Another try with his hands reversed, right pressing left. People are watching, gathering.

Nash jerks again, harder. His face is next to Adele's and he recognizes, in his growing panic, a familiar and pleasing scent from his youth, her perfume. "Oh, God," Nash cries. He thinks he is breaking her bones under his hands, rupturing organs, but he doesn't stop. "Do something," Richard is yelling. Nash answers with his best upward thrust. He hears a sound, a pop, from inside Adele, and at the same time the morsel of steak flies out of her mouth. It lands—more humiliation—in plain view on a white square of tile. Adele inhales noisily and exhales with a sob. Nash tries to turn her into his embrace, but she is in her brother's arms now. Richard is crying and smoothing her hair.

Nash stands to one side, stunned. Someone tries to shake his hand, but he waves theirs away. Richard is beseeching Adele to speak, to take a deep breath, to sit. A waiter hands him a clean linen napkin and leaves quickly with the offending platter of steak. Richard wipes her mouth and her tearing eyes, studying her face for signs of the old Adele.

"Let's get her out of here," says Nash. "Let's get a cab."

"The bill—" says Richard.

"Fuck the bill," says Nash.

The maître d' is begging their pardon, picking Nash's jacket off the floor and smoothing it with a solicitousness meant for a human casualty.

Richard takes the first step toward the door, one arm around Adele. "My purse," she says weakly. A man, another diner, grateful to be of help, jumps forward and offers the pocketbook tenderly as if placing a wreath at a headstone.

"I'm okay," Adele murmurs.

"Does your stomach hurt?" asks Nash. "Or your ribs? I might have done some damage. You're as white as a ghost."

"She seems to be fine," says the maître d'. "Absolutely I'd say so."

"Maybe you should be checked out," says Richard.

"No," says Adele.

"Not now. At some point . . ." says Nash.

"Should I call Kathleen at work?" asks Richard. "She'll kill me if I don't. I know she'd want to come home early."

The suggestion annoys Adele, and thereby restores her: "What the hell will Kathleen do? Besides bawl all over her silk underwear?"

Nash is also revived. Kathleen? he wonders. Which one is Kathleen?

Six

Richard drives, and Nash sits in the back seat, trying to minister to Adele, who is having none of it. She leans against the window, as far away as she can slide from Nash, who reaches over paternally, and locks the door. "Don't want you falling out," he says with a wink.

"Of all the hotels in Boston . . . ?" She closes her eyes. "On one hand it's unbelievable. On the other hand, classic."

"What happened to the Holiday Inn, by the way?" asks Richard.

Nash considers where he'd like to lead this conversation, and chooses unwisely. "Something drew me to the Copley Plaza. I know that now. On some unconscious level I must have wanted to go back and fix things."

"Please," says Adele. "Whom do you think you're talking to?"

Nash says to Richard, "I understand how she feels. I really do. A Heimlich maneuver can only fix so much."

"She's tough," says Richard. "Probably the toughest."

"Of the girls, you mean?"

"*Women,*" Adele snaps.

Nash settles back, belatedly buckles his seat belt, and sighs. "How about you?" he asks Richard. "What are you up to these days?"

"I work for the Sheriff's Department," he says. "Suffolk County."

"He delivers subpoenas," Adele says, in a tone that tells Richard she resents his easy conspiracy with the enemy.

"No kidding? Full-time?"

"Lots of cases, and lots of asshole witnesses out there," he says.

"How does someone get into that line of work?"

"By accident."

Adele clicks her tongue in annoyance.

"What?" says Richard. "Am I being too nice to him? Maybe a little too grateful for saving my sister's life?"

Nash asks humbly, "Is my going back to the house out of the question?"

"You *are* going back to the house," says Richard.

"No, he's not."

"Ever see anyone bounce back from death as fast as this one?" asks Richard.

"I'm in pain," says Adele. "I'm in no mood to be teased."

"What kind of pain?" asks Nash.

"Are you having trouble breathing?" says Richard.

Adele is looking out the window, refusing to answer. She touches her midsection and Nash notices.

"It's sore?"

She nods.

"Sore like it's bruised from the punching, or like I broke something?"

Adele shrugs.

Richard asks what she said.

Adele snaps, "Just sore. I'm not a doctor."

"We'll call him when we get home. Maybe he should see you."

Adele is feeling under her ribs. Something hurts, but she doesn't speculate aloud on what. "I should go back to work," she says.

⌐ The X-ray shows a broken rib, which the doctor says can, on the rare occasion, result from a misapplied Heimlich. But still, he points out, Adele is a lucky woman. Go home and have a glass of wine and count your blessings; if you cough or sneeze, splint your side with your hand.

Richard and Nash are waiting in molded blue chairs, sharing a package of peanut-butter crackers. Nash spots her first.

"I'm fine," says Adele. "One broken rib—an 'undisplaced fracture.' "

"Did I do that?" asks Nash.

"A small price to pay," says Richard.

"Does it hurt like hell?" asks Nash.

Richard says, "Only when she laughs."

Nash says, "I want to pay any and all of your medical bills."

"That's ridiculous. I have insurance. Besides, they don't do anything for a broken rib. It heals itself."

Richard says, "He saved your life today. Maybe *you* can't say thank you, but I can."

Adele says without expression, "Thank you for saving my life. My brother is very grateful." She turns to Richard. "Where did you park?"

He points out the plate-glass window to a cylindrical garage and says he'll bring the car around.

"Don't be ridiculous. I'm not an invalid."

Nash asks Richard, "Don't you have to work? Don't you have subpoenas to deliver?"

Richard says, "Yes, but—"

"We'll take a taxi," says Nash. "If that's okay with your sister."

"It won't be," says Richard.

Adele sits on an adjacent green chair, wincing. "I have no say in anything, apparently. You two work it out. I just want to go home and forget this ever happened."

"At least she's given up the return-to-work crusade," says Richard.

"I have to call them," says Adele. "They'll think I fell under a train."

"I'll call," says Richard.

"And say what?"

Richard knows what she'd like him to say: *I came down with something at lunch. I had to go to the emergency room.* "It's best to tell them exactly what happened," he says. "They're your friends. They should know you almost choked to death, and now you have a broken rib, in case someone wants to wrap you in a bear hug when you get back."

"Unlikely."

"Near-death experiences," Nash says solemnly, "are the kinds of things that can change a person's whole outlook. People leave jobs, marriages, go start new cults. Books have been written on such topics."

"Whole hours on *Larry King Live* have been devoted to such survival stories," says her brother.

Adele says, "I don't find either of you remotely funny."

⌒ Nash is skilled at reducing chapters of his history to short paragraphs. "Her name was Dina," he narrates on the short taxi ride back to the Dobbin apartment. "We stayed together much longer than was good for either one of us."

"Then what?" asks Adele.

"That's it. There's no more to tell."

"I meant, Did you get your own place? Did you move onto a friend's couch? Did she?"

"Oh, you mean real estate. Of course I let Dina have the house. She's what they call a reflexologist—she massages feet for a living—and she has an office there, and a big table. Also, she wouldn't have to change her phone number or get new cards printed up."

Adele leans forward, holding her side and a five-dollar bill, to tell the driver that it's the apartment building with the slate face, just ahead on the left.

"I'll take you up," says Nash. "I promised Richard." He rushes around to her side, opens her door, and extends his hand. Adele ignores it. He takes her elbow just the same.

She says, "If it appears to you that I'm being hospitable, I'm not. I'm waiting to hear the rest of your life's story, and since you haven't told me one damn thing that explains why you ran away and why you came back, I figure this might be an opportunity to interrogate you."

"I welcome it," says Nash.

"I expect my sisters will turn up before long. I'd like you to be gone by then."

"Of course," says Nash.

"You have a way of charming people," says Adele. "I seem to be the only one immune to it, but I don't think my sisters will be. If you're here when Kathleen comes home, she'll be weepy with gratitude and invite you to dinner."

He hesitates, letting Adele walk onto the elevator first, then says wryly, "Which would never do."

"I agree."

"Even though I haven't eaten all day."

Adele says, "Third floor."

Nash asks where these sisters work.

"Lois works for the state, and Kathleen owns a shop downtown."

"One at a time. What does Lois do at the State House?"

"Not actually at the State House. She works for D.E.S."

"Which is?"

"Division of Employment Security—'Unemployment' in the vernacular."

"And what kind of a shop does Kathleen own?"

"Lingerie. High end."

Nash conjures crude images of low-end lingerie, but doesn't share them with Adele. "Does she enjoy that line of work?" he asks.

Adele ignores the question, which sounds insincere to her, and suggestive. When the doors open, she leaves the elevator as purposefully as her sore midsection allows. Nash follows her to the end of the hallway. He can hear the phone ringing, but it doesn't seem to incite any urgency in Adele. Nor does she rush for the phone when they get inside.

"Is your machine on?" he asks.

"We don't have one."

Nash doesn't know anyone without an answering machine. He asks how people living together—women, he means, single women who need to know which men called—get by without an answering machine.

"People know we're at work during the day, so they call when we're home." He is standing in the foyer, waiting to be invited deeper into the apartment. He asks, "How long have you lived here?"

"Four years." She doesn't volunteer the circumstances: We kept the house after our parents died, but sold it when Lois married, thinking it was just Kathleen and I.

"It reminds me of your house," he says.

"All the furniture is from Dean Road. We didn't buy one thing." He follows when she walks through one predominantly blue parlor into a second rose-colored parlor, which leads into a green-flowered dining room, and finally a yellow kitchen.

"Nice place," says Nash.

"It's not very interesting," says Adele, who has opened the refrigerator door and is staring inside.

"Can I help?"

Adele says, "Help how? I'm not making you lunch."

"No," says Nash. "Of course not."

She takes a carton of brown eggs from a shelf, and says, "Here. You be the chef. Scramble yourself some whites."

Nash doesn't know how to cook, let alone get the whites out of an egg. "Got anything else?" he asks.

"Look for yourself. Take whatever appeals to you."

"Where are you going?"

"To change into something loose," she says, but without a trace of the usual innuendo Nash associates with the phrase.

"Could I run you a hot bath?"

"I run my own baths," she says.

Nash takes an apple from a fruit bowl on the kitchen table and bites into it.

"They're not washed," she says.

"If you're lucky," he says, raising his eyebrows, "I might get poisoned."

Adele doesn't answer. She rearranges a few bottles in the refrigerator, exposing a covered earthenware casserole. "Here—last night's leftovers," she says. "We had some kind of veal. Kathleen always makes too much."

"Really?" he asks. "I wouldn't be taking someone's dinner?"

"So what? She'll be honored. Put what you want in the microwave. Plates are in the cupboard over the dishwasher."

He slides the casserole from the shelf, compliments its Japanese glaze, takes its lid off, and smiles happily at the congealed, monochromatic lumps of meat and potatoes. "Looks fabulous," he says.

Adele says, "It's not. We gave it a B-minus, which means we won't see it again."

Nash seizes on this conversational gambit. "B-minus," he repeats. "You mean, a grade?"

"We grade new recipes—Kathleen insists—and she only introduces it into her repertoire if it gets an A."

"Fascinating."

"No, it isn't. It's mildly interesting. We find it endearing because it's so Kathleen."

"Is she the only one who cooks?"

"I can cook, but I don't like to, and Lois is hopeless, except for one pot roast made with dehydrated onion soup."

Nash has been holding the casserole by its two handles. "Can I zap this?" he asks.

"I think so."

He doesn't move. Adele says, "I'm going to change. Just put it in and give it a couple of minutes." When he doesn't move, she opens the microwave door. Nash puts the casserole inside, and Adele hits "4-0-0" and "start."

"I appreciate it," he says.

"You might want to rotate it halfway through the cooking."

"You're very kind," he says.

Adele says, "I certainly don't mean to be."

Nash laughs.

"Richard would be appalled if I didn't feed you."

Nash tries a half smile. "I think it's an old Indian custom—feeding the person who saved your life."

Adele takes an oval straw place mat and a sunflower cloth napkin from a kitchen drawer, and sets one place.

Nash tries again. "Not that someone else in the room wouldn't have known the Heimlich maneuver. You were probably never in any real danger of dying unattended."

"I wonder," Adele murmurs.

Nash says, sensing an opportunity, "What *I* wonder is what exactly made me come back at this exact moment in time? I mean, all these years, and suddenly I have to come back to Boston. Do you believe in stuff like that—fate or karma or some larger force moving us around on a big board?"

"I find that kind of thinking idiotic," says Adele. She raises her voice. "Was it some larger force that made you run away and humiliate me all those years ago? Was it karma that made me choke on a piece of steak today? In front of you, of all people?" To Adele's horror, her voice cracks. "I hate you," she says. "I always have and I'm not going to stop now."

" 'Always'?" he repeats. "You agreed to marry someone you hated? That can't be true."

"I can't remember ever feeling"—she considers employing the word *love,* but can't in front of him—"anything but hate."

Nash shakes his head throughout her speech, then says woefully, "You loved me."

"If I did, I stopped in one night, and every single member of my family feels the same way."

"You loved me," he repeats.

The microwave beeps. Neither moves toward it. Nash thinks, This is hard; harder than usual. In most cases, such anger can be soothed by holding the subject in his arms until she gives up the fight. But Adele looks icy, not disposed to thawing, and has a broken rib. Besides, under fluorescent light, without lipstick, she looks her age. "Do you want me to leave?" he asks.

She nods.

"Love and hate," he muses. "It sounds a little childish, doesn't it? To be using such extremes about something that happened a lifetime ago?"

"Get out," says Adele. "Take the whole goddamn thing with you. I hope you choke on it. And I hope no one's around who knows the Heimlich maneuver."

He accepts the casserole dish and walks past her to the front door, looking wounded but dignified like the better man he has become over the intervening thirty years. The earthenware casserole is a nice prop, he thinks: He will have to return it, and Adele will have to explain to her outraged sisters why it's gone.

⟳ Kathleen sees a stranger in her vestibule holding a glazed casserole identical to the one she bought at a seconds sale in

Woodstock, Vermont. Her first thought is, I have a pot like that. But as soon as the glass door between them opens, she smells Veal Marengo.

"Excuse me?" she asks. "Where are you going with that?"

Nash recognizes immediately what has happened: The sister with the soft heart and the lingerie shop has been summoned, and has rushed home to tend to Adele.

"I feel so foolish," he says. He puts the casserole on the floor at her feet and puts out his hand. "I'm Nash Harvey," he says. "You don't have to tell me who you are."

"Kathleen—"

"The baby," he says.

"Where are you going with my dish?"

Nash says, "I'm not stealing it. I was going to return it as soon as I thought Adele would let me."

"Is she okay?"

"She has a broken rib."

"I know. Richard told me."

"So he told you about the choking in the restaurant?"

Kathleen presses her hand to her chest, and swallows. "I can't believe it. She could have *died*."

If you weren't there, Nash silently prompts. *If you hadn't come to the rescue.*

"I can't believe Richard went back to work," says this sister.

"I insisted."

She stoops over to get the casserole, but straightens up to say, " 'Insisted'? What gives you the right to insist on anything having to do with my family?"

This sister has a heart-shaped face, and no gray in her red hair. "I'm sorry. I hadn't eaten anything all day. Adele heated it up for me. She asked me to leave so she could get more comfortable, but said I should take this."

"It seems funny she would have given you my casserole dish instead of Tupperware."

"I'll return it, washed, of course." He waits a few beats then says, "Kathleen, you do realize who I am?"

"Of course I do."

"The Harvey who used to go out with Adele? Because I haven't seen you since you were a little girl."

Kathleen repeats scornfully, " 'Used to go out with Adele'? I wasn't *that* little. I was sixteen. I was there that night. And I was old enough to take her home and put her to bed."

"Of course you were," he says. "Which makes it all the more astonishing when I look at you right now."

Kathleen stares, waits.

He smiles. "Well, if my math is right, and if you'll allow me, your driver's license must say forty-five, but your face says thirty."

She hears her own voice say faintly, "I'm forty-six."

"And I understand you're in ladies' . . . apparel. Adele told me. I'd love to see your shop while I'm in town."

Later Kathleen will say it happened like a crime of passion, without premeditation. She won't be able to pinpoint which inflection, which inch of his face infuriated her—or what made her raise her arms and bring the veal-filled casserole down on his astonished head.

Seven

Nash is not knocked out by Kathleen's assault, but does recognize, as soon as he hits the tile floor, the possible advantages of playing near-dead. The casserole lies broken in jagged pieces, its contents smelling of onions, splattered on his pinpoint-check jacket. He slumps against the door, affecting what he hopes is the slack jaw of a man seeing stars. His head genuinely hurts from a sharp, localized pain, as if he'd walked into the corner of a cabinet door, and he thinks there may be blood mingling with the gravy on his face.

Kathleen is whimpering, a stream of *Oh no*s and *Oh my God*s. Nash can tell she is coming closer, about to do something caring and diagnostic, kneeling without regard to the glop under her knees. A good actor, he doesn't flinch when she slides her fingers onto his carotid artery. "Oh, Christ," she murmurs. She repositions her fingertips and says more urgently, "Oh, shit." Nash feels a poke in the shoulder with a finger that has a sharp fingernail. He flutters his eyelids once, twice, but leaves them closed.

"Harvey!" she shouts like a cop trying to rouse a drunk. "Harvey?"

He thinks he shouldn't answer any too soon. He hears her high heels click on the tile, then the buzzer sounding a long blast. He opens his eyes a few millimeters. He can see up Kathleen's skirt to the hem of something black and lacy. Adele's voice answers after what seems like a full minute.

"Yes?" she says crisply.

"Can you come down?"

"Why?"

"Harvey! I hit him and I knocked him out."

It sounds to Nash as if there is a laugh traveling through the intercom, but he can't be sure.

"Dell! Please! It's no joke. He's out cold."

"You *hit* him?"

"Not with my fist. With the pot. Bring some paper towels."

Kathleen must have released the button because she is returning to his side. Plenty of time, he thinks, to come to.

"Harvey!" she yells again. "Can you hear me?" The toe of her shoe prods his outer thigh. He doesn't react. She takes his hand and feels the inside of his wrist. "Good," she murmurs after a few seconds. "Good." She smells nice, he thinks. Something floral and powdery. Dina wears perfumes and emollients extracted from vegetables and seaweed. Kathleen pats the dry side of his face, tentatively at first, then with increasingly harder slaps. He murmurs so she'll stop.

He hears the elevator whirring and a bell dinging.

"Here!" yells Kathleen.

Nash doesn't open his eyes, and can't hear footsteps. He allows one flutter to assess the situation: It is Adele in a navy blue fleece bathrobe and crew socks, her hands on her hips, staring down at him.

"He's certainly not dead," she says.

"He won't wake up," says Kathleen. "Maybe we should lie him down flat."

"You're not supposed to move someone who's been injured," says Adele.

"Are you okay?" Kathleen asks her sister, annoying Nash with her misplaced tenderness.

"I choked on a piece of steak, and broke a rib. He broke it doing the Heimlich maneuver."

Nash groans.

"Harvey?" says Kathleen.

"Nash?" Adele says more sternly. She asks Kathleen if the pot broke in the act or when it hit the floor.

"Both. I think the pot broke on him, and the lid broke when it hit the floor."

"I meant, did it cut him? I don't see any blood."

Disappointed, Nash moans.

"Do we have smelling salts?" asks Kathleen.

"Smelling salts? Who has smelling salts?"

"He might have broken his neck. He looks a little off-center."

"How did he fall?"

"He just crumpled."

"Did he hit his head?"

"He just sort of sat down."

Adele says in a louder voice than before, "There's no question we need an ambulance. He'll need to be seen by a doctor and get a spinal tap. Don't touch him. I'll call nine-one-one."

Nash stirs. He blinks hard a few times, works his jaw in a circle and says, "Whaah happen?"

"You got conked with a casserole," says Adele.

Kathleen asks, "Can you touch your chin to your chest?"

Nash blinks again, then slowly lowers his chin.

"Good," says Kathleen.

"Can you move your legs?" asks Adele.

Nash lifts one leg at a time, an inch off the floor.

"What about your arms?"

"He's fine," Adele snaps. "If the legs work, the rest will."

"Do you think you could get up if we helped you?" asks Kathleen.

"Maybe," he whispers, staring hard as if he's not sure who these Good Samaritans are.

"Where does it hurt?" asks Adele.

He touches the spot on his head where it really does hurt, and feels, to his relief, a bump the size of a new potato. "Oww. I've got a doozy."

"You're not bleeding," says Adele. "See if you can get up on your feet."

Kathleen takes an elbow. Adele says, "I certainly can't help."

"Give me a sec," says Nash.

"If you can't get up, we have to call an ambulance," says Adele.

"What's their name?" says Kathleen. "The doctors? The couple? I can ring their apartment."

"I don't need a doctor," says Nash.

"They won't be home in the middle of the afternoon anyway," says Adele.

"I think I may be able to get up now," he says. "As long as I can use you for balance."

Nash rolls over to his knees and slowly rises to his feet. Uninvited, he puts one arm around each woman's shoulders. Kathleen slides her arm around his waist but Adele slips out from his clutch. "I have a broken rib, remember?"

"Let's try to walk," says Kathleen. "One step at a time."

"Which way?" Nash asks.

The sisters exchange looks.

"I think we have no choice," says Kathleen. "Even if he just stays for an hour. And then if he's steady, we'll call a cab."

"I don't think I have a concussion," Nash offers.

"You should go to the emergency room if there's even a possibility of that," says Adele.

"I think a bump is a sign that it's not a concussion," says Kathleen.

Adele says, "I forgot the paper towels."

"I'll do that," says Kathleen. "We'll clean him off, and I'll come back down with a mop and pail. You're in no condition to be washing floors."

"Besides," says Adele, "I couldn't look at these chunks of meat."

"Poor Dell," says Kathleen. "I'm sorry, hon. You'll take a nap, too, while I clean up. Do you want Lois to come home?"

Nash fingers his bump, and produces a sharp intake of breath. He expects an echo—a "Poor Nash," or, more likely, a "Poor Harvey."

"We have ice," says Adele.

"I don't know what possessed me," says Kathleen.

⟶ There is a diagonal welt on his cheekbone, which Kathleen recognizes as an imprint of the casserole's bamboo-inspired handle. Not that she is fussing over him. While Adele rests behind a closed door and waits for a Valium to kick in, Nash is ordered to a kitchen chair, given tea, raisin toast, and ice cubes wrapped in a facecloth. Kathleen works on his stained jacket with lighter fluid and a rag. She looks up at him, and says, after a diagnostic stare, "Does your eye hurt?"

"Why?"

"It looks . . . there's a little half-circle of purple—here." She touches the corresponding skin under her own eye. "Not big. A thumbprint."

"I have a black eye?" Nash asks, enchanted with the development.

"It seems so."

Nash touches his face, and pronounces it tender. He says, "In the movies they put a steak on a shiner, but we know *that* doesn't work any miracles."

Kathleen doesn't smile.

"The veal," he explains.

Kathleen shakes out his jacket, then places it on the back of an empty chair without comment.

"Under the circumstances," Nash tries, "most people would apologize for assaulting another human being without provocation."

Kathleen says, "My position is that I was provoked."

"You're lucky you didn't kill me: 'Your honor, he paid me a compliment; said I looked thirty. What choice did I have?' "

"I wouldn't take the stand," says Kathleen.

Nash says, "Aren't you being a little childish? I saved your sister's life, and now I can't even get a modicum of sympathy from the person who knocked me senseless."

Kathleen says, "Okay: I'm sorry I hit you with the casserole."

Nash tries to look aggrieved as he sips tea from his clear glass mug.

Kathleen says, "It was my favorite pot. Dishwasher-safe and ovenproof."

Nash inspects Kathleen's expression for signs of irony, but doesn't find any. Instead he thinks, Why haven't I noticed her eyes until now—pale green with a ring of pure yellow at the outer edges.

She says, "If I'd been the one who answered the doorbell last night, I'd have told you to get the hell off my property and never come back. And if I had been Richard, I would've knocked your block off."

"You did knock my block off," he says. "My block is throbbing, and probably bleeding internally, and now I have a black eye."

Kathleen sighs, and asks if he'd like some Tylenol.

"I'm feeling a little dizzy. Do you think it's okay to take something if I'm light-headed?"

Kathleen takes the facecloth, rewraps it around new ice, and repositions it on his sore lump. When he smiles gratefully, she doesn't scowl.

Now? he wonders. *Now* can I comment on the color of her eyes? Sea foam? Spring grass? Lemon and lime cat's-eye marbles?

"Aspirin, no," she says, "but Tylenol's probably okay."

Nash takes two red-and-yellow capsules from the bottle she's set in front of him, and swallows them with a gulp of tea. "I remember once when I was a kid and I got hit in the head by a pitch, and the doctor told my mother to keep me awake."

"So?"

"Which is why the thought of spending the night in a hotel scares me."

"You're afraid you'll slip into a coma?"

Nash shrugs. "I suppose I could ask the desk to call upstairs every ten minutes."

After an unhappy pause Kathleen says, "I could ask Richard."

"Ask Richard what?"

"If you could stay at his place."

"Isn't there a trial separation going on?" asks Nash. "Or did I get that wrong?" He puts down the ice pack and explores his bump as gingerly as if it were a newborn's fontanel. He bites his lip—the pain and the indignity of it. "If my folks were alive, I'd stay there," he says.

Kathleen sits down opposite him. "Why come back now? Why

not the morning after you ran away? Or when you turned thirty. Or forty, or *fifty*?" Kathleen leans across the table, forcing Nash to notice that she has a young woman's breasts—not large but high and alert.

"I felt this pull," he says. "I was asking myself, 'Why can't I get it right with any woman? Why do I keep moving on instead of settling down?' And slowly the answer dawned on me: Adele Dobbin." Nash is pleased with his answer, and with what he hopes is the weight of it.

"Tell me what you want from her," says Kathleen.

Nash can't say what he wants from Adele because he has again moved on, fixing Kathleen's heart-shaped face and yellow-green eyes in his field. Luckily, the front door opens. Someone new, someone requiring Kathleen's attention, steps inside.

"Richard?" Kathleen calls.

"No," says a woman's voice, coming toward them, heels clicking. "It's me."

It's a new sister to Nash, the tallest and most formidable one, broad-shouldered and rangy, with a barrette in her pageboy.

Kathleen says, "Shhh. You'll wake Adele. Lois—this is Harvey Nash."

"Harvey," she breathes.

Nash stands up, switches his ice pack to his left hand, and offers his right. "Lois," he says. "Long time."

"Harvey did the Heimlich maneuver on Adele," Kathleen explains.

"I heard," says Lois. "Richard said it happened so fast that he didn't even know she was choking. Thank you *so* much. We're so grateful." And with that she throws her long arms around Nash's neck.

Nash says happily, "Watch my injury!"

"Where?" she cries. "What happened?"

Nash gestures, palm upturned, toward Kathleen, who says flatly, "Nash was leaving the apartment and I was coming in. He said some things, and I flew off the handle, and I whacked him with the casserole we got in Woodstock."

"Tell me you didn't," says Lois.

"I did."

"After what he did to Adele?"

"Exactly," says Kathleen.

"I meant after he saved her life? What's wrong with you?"

Nash smiles. This one has presence, he thinks. She doesn't have Kathleen's femininity or Adele's looks, but there's empathy here and some kind of good strong . . . something.

"I am *appalled,*" says Lois. "What were you thinking of?"

"I wasn't thinking. It was pure adrenaline."

"Don't be mad at Kathleen," says Nash. "She had her reasons. I deeply regret the pain I've caused this family."

Lois says, "You saved my sister's life! She'd be dead now if it weren't for you. What kind of family holds on to a grudge after that?"

Finally, Nash thinks—a Dobbin sister who knows how to accept an apology.

"He says he has to lie down," says Kathleen. "He's feeling dizzy."

Nash notices that Lois has slashes of too obvious color on her cheekbones, and eyebrows redrawn with auburn pencil. As a student of the sisters, of the various shades of their red hair and their various endowments, he finds Lois a bit . . . well, hard. But then again, "hard" carries its own possibilities: a divorcée in the old-fashioned sense of the word, his mother's quaint bias—single and sullied through every fault of her own.

"Follow me," Lois orders.

"He wants to spend the night," says Kathleen.

"He can have my room," says Lois.

"Lois—" says Kathleen.

"What? Are you going to remind me that he ruined Adele's life, therefore we have to make his as difficult as possible?"

Kathleen purses her lips into a tight "No."

"Are we eating in?" asks Lois.

"I haven't given it a second's thought."

"You rest," Lois says to Nash, "and we'll wake you for dinner. We'll get Chinese food. Do you like Chinese?"

"Yes, I do," says Nash. "Although I'll understand if you want it to be sisters only, a family dinner. A celebration of life. I'd be happy with a tray in my room."

"Don't be silly," says Lois. "Richard will be back and he'll want a report."

Kathleen shakes her head. "Harvey Nash. In our house. At our table."

"May I use your phone?" he asks.

Eight

Senior Deputy Sheriff Dobbin has spent the second part of his afternoon trying to serve divorce papers to a psychiatrist who is never home and who has no receptionist at work. He waits in a hallway outside her modest office, through two cycles of patients: a college-age student, female, kohl-eyed and hostile, then what appears to be a bag lady, who leaves with several waiting-room magazines.

Richard politely asks a wire-rimmed young man in a suit and ponytail—the doctor's four o'clock—to tell her she has an official visitor from the Commonwealth. The patient looks suspicious, then annoyed: It's his fifty minutes with Dr. Hornick, so fuck off, pal.

As the ponytailed four o'clock leaves, Richard slips into the beige waiting room. At five past five, he calls out, "Hello?" and gets no response. At eight past five, a plain woman with lank brown hair, parted in the middle, comes out carrying a briefcase and a lumbar-support pillow.

"Dr. Deborah Hornick?" Richard asks with a pleasant smile.

She hesitates—a strange man in her waiting room, after all. But she has done enough psych rotations in jails and hospitals to feel that this rather dashing man in the camel-hair overcoat and leather watch strap is no threat; is merely a new detail man, possibly a regional manager for Burroughs or Pfizer.

"And you're . . . ?"

"Senior Deputy Sheriff Dobbin. Are you Dr. Deborah Hornick?"

"Yes," she says, frowning after a long pause.

Richard reaches inside his overcoat and brings forth folded documents.

"No!" she says, stepping away. "I'm not taking those."

"Take them," he says. "You've been served. Even if I drop them at your feet, you've been due-delivered."

"I'm refusing them," she says.

"Which is pointless."

The doctor stamps her foot. "I'm not giving him the Wellfleet house. He thinks it's his because he bought it before we were married."

"Which has nothing to do with when you take these papers." He leaves them on the coffee table and moves toward the door before stating—his standard advice to those who argue their case before him—"I'd get myself an excellent divorce attorney, and I'd be sure I showed up in court."

Now Dr. Hornick takes the papers with a purpose, and that is to shake them in Richard's face. "This is what you do? Ambush people in their private offices without their permission?"

"I left you messages," he says evenly. "You could have called me back. If you had said, 'I leave for work at six forty-five A.M.,' I'd have been at your house at six-thirty, at your convenience. That's what I do."

"Sneak up on people?"

"If necessary," he says. "And most people are a lot less gracious than I am."

The doctor's voice turns even shriller. "Do you get pleasure from this? Does it make you feel important, like a private eye?"

Richard says, "What're you so angry at me for?" He stops, smiles at the prospect of what he'll say next. "Isn't this what the psychology books call displacement?"

Dr. Hornick opens her mouth, but is momentarily silenced.

"You're a psychologist, right?" he continues.

"Psychiatrist—"

"Same thing. You should be a little nicer to people, Doc, especially complete strangers who are just doing their jobs. There are a lot of nut cases out there, and one of them might want to run a key along your paint job while you're inside helping your patients feel better about themselves."

Dr. Hornick says, "Fuck you."

"Mark your calendar," says Richard. He reaches over and gives the papers a little pinch and shake as if they were the cheek of an adorable baby.

⌐ Imperturbable Deputy Sheriff Dobbin is furious—*furi-ous*—with Kathleen over her assault on Nash.

"You're like a punk who can't control himself," he yells. "You acted like a thug. Like a crazy woman. Like a crackpot. Literally."

"*Okay*, Richard," says a weary Adele. "We get your point."

"Kathleen! Of all people. I don't get it. I do *not* get it."

"Why get hysterical? There's nothing you can do now, and she's not going to do it again."

Lois is sitting apart from her sisters and brother at a stool next to the phone, studying a take-out menu. "That's the same argument people make when a wife murders her husband," she observes. " 'She's no threat to society because he was the only one in danger.' "

"You keep out of this," says Adele. "You waltz in here without a clue to what calamities have occurred, you take sides, and appoint yourself the family spokesman: 'Stay for dinner, Harvey. I insist.' "

Kathleen is keeping silent, because she knows she is guilty as charged. Another thought bothers her and that is: How will I spin this tale for Lorenz on Monday? What version of today's assault will paint me as a reasonable and amiable woman, rather than one who throws things?

The phone rings, and it's for Adele. Richard gets up from the table and crankily takes his six-pack of beer from grocery bag to crowded refrigerator. Adele murmurs into the receiver that she is fine, and will be in on Monday.

"You're lucky," Richard starts in again when he sits down. "You're goddamn good and lucky that you didn't give him a concussion."

"Or kill him," says Lois.

"I know," says Kathleen. "We've been over this."

"Don't you have any impulse control?" asks Lois.

"Apparently not."

"I'd expect this from the other two," says Richard. "But you? It's like hearing that Gandhi threw a punch."

"It's beyond ridiculous," says Lois.

"I must have had my reasons," says Kathleen, "even if I can't explain what they were right now."

Richard lowers his voice to a whisper. "Seriously. I don't know what we're dealing with here, temperamentally. He could be lying on Lois's bed right now planning his lawsuit."

Kathleen shakes her head with conviction.

"You don't think so? You don't think I've seen every cocka-mamie suit filed against another person that could possibly be dreamed up? A guy who sits on a wad of gum in the Fleet Center and sues for damages?"

"I know that's what you see on a daily basis," says Kathleen, "but it wouldn't be the case here."

"Because?"

"Because—" She checks behind her before answering. "Harvey wants to ingratiate himself with us, and he isn't about to have me arrested."

Adele is off the phone, announcing that that was Marty Glazer from Legal calling. Kathleen asks if she's mentioned him before, and Adele says, "No."

Richard says, "Another admirer?"

Adele snaps, "His secretary happened to be in Development when you called, so she told him about the incident."

"See," says Richard, finally smiling. "Legal: an ambulance chaser. He probably heard 'Maison Robert' and thought, 'Hmmm. Maybe we can turn this into a corporate sponsorship. Or, at the very least, get them to send some croissants over during the fund drive to feed the volunteers.'"

"Not Marty," says Adele. "He's a mouse."

"It was nice of him to call," says Kathleen.

"Were you civil?" asks Richard.

Lois is disappointed. She'd been enjoying Richard's display of temper, and doesn't want the conversation to slide back to good-natured brotherly chatter. "Do you think he's in any danger?" she asks.

"I doubt it," says Kathleen.

Adele says, "Perhaps you should go in there and lay your hand on his brow?"

"Or just lie down next to him," says Kathleen, "so you'll be the first thing he sees when he opens his black eye."

Lois rustles the menu and ignores her sisters. Richard returns to the refrigerator and takes one of his beers. "Anyone else?" he asks. Adele says, "Me."

Kathleen says, "Me, too."

Lois is ignoring everything but the take-out menu from Sze-chwan City Limits. "How many dishes?" she asks.

"I'm not hungry," says Adele.

"Don't go overboard," says Kathleen.

"Go overboard," says Richard. "I'll take the leftovers."

"I'm wondering if we should get Peking duck, since there's five of us," says Lois.

"In celebration of the return of Harvey Nash?" Adele asks.

Lois turns to Richard for the appropriate riposte, but gets only a shrug and a view of the base of his brown beer bottle. "I'm calling it in now," she says.

A door opens down the hall. Adele, Kathleen, and Richard sit up straighter. For a minute, they hear only Lois, in loud, patronizing syllables, articulating her choices into the telephone.

Nash walks into the kitchen. The black half-circle under his eye is turning colors, and the welt on his cheekbone is weeping.

"Ladies," says Nash, nodding formally. "Richard." It is the first time he is viewing all three sisters together, and though he wants to weigh them against one another—to rate hair and freckled skin and three distinct bustlines on the same scorecard—he resists.

"Heard you had a little brush with the ferocious Kathleen," says Richard.

Nash smiles charitably, the bad eye swollen out of alignment. "We've all done silly things in the heat of the moment that we regret."

"You look like hell," says Adele.

"And you'll be sure we get the pancakes and the plum sauce?" Lois barks into the phone.

Richard points with his beer bottle. "Did you put ice on it?"

"Your sister did."

Lois greets Nash, then asks brightly, "Who's picking up the food?"

Richard says, "I just got home."

"Don't they deliver?" asks Nash.

"Let's you and I go," says Adele to Kathleen. "I could use some fresh air."

Nash says, "If you'll permit me, I'd very much like this to be my treat."

"Forget it," says Richard.

Kathleen and Adele leave the kitchen with exaggerated dignity, chins held high like ballerinas playing soldiers.

Nash points to a vacated chair. Richard says, "Sure. Sit. She feels pretty bad. And it's so unlike Kathleen—"

"Why are you speaking for Kathleen?" asks Lois. "She should be saying this, not you."

Richard wants to say, "Shut up, Lois," but says only, "Lo? You weren't there today when Adele almost choked to death."

"That's exactly—"

"And you weren't there when I called Kathleen to tell her what happened at the restaurant. You didn't hear her weeping into the phone."

Nash produces a small gag of physical or emotional distress. "I envy you," he explains.

"You do?" asks Richard. He slides Kathleen's untouched bottle in front of Nash.

"A big family, still close. Lots of siblings."

"Sisters," corrects Richard. "*They* have siblings. I have sisters."

"How often do you get together like this?" asks Nash.

Richard smiles. "It depends on how much they like my current girlfriend."

Nash is all ears. "You mean their standards are a little high?" he asks.

"Higher than mine."

"He meets them on the job," says Lois.

"And that's not good?"

"Serving papers?"

Richard grins. "Perfectly nice people get served. Eighty percent of the population will at one time in their life come into contact with a deputy sheriff."

"Blah, blah, blah," says Lois.

Nash likes the sound of this outlaw dating pool. "Like who?" he asks.

"You mean, who gets served, or who have I ended up dating?"

"We like Leslie," says Lois.

"Leslie's a writer," says Richard. "She was being sued by an old boyfriend who claimed he was the model for the asshole husband in her novel."

"Is Leslie the woman you're currently . . . on hiatus with?"

"Correct."

"He says he doesn't flirt with them when he serves them," says Lois. "But there's no other explanation for why they call."

Richard raises his eyebrows. "*No* other explanation?"

Lois turns to Nash. "Would you ever think of calling up someone who served you papers, or notified you that there was a bench warrant for your arrest—"

"Wrong," says Richard. "I've never called or dated anyone I've served a bench warrant to."

"They call *him*," says Lois.

"I serve dozens every day. Most are debtors and lowlifes. Once in a great while I ring someone's doorbell, and they answer it, and we have a nice conversation, and I get a sense of what her situation is, and maybe she'll ask for my card."

Nash now recasts Richard's life as that of a dashing door-to-door salesman calling on housewives who are naked and perfumed under their dressing gowns. "Deputy sheriff," Nash muses. "I wouldn't have thought . . ."

"Richard could have gone to law school," says Lois. "He was accepted at Suffolk University."

"Nights," says Richard.

"You obviously like your work," says Nash, messy eyes shining over the imagined perks.

"It's interesting. And no two days are the same."

"Can you arrest people?"

"I can."

"He can get beeped in the middle of the night," says Lois.

House call, Nash thinks. Housewife. Housecoat. "For what?" he asks.

"Last time it was a custody case. I got a call from Florida—"

"When was this?" asks Lois.

Richard answers in shorthand: Florida Highway Patrol called Suffolk County. The father had custody. The mother took off for Boston with the kid. We got him back. Four years old.

"Wow," says Nash.

Lois asks if she can get anything. Peanuts? Crackers and cheese? Chips and dip?

"Not a thing," says Nash.

"All of the above," says Richard.

"So you had to find the kid and return him to Florida?" asks Nash.

"The father followed them up to the grandmother's, so we turned the kid over to him."

Lois smiles, and asks, "Do you visit Boston on a regular basis?"

"Unfortunately, I don't."

"Not since your folks died?"

"Longer than that. They'd come out to escape the winters." *For a week in January.*

"I'm certainly not going to spend many more winters here," says Lois.

"Since when?" asks Richard.

She turns to Nash. "Are you still writing for the movies?"

"Music," he says. "But more for television these days."

"That must be so interesting. And creative—to be surrounded by music all day."

"That part's true," says Nash.

"I love music," says Lois. "I don't know if you remember, but we all had piano lessons."

Nash says, "I noticed the Chickering. I wondered which one of you played."

"I'm the only one who stuck with it past junior high school. I'm not very good, but I love it."

"Which is the most important thing," says Nash.

Richard says, "Where are we eating?"

"Dining room," says Lois. "We'll need bowls and soup spoons."

"Do we have chopsticks?" he asks.

"No we don't," says Lois, as if it's further evidence of his annoying lifestyle. She turns to Nash. "Maybe you'll play for us later."

"How about now?" says Richard. "Unless you think you've been sidelined by Kathleen."

"That reminds me of a joke," says Nash. "A man asks his doctor—"

"Cloth napkins, please, Richard," says Lois. She turns to Nash. "I insist on having the piano tuned once a year." She stands and gestures toward the rooms beyond. Limping slightly, Nash follows her through the green dining room, into the rose-colored parlor, to the end of the needlepoint piano bench.

"Play something of yours," she says.

"No," he says. "I'd rather hear you."

Without further coaxing, Lois moves toward the center and tries the pedals. She arranges her pleated skirt once, twice, until her right hand grazes his trouser leg. "Let me see," she murmurs. "Do you want to hear popular or classical?" She shifts pages of sheet music. "Classical, am I right?"

"Of course," says Nash.

Lois returns her hands to her lap, then up again to the keyboard in a graceful arc, reminding Nash of his first spinster piano teacher—two dollars a lesson, by the forty-watt glow of a plastic candelabra. Lois's right hand begins tinkling out the opening notes of Mozart's "Turkish March," as her shoulders hunch with artistic endeavor.

"Ahhh," Nash murmurs.

He hates this piece. He doesn't notice that her lipstick has been refreshed while he napped, or that she's exchanged a velvet headband for her daytime barrette. He does notice a substantial diamond ring on her left hand, and nail polish on her fingernails, which are too long for the serious pursuit of piano. As she approaches the last notes on the first page, Nash reaches up to turn it. Lois smiles with the gratitude of someone who's been chronically unaccompanied and, without apparent talent, plays her heart out.

Nine

*B*yron Sprock thinks they should eat a therapeutic dinner and drink a restorative bottle of wine. "You could tell your girlfriends, 'After the two-car pileup—me entirely at fault—he treated me to dinner. Imagine. That's when I knew he was a prince.' "

Dina doesn't know how to respond to this campaign. She hasn't experienced anyone like Byron Sprock before—this utterly dry delivery of rather charming thoughts. It must be what people from New York are like, she thinks. Or maybe New York intellectuals. "I'm sure you *are* a prince," she says, "but it's been such a horrible day that I can't even think straight, let alone evaluate your character."

"Mine is spotless," he says. "And I can give you references."

Dina takes several sips from her teacup before answering. It occurs to her that Nash could walk through the door any minute and find what he deserves—the woman he spurned drinking green tea with a tall, distinguished, Obie-acclaimed stranger. "Ordinarily I'd have a comeback," she says finally, "and I might even call your bluff, but this has been the worst day of my life, so I'd just as soon not have supper and a drink with you."

"But?" he prompts.

"But nothing," says Dina. "I'm exhausted."

"Have you eaten?"

"I'll make something here."

"Such as?"

"I have things in the freezer."

Byron walks to her side-by-side refrigerator-freezer, and asks, as he opens the left-hand door, "Mind if I see if you're telling the truth?"

Dina, from her stool at the Formica island, lets him survey the frozen foods. "Lean Cuisine Fiesta Chicken," he says. "Cascadian Farm Organic Gardener's Blend. . . . Pot-stickers. I like those. . . . Nutri-Grain Waffles. . . . Look at this, will ya: 'Vegetarian Pad Thai.' *Très exotique.*"

Dina's never seen such conduct. It reminds her of something she can't pinpoint, until he catalogs a few more items: bagels, Birds Eye Sweet Peas and Pearl Onions, Five Alive. Then she remembers: As a little girl, she'd watch Art Linkletter rifling through an audience member's pocketbook, making everyone laugh as he brought forth the unexpected—an alarm clock, a tiara, a bottle of Wite-Out.

"You're funny," she says.

"I know."

"Without cracking a smile."

"It's charming, isn't it?"

She doesn't know and can't decide.

"What about eggs?" he says. "It always makes the romantic hero look tender and affectionate. Whipping up an omelet on stage works well because any feeb can break eggs into a bowl and use a whisk, and if you have any kind of run at all, he looks better and better each night."

Byron closes the freezer and opens the refrigerator. He checks the cheese and butter compartments and all four crispers. Paper towels line each empty drawer. After a moment he says, "Is this the usual state of things, or did you forget to go shopping?" He opens the freezer again and says, "How are Juice Only Fruit Bars?"

"Good," says Dina.

Byron helps himself to a bag each of chopped onion, chopped bell pepper, and broccoli spears. "Have any protein?" he asks.

Dina finds foil-wrapped portions marked "chick. patty," "chick. breast," "f. of sole."

Byron says, "Is this how you eat?"

"I eat salads," says Dina. "Rice cakes, bagels, fish, chicken."

"Do you cheat?"

Dina says, "Not with food."

"I hope when we do get out to a restaurant you don't do that thing that anorexic women do—push their food around on their plate instead of putting it in their mouth. Sometimes I stick my fork in whatever it is they're pushing around, and pop it in my mouth."

"You date a lot of anorexics?"

"Actresses in my plays," he says. "Same thing. Working lunches, though, not dates."

"I don't have an eating disorder," says Dina. "I just watch my fat grams."

Byron tosses the bags of frozen vegetables into the kitchen sink, and walks to a cupboard.

Dina asks what he's looking for.

"Oil."

"I have Pam," she says.

Instead Byron finds an unmarked plastic bottle with an inch of yellow liquid left. He sniffs it and says, "Stale."

"It's the best you're going to do."

He asks Dina for a big sauté pan, a wok would be even better, and could she zap those chicken portions, then hand them here? He'll approximate a stir-fry. Cutting board?

"This knife is pathetic," he says after a minute's work. He presses the minced onions and peppers into the sides of the oiled wok, then shakes it by the handle so that the morsels jump around impressively. "You must have garlic," he says. "Don't you people think it's imbued with healing properties or some such horseshit?"

" 'You people'?" Dina repeats.

"Californians," he says. "Granola eaters. Volleyball players."

"That's a little harsh," says Dina. "Especially for someone who's talking about a future together."

"I'm having second thoughts, though. It says a lot about a person when she shies away from food. I mean, as much as I'd like to stay here tonight, I'm not sure I want to sit down at a table and have a slice of dry toast tomorrow and call it breakfast."

Dina is startled. Which piece of this arrogance should she rebut? The "stay here tonight"? The character analysis? The breakfast menu?

"Only kidding, cookie," he says, stirring and flipping expertly. "The idea of sleeping over never entered my mind. I'd hate myself in the morning."

"So would I," says Dina.

"You have this face that begs to be teased. This born-yesterday quality which I find, quite frankly, irresistible."

"I don't think you can judge someone on the basis of one survey of her refrigerator," says Dina.

"You're absolutely correct. Or freezer." He points with his chin toward a cupboard. "See if you have soy sauce."

Dina locates a low-salt soy sauce that looks somewhat evaporated. "Give it here," says Byron, "then find me some cornstarch."

Dina doesn't even bother hunting for the cornstarch. She returns to her kitchen stool at the island and watches. Byron adds another splash of oil to the wok. He starts scrambling the stir-fry once again with confident turns of his wrist. "I'm going to need plates in a second," he says.

Dina supplies an oval platter painted with the head and skeleton of a fish.

"Two dinner plates are fine. I'll divvy it up."

"Where did you learn to cook?" she asks.

"In the poorhouse."

Dina's eyes widen.

"Not literally. I meant, playwrights don't have a lot of discretionary income to spend on dining out. Among other things."

"I would imagine," murmurs Dina.

Byron says, "I can see exactly what you're thinking: 'He's nice. He's not bad-looking in a geeky, valedictorian kind of way, but if he's penniless . . . no, thank you.' You looked crestfallen when I said 'not a lot of income.' "

"I did not."

"I disagree. An open book."

Dina says, "If my face fell it was because I thought that you were really in a poorhouse. As a kid or something."

Byron points his spatula at a snapshot on the refrigerator. "Speaking of faces, is that him?"

Dina says, "On Christmas."

"I'm guessing late fifties."

"Fifty-five," says Dina. "That's not a great picture."

"Handsome," says Byron. "If you like that older, matinee-idol kind of devastating good looks."

"How old are you?" she asks.

"Forty-one."

"You're almost bald."

"But look: no gray hairs. If I had a full head of hair I'd look twenty-five."

Dina smiles.

"How old are *you*?" he asks.

Dina says, "I usually lie."

"Don't lie," says Byron. "You're going to eat more, and you're not going to lie."

"I'm forty-two," says Dina.

"Excellent," he says. "Excellent truth-telling, and an excellent age."

"I'm older than you," she says.

"I'm more mature, though." He shuts off the burner with a snap. "And a much better driver."

"Aren't you going to tell me I look thirty-five?"

"I would, but I think that's what all the guys tell you."

Byron divides the stir-fry into unequal mounds on two blue plates. Dina pinches a taste from one and says—an experiment in how this willful contrariness feels from her own mouth—"This isn't so hot."

"I'm not a magician. You had no ginger and no spices. I didn't even ask for sesame oil."

Dina carries both plates to the dining room. Byron follows with the teacups, and switches the larger serving to her place. "Where were you headed tonight when I hit your car?" she asks.

"Nowhere. I heard the crash and came out to see what all the racket was."

"Whose house did you say it was?"

"A friend."

"A male friend?"

"A woman friend who used to be my roommate in New York, and her husband."

"An old girlfriend?"

"Actually not. Just a roommate."

"Are you gay?" Dina asks.

Byron says, "As it happens, I'm not, but I know exactly why you asked."

"I didn't think you were—"

"You were starting to add up the stereotypes: He's in the theater. He's forty-one and single. He lived with a woman but they were not romantically involved. Her husband is not threatened by him. He has a sardonic sense of humor. He has those pretty-boy good looks."

Dina says, "I guess that puts me in my place."

"Seriously. Would I be courting you if I were gay? Right under the nose of my friends? Your neighbors? Wouldn't they report me to my lover back in New York?"

"You could be married with a wife back in New York. People cheat all the time," says Dina.

"Like what's-his-name?"

"Nash."

"When does Mr. Nash come back?"

"He's not," says Dina.

"You know that already?"

"I'm almost positive."

Byron waits a few beats before asking, "Is that a heartbreaking thought?"

She shrugs.

"Is it another woman?"

"Yes and no. He went off to Boston to find some woman he used to be engaged to."

"When?"

"Ages ago. In his twenties."

"Otherwise, has he been faithful?"

Dina says, "Is that any of your business?"

"I'm a playwright," he says. "I need to know how the world works."

"We weren't married."

"And you think that's pertinent?"

Dina drones, "Unmarried means single. Single means not coming home occasionally."

"Is that what happened last night?"

"No," says Dina. "This is a breakup."

Byron says, nodding as if rendering a serious and thoughtful verdict. "Clearly, he's the wrong man for the job."

"Maybe."

"Too old and too randy."

Dina laughs.

"Whereas I'm young and true blue."

She smiles. "And full of shit."

"In a good way, right? You use 'full of shit' to mean 'silver-tongued' and 'expressive.' "

Dina hesitates. "You have an answer for everything."

"I do, but I'm not being glib. It's eloquence. If it were another century I'd be a great orator, debating and running for president."

"You could run for president in *this* century."

"No," he says. "I take my God-given talent and put it into monologues. Or dialogue."

"See," says Dina. "Yak, yak, yak."

Byron asks, "Will you take me around to see the sights of Orange County tomorrow?"

"Why?"

"To thank me for my Zen-like composure in the face of vehicular mayhem."

"You don't know me," she says. "This crap about loyalty and 'if we fall in love,' is just that—crap. I know a line when I hear one. Yours just happens to be one I never heard before, probably because I've never been to New York, and never seen one of your plays."

"How about Laguna?" he asks. "We could have dinner. Or lunch, if that suits you better."

"I have clients tomorrow," says Dina.

"When?"

"All morning."

Byron says, "Me too. Meetings."

"Then I have stuff to do in the afternoon."

"I'm sorry," he says, "but you can't give me the brush-off. I have a couple of more weeks left, and then they send me home. I have to forge a bond with you before I get on the plane."

"This is a bond," she says. "We've bonded."

"Dinner, then?"

Dina looks away, out the window, then back at Byron Sprock's freckled face and pink eyelashes. "I don't think so," she says.

"I'm basically irresistible," he tries, "but sometimes it requires an investment of time to detect it."

Dina says softly, "I don't understand why you're trying so hard."

Byron Sprock's East Coast heart contracts then expands. "I know you don't," he says.

"I'm fine. I've recovered from the shock of the accident."

He puts his fork down and pushes his plate away. "I'm serious now," he says.

Dina puts her fork down, too.

"Where I come from," he begins, "accidents are random. Ice melts, frost heaves, pavement becomes potholes. We have fender benders. We call the police and Triple A. In other words, our accidents have no subtext. But here, it may be something else. Chance. Fate. The gods. For example, what made me park in that exact spot, on this night? And what saved you from getting killed crossing four lanes so that you'd live to hit my driver's-side doors?"

Dina says, "I checked to see no one was coming in either direction, but I didn't expect anyone to be parked opposite the driveway."

He resumes eating, because Dina is looking more puzzled, and no more sympathetic, and scolds himself for indulging his own voice. Unless you're Shakespeare, he reminds himself, soliloquies rarely work.

Ten

*B*ecause she feels bad about declining whatever it is that Byron Sprock is offering, Dina sends him back across the street with a gift certificate for a half-hour reflexology session.

She consults her calendar, and says she doesn't usually see clients Saturday afternoon, but would make an exception. Say, one P.M.?

"And then I take you to lunch?"

"I'd love to," she lies, "but I can't."

Dina sees things slightly differently in the morning. She changes outfits between her last client and Byron, from her New Age clinician's look of a white lab coat over Mao pajamas to a short, stretchy skirt and jersey top that shows an inch of midriff. When Byron arrives on the dot of one, Dina explains the drill: foot bath, diagnostic stimulation to determine which organs or areas of the body are in a state of disorder, then the actual reflexology treatment, which she combines with aromatherapy. Does he have any particular aches or pains?

"In my feet?"

"No, anywhere. Back? Head? Gastrointestinal tract?"

"Why?"

Dina explains: He knows, doesn't he, that all organs, nerves, and glands are connected to certain reflex areas in the hands and feet?

"I certainly did *not* know that."

Dina tells him to look up there at her chart: Toes correspond to the head and brain, with his pituitary gland here. His sinus here. His gallbladder, kidneys, and transverse colon there. "I have patients I treat for migraines, for infertility, glaucoma, cataracts, neuritis, shingles, arthritis, sinus trouble . . ."

Byron asks where his private parts are on the chart.

Dina traces a line on his foot, between anklebone and heel.

"Wow," says Byron. "If only I'd known."

"Now you're going to hop up on the table, and lie down, supine. I want you to relax completely." Dina begins pinching and stroking and kneading his feet with the upper-body gusto of a varsity rower.

He asks if people talk during their session the same way they do to their barbers.

"Sure."

After a few minutes he says, "Very relaxing. Is that what I'm supposed to be feeling?"

Dina smiles. "Harmony. Relief of stress and tension. Increased concentration. Maybe not right away, but over time."

"Can I do this myself at home?"

"Somewhat," says Dina.

"But it's not the same as having your feet caressed and squeezed by a woman?"

Dina says, "The theory is that there's a transference of energy between the therapist—"

"A *beautiful* woman, if you don't mind me saying that."

"Why should I mind?" she says. "I never understand these women who don't like compliments."

"Me neither. And it's not like you'll ever have to see me again."

Dina pumps another squirt of almond-scented lotion into her hands and rubs them together thoughtfully. "Really? You think we'll never see each other again after this session? With your friends right across the street?"

"Have we had a change of heart?" he asks. "Because lunch was discussed without success."

"Was it?" she asks. "I must've been more tired than I realized."

Byron makes a V of his feet, and studies Dina between them. "Have you decided that I have some redeeming social value?"

"I think you're smart," she says, "and I like hearing you talk."

"Which you've realized is no small set of attributes."

"I've been adding them up, as a matter of fact," says Dina. "Your brains, your height, your nice coloring, your apparent good physical and mental health."

"All true," says Byron. "I'm quite the specimen."

"I think you are," says Dina.

"And you would know because you see a lot of specimens. And the feet never lie, correct?"

"That's correct," she says.

"How do I stack up in the feet department? Top third of all feet? Top ten percent?"

Truthfully? Byron's feet could appear in magazine ads. He has unusually regular, attractive toes, and beautifully defined arches and soft skin. His nails are a healthy pink and there isn't even the suggestion of a bunion or a callus. "Yours are probably in the top ten pairs I've ever handled," she says. "If you lived here, I'd use you in teaching."

He asks how often her clients have these sessions.

"Usually weekly. Sometimes more often." She explains that what she is doing now, if it hurts a bit, is breaking up the deposits of waste—lactic acid, uric acid, calcium—along his nerve pathways. With stress, they build up. And of course gravity carries the wastes along the nerves to his extremities.

"Of course," he says.

Dina moves to an ankle and its neighboring indentations.

"What's this called?" he asks.

"Finger-walking," says Dina. "Sometimes I say 'moon-walking.' "

"Aren't you in the vicinity of my private parts?"

She frowns as she works the medial side of his foot between ankle and heel, exactly what one is supposed to do to rev up and clean out the pathways that carry sperm and related fluids.

⟶ At the door he asks, "Did he call last night?"

"Nash? He left a message."

"Can you tell me what he said?"

"Nothing: the name of his stupid hotel."

"That's it? Nothing personal?"

" 'Take care, Deenie.' And that was all."

"Did you want to talk to him?"

"No," says Dina. "Well, maybe. It wouldn't have killed him to leave his number. Or to call on the other line."

"I told you he's no good," says Byron.

"He deliberately called my work number because he knows I don't pick that up at night."

"Shmuck," says Byron.

"It's not like he can avoid me forever. Most of his clothes are still here, and all of his equipment."

Byron asks if the Miata was his.

"His name is on the lease, but I make the payments."

"Then maybe it's better this way. You'll talk to him after the dents are fixed and you're over the trauma. Last night you might have felt compelled to blurt out the whole story."

Dina bites her lip.

"Are you going to cry?" he asks.

Dina shakes her head no, bravely, but Byron doesn't believe her. It's his own fault. He sees how indelicate he has been, and how inappropriate. A person doesn't break up with a long-seated boyfriend one minute and engage in a flirtation the next. It's time for him to be sincere, to admit that a certain amount of creativity went into his speech making of the night before. He should tell her: Inadvertently, he had slipped into the joke maker–sidekick–Gig Young role of the romantic comedies of his youth, in which insincere and halfhearted bids for the leading lady result in warm feelings, even lunches, but not sex or love. They are great guys, these old movie frat brothers and army buddies. Theatergoers love these characters. They express it at curtain with a burst of fond enthusiasm as the best friend of the leading man takes a witty, acrobatic bow, and brings the house down.

Byron puts his arm around Dina's shoulder for a consoling, platonic squeeze. He thinks, I'll send her flowers when I get back to New York with a card that confirms my demotion to friendship, and full acceptance thereof.

Dina does not move away. Byron croons, "I know. It's hard. It's like a divorce." She doesn't break down, nor does she prop herself against him in any body language that suggests grief. To the contrary, she tilts her face upward, closes her eyes, and kisses him full on the lips.

Byron is surprised and amenable. He hasn't been kissed in weeks.

When the kiss ends he says, "That was an unexpected thrill."

"I don't know what came over me," she whispers, patting her neckline and smoothing her hair.

"I like to be kissed," he says. "I especially like it when the woman takes the initiative."

Dina asks if the earlier offer—dinner, was it? In Laguna?—is still on the table because she has a favorite restaurant there that she thinks he'd like: Mexican seafood and the best margaritas.

"What time?"

"Eight?"

"It's a date, cookie," he says, "as long as you don't mind driving."

"Wonderful," says Dina, finding his hand and squeezing it.

This is great, thinks Byron. Travel is great. I must be great. I love the culture out here. I haven't even known her twenty-four hours. We'll have fun while I'm here and I'll send her flowers when I get home. Now the card will have to be entirely different—sensitive and appreciative instead of brotherly; sexy but not rhapsodic; enough to pave the way for more lovemaking on future California trips, but not enough to lure her to New York. *Carpe diem,* he reminds himself. Call later and tell her you're counting the hours. Read up on reflexology. Find an A.T.M. Walk to Balboa and buy rubbers. And tonight, God willing, after dinner and a short mood-enhancing walk on the nearest beach—unless you've woefully misread the cues—get laid.

Eleven

Cynthia John has been hearing the name "Adele Dobbin" in her head all day, and suddenly remembers why: It's the woman with the patrician accent and dark red hair, well cut, who asks for money on Channel 2. Cynthia reflexively calls the station and asks if Adele Dobbin works there. The answer is nonverbal, a click and a connection, then a new voice saying, "Development."

"Oh," says Cynthia. "I'm just confirming that Adele Dobbin works there."

"Yes, she does," says the friendly male voice, "but she's not in."

Cynthia, without a plan in the world, asks when Ms. Dobbin *will* be in?

"We don't know."

"Later today?"

"She's sick," says the voice. "She went home after lunch and isn't coming back today. Can Scott or I help you?"

Liar, thinks Cynthia. She's taking a personal day, revisiting her haunts and her youth with Nash. "It's about gift giving," she tells him. "But I'll call back."

Cynthia buzzes her secretary, Philip, and asks, "If I'm out sick, what do you tell people?"

"It depends. Why?"

"I just called someone's office and was told, 'She went home sick today and won't be back.' It struck me as extremely unprofessional."

"I'd kill that person," says Philip dryly. "Then I'd fire the corpse."

"I mean, if it's my sisters, that's one thing."

"Or your mother, right?"

Cynthia thinks this over. "Maybe I'll make a list of who that would include."

"I think I know that, Cyn," says Philip.

"Let me add a name." She waits a few seconds. "First name, Nash. Last name, Harvey."

"Got it. Nash, like the car. Phone number?"

"Really? The car? I'd forgotten about that."

Another line lights up, and Philip repeats with more urgency, "Phone number?"

"Not at this time," says Cynthia.

Lorenz calls the Dobbin home, using the excuse that Kathleen, in her haste, left the "open" sign in the storefront. Would she like him to unlock the door and flip it to "closed"?

"Don't bother," says Kathleen. "I think people will get the idea. And I'll be in first thing."

Lorenz asks, with the authority of a man in possession of skeleton keys, Does she need anything from the store? From her desk? Could he make a deposit for her? Did she turn off her computer and activate the alarm?

"I think I'm all set."

"Is your sister okay?" he asks. "Do you feel like talking?"

Kathleen says, "Not right now. I'll fill you in tomorrow. But I will say this: I've been behaving badly."

Lorenz is overjoyed to be the receptacle of a confidence. "That's hard to believe," he says.

"Wait'll you hear what I've done," she continues. "You're going to have to promise you won't think I'm a crazy woman after I tell you."

Lorenz waits.

"Lorenz? Are you there?"

"Of course! I'm all ears."

"I didn't mean now. Everyone's waiting for me. I'll tell you when I see you."

Lorenz swallows, checks his watch, and feels a trickle of sweat leave his sideburn and drip down his cheek. "Would it be possi-ble—" he begins, "would it be *agreeable* to you to discuss it over dinner tonight?"

Kathleen says, "I can't over dinner. Not tonight, anyway. There's a houseful of people—"

"I understand," Lorenz says too quickly. "Of course. It's very short notice."

"It's not that," says Kathleen. "It's what happened today. The man who did the Heimlich is here—Lois invited him to stay for dinner—and Adele and I just walked in with a ton of Chinese food. . . . What about coffee later? Say, eight o'clock?"

The question squeezes the breath out of him, but he manages to ask, "You mean tonight?"

"We're sitting down now, then after we eat I'll make sure Adele is settled, then I'll excuse myself. Eight should be fine."

"Or eight-thirty," he suggests out of joy and generosity and con-fidence.

"Let's do eight."

Lorenz composes himself enough to ask for directions to her house. Kathleen asks if he'll be arriving by trolley or by car.

"Car!"

"Do you know Coolidge Corner?" she asks.

Lorenz says he knows how to get there, but not the specifics of the neighborhood.

Kathleen describes where he can make a legal U-turn on Beacon Street, and how to find Stearns Road from there.

Lorenz mentions the famously restricted Brookline parking.

"No!" says Kathleen. "Don't park. I'll be waiting downstairs. It's too complicated here."

Lorenz says, "I'll be here until seven-thirty, in case you want to change the time or if Adele objects."

"I won't and she won't," says Kathleen.

⟶ Adele sips only broth spooned from the top of her House Special Soup. Kathleen and Richard, who notice the pained look on her face as she swallows, exchange worried looks around and over the jubilant Lois.

"Tell us," says Lois, "when did you reverse the Nash and the Harvey?"

Nash says, "Exactly? You mean the year?"

Lois nods eagerly.

"I was always called Nash in school by friends, so it wasn't that big a deal."

"*Nash,*" Lois repeats as if sampling the most appealing entry in a book of baby names. "It is distinctive."

"Did you change it legally?" asks Richard.

"Somewhere along the line, I did."

"Harv," says Richard, "I'm betting that you never made it official. I bet you pay your taxes as Harvey Nash."

"Which would make it a stage name," says Lois. "Nothing wrong with that."

"And it isn't like you had a college diploma that needed altering," Adele says.

Nash's voice suggests that the strain of diplomacy is beginning to show. "I think you forget that I studied at the New England Conservatory after I graduated from Boston Latin. On the honor roll."

"I didn't forget." Adele signals to Kathleen that something only she will appreciate is forthcoming. "But at the same time I don't remember any bachelor's degree."

"And that, of course, is more important around this table than any of my subsequent accomplishments."

"I don't think she was saying that," Kathleen murmurs.

"Look at Bill Gates," chirps Lois. "Dropped out of Harvard his freshman year. Richest man in America."

Richard says, "How about you, Harv? Are you rich?"

Only Lois laughs.

"I'm serious," says Richard. "What kind of money do you make writing jingles?"

Nash asks, "Are you asking how much money one makes in my field, or—"

"No," says Richard. "How much does Harvey-Nash-Harvey make?" He reaches for a flour pancake, but doesn't break eye contact with his subject.

Nash says, "Enough."

"Enough for what? A guy with no dependents and rent on a studio apartment, or a guy with a big house on the beach?"

"Enough for a small house on the beach and two hundred grand in studio gear."

Only now, after she's heard his answer, does Lois emit a scolding, "Richard!"

"I don't mind," says Nash. "It's what your father would be asking, God rest his soul."

"Don't encourage him," says Lois. "He thinks his badge gives him the right to cross-examine everyone who crosses his path."

"You have a badge?" asks Nash.

"Show him," says Lois.

"If you've seen one, you've seen 'em all," says Richard. "Besides my wallet's in my jacket."

"When would I have seen a badge close up?" Nash asks. "I've led an exemplary life with no sheriff ever knocking on my door."

Adele looks up. She repeats the words "exemplary life" disdainfully.

Lois announces that she ordered the Buddha's Delight, this time with garlic sauce.

"So?" says Richard.

"I meant it's not as bland as usual."

"Pass it this way," says Nash.

"What beach do you live on?" Kathleen asks.

"I live on the bay in Newport Beach. It's on the water but it's not a beach."

"We've covered this," says Adele.

"And is most of your work in Hollywood?" asks Lois.

"Actually," says Nash. "Have I not mentioned this to anyone? The middle years? After I tried to compose for the movies—some bites but eventually striking out—I ended up freelancing for jingle houses."

"Jingle houses?" repeats Lois.

"A music company that does sound tracks for commercials," says Nash. "A friend got me in."

"Where?" asks Richard.

"Why should he say?" says Kathleen. "It might put his glamorous missing-person status at risk."

"My parents knew where I was," says Nash. "And certainly the I.R.S. knew where I was. And the A.F.M. I was hardly a missing person, Kathleen."

"Is that your position? That you *weren't* hiding from this family?"

"Kathleen," says Richard. "This is a guess, but I think you're working up to something, and I'd rather it didn't get physical again."

Lois laughs another brittle laugh.

Kathleen says, "I happen to be going out after dinner. I want a few answers before I leave, on the theory that I may never see this character again."

Richard coughs into his fist, telegraphing that this may be a matter of some delicacy.

"What?" asks Kathleen, annoyed.

"Maybe this isn't the best time."

"Pretend I'm not here," says Adele. "Just as you have been."

Kathleen pushes her plate in from the edge of the table, and says smartly, "Harvey?"

He is brushing plum sauce onto his pancake with a feathered scallion. Instead of answering, he reaches for the platter of sliced duck.

"My question," says Kathleen. "*Our* question, all of the Dobbins', including our late parents', question is, and has always been . . ." She stops, suddenly realizing that she knows all the answers in this inquiry, and sees that every explanation will only humiliate Adele.

Nash reads the look on her face, and decides to help. "I think you want to know why I left," he begins. "And the reason is patently obvious: I was immature and brainless, not to mention scared. I was thinking only of myself. I was so selfish that I couldn't even imagine what was taking place back at the engagement party, let alone the hatred it would spark."

Kathleen feels immensely grateful for his spin, and relieved. But she is not the commander of this campaign, not invested with the power to wave a white flag. She asks her sister if this explanation and *mea culpa* is satisfactory.

"He's never said a sincere word in his life," Adele replies.

"My *life?*" Nash repeats with a new impatience. "You haven't known me my whole life."

Adele stares, as if Nash has finally said something interesting.

"I may have been raised by two socially inferior parents," he continues, "but they always taught me that when someone is a guest in your home, you don't attack them or insult them or do anything other than act like a good host. Here, apparently, it's just the opposite: I get shoved out the door by the person whose life I saved, then brained by this one who doesn't like the way I said hello. I saved your life, Dell; I'm sorry I broke your rib, but I'd do it again if it meant dislodging the steak. I'm not such a terrible guy, and I think it's time you stopped glaring at me."

"How dare you," breathes Adele.

"She almost died today!" cries Kathleen.

"And she's not the one who knocked you out," says Richard.

"I'd like you to leave," says Adele.

"He came all this way to set things right, and now he's going to walk out the door and you'll never see him again!" wails Lois.

"I'm in no condition to leave," says Nash. "My vision is blurred, my head is throbbing, and I think I may be running a temp." He turns to Richard, old hand at vain claims. "I was injured under this roof, and I think it's only fair that I recover here." He returns to his food, rolling up his bulging pancake expertly.

Adele says, "Absolutely not."

"You know, Harv," says Richard, "I'm sympathetic up to a point, and I am grateful for that business in the restaurant, but I see problems with your spending the night here."

"Would you want to be seen looking like this? Have I ever looked less presentable or more unappetizing?"

"C'mon, Harv," says Richard. "You know we don't have room. You've made your point. The girls can't have you underfoot."

"They should have thought of that before they assaulted me—"

"*They?*" repeats Lois. "I came home at five forty-five."

"Assaulted me and showed no remorse."

"Where will *I* sleep?" asks Richard.

Each sister silently assigns beds, but only Lois articulates the plan: Nash can have her room. She'll sleep with Adele, freeing the daybed for Richard.

"I have a broken rib," says Adele. "I'm sleeping alone in my own bed."

"Then let this one get a roommate," says Nash, jerking his thumb at Kathleen. "It seems to me that if anyone should be inconvenienced, it's Red here."

Kathleen looks at her watch and frowns. "I don't consider this settled. I should be back from my date by ten, ten-thirty."

Adele smiles—Kathleen sees she is pretending Nash is invisible and hasn't asserted a preposterous claim—and says, "May we ask who this date is with?"

"Someone at work."

Richard laughs, which everyone understands to mean, There's no one at work except ladies trying on underwear.

"His name is Lorenz," says Kathleen. "He's with the building's management."

"Lorenz?" repeats Nash. "Like Lorenz Hart?" He leans back in his chair, fixes Kathleen with an impudent expression, and sings the first line of "Bewitched, Bothered and Bewildered."

"Must you?" says Adele.

"His words, not mine. Music by Richard Rodgers."

"From *Pal Joey*," offers Lois.

"He also wrote 'Blue Moon'—talking about American classics."

"Are we going to meet this guy?" Richard asks Kathleen. "I mean, isn't that my role as man of the house?"

"He's not coming up," says Kathleen. "I told him I'd wait downstairs."

"Lorenz *who*?" asks Lois.

"You'll set the bottles when you get in?" asks Adele.

"We're just going for coffee," says Kathleen.

"A coffee date," says Richard. "I do that, too. It's a good icebreaker. No big commitment."

"Which is exactly your problem," says Adele. "No big commitment, ever."

"Let's not argue," says Lois. "We have a guest. Let's just have some coffee now, and stop bickering, and let everyone get on with their evening plans. Who wants decaf?"

"Not me," says Kathleen. She stands up, and clears her plate and Adele's.

"Leave it," says Adele. "You don't want to keep the gentleman waiting."

Lorenz, muses Nash. Young? Old? European? Puerto Rican? He knows he can't say anything that will reveal he is unsettled by the fact that Kathleen, the youngest and dewiest, has the beginnings of a boyfriend. "Don't stay out too late," he says. "I don't think I'll be able to fall asleep until everyone's home safe."

"Are we supposed to let you fall asleep?" Lois asks.

Reluctantly, Nash turns to this less appealing voice and presence.

"Remember? We were going to check you every few hours so we know you're not comatose? Like your mother used to do?"

"In shifts, I hope," says Nash. "I wouldn't want that burden to fall on just one person."

"Adele can't help, and Kathleen's going out—"

"And I'm not sticking around," says Richard.

"I think at this point," says Nash, "that sleep would be the best medicine."

"*Go*," Adele tells Kathleen.

Nash kisses his fingertips and wiggles them like a doting uncle. "Lucky Lorenz," he calls after her coyly. Kathleen flinches but doesn't stop.

⌐⌐⌐ It is twenty-four hours since Cynthia has had sexual intercourse with Nash, and she thinks she should have heard from him by now. She is positive that she knows where he is, and has the computer printout from her *Street Atlas USA* CD-ROM to prove it. The phone book lists only a "Dobbin, Lois," but the address is right. Her plan is this: Give Nash Harvey until nine P.M., possibly five past, at which time she will feel free to embarrass the man who will have proved himself insincere beyond all her powers of detection and defense.

At six forty-five, she orders an artichoke pizza with extra cheese, which is announced at seven-twenty by the doorman. "Could you send him up?" Cynthia tries. "I'm waiting for an important call."

"Can't, Miss John," says Lorenz.

"Could you bring it up?"

He says kindly, "And who would watch the front door?"

Cynthia doesn't want to leave the apartment because she thinks her social luck is tainted by a force that makes the phone ring during the one minute she is getting her mail or picking up her takeout or rinsing her hair in the shower.

"Tell him I'll be right down," she says.

She finds Lorenz in street clothes—wool trousers, gray pullover, and loafers—the first time she's ever seen him out of uniform. "Don't you look smart," she says.

He tells her he is off duty in seven minutes.

"And I think you have a date."

Lorenz's olive skin doesn't blush, but changes tone. "Just dessert," he says after a pause.

"A lady friend?"

Lorenz smiles. "I wouldn't want your pizza to get cold."

"That must be a *yes*." She takes a step toward the elevator, then says, "I know, it's none of my business. But you, Felix, and the others know every detail of our lives—who comes and goes, at what hour. So it doesn't seem particularly nosy to inquire about a Friday evening."

"We *have* to notice who comes and goes," says Lorenz. "It's the most important part of our job. Every person who comes in has to be accounted for. Even pizza deliverymen."

"Which is overkill," says Cynthia.

"Is it?" asks Lorenz. He takes keys out of his pocket, not his work-related master set. Cynthia thinks, Lorenz has a car! A home that he drives to; a life beyond this lobby. "All it takes," he continues, "is one impostor holding an empty pizza box or a brown bag with a Chinese menu stapled to it."

"I know," she sighs.

"Remember what happened at the Towers? The guy posing as an exterminator? That's when our board made the rule."

"You win," she says. "And the truth of the matter is, I voted for this stupid rule." She walks back to the elevator and waves with the two fingers she can spare from the grip on her pizza box. "Have a great time, whoever she is."

He says thank you, formally and sincerely. He is fond of Cynthia, and he is sympathetic to her need to chat. It reminds him of the children in the building who draw him pictures and invite him to their birthday parties. He guesses why she didn't want to leave the apartment—a hoped-for phone call from the tanned man in the raincoat who left the building at ten-fifty P.M. the night before—"w/suitcase," Felix had jotted under "Comments."

"You enjoy your evening, too, Miss John," he says.

Lois is not stupid. Adele and Richard are a team, the oldest and the youngest Dobbins, united forever by today's near tragedy. Their tight circle has squeaked open one body's width to include Kathleen—nurse, mother, cook, companion, and everyone's pet. Lois knows her sisters view her as a defector prone to boy-craziness, but too bad. She's the one with manners, not Adele, who is recognized on the street by supporters of public television for being professionally gracious; not Richard, who is acting like their father; and certainly not Kathleen, who today has revealed a side that disqualifies her as anyone's darling.

Lois feels that she alone is right. She can't help being grateful to Nash. And who wouldn't be curious about where he's been and why? History is filled with truces and with swords being turned into ploughshares. The Cold War is over. Russians and Americans room together in space. Yasser Arafat made a condolence call to the widow of Yitzhak Rabin. And, really, when the layers of anger and hatred are peeled away, shouldn't *one* of the sisters embrace the man who's come to make peace with the Dobbins?

Tonight, things are falling into place. Adele excused herself as soon as Kathleen left the table. Richard and Nash are watching CNN with bowls of ice cream on their laps. Richard has already announced his plans to return to his friend's couch in Newton—Nora, the lesbian, who has Surround Sound. When he leaves, Lois will take off her WGBH apron, change into the hostess outfit of champagne-colored shantung with the mandarin collar, and bring a selection of after-dinner drinks and two cordial glasses into the den. She'll sit. Then she must tell Nash her story, even if he doesn't ask: her short marriage to a divorced man, a patent attorney. The whirlwind courtship. Their being deeply, passionately in love. The sparks that flew, and the attraction that was obvious to everyone who saw them together. Here, she will pause and smile ruefully. "One never knows someone until one gets married. I mean, things were normal—in private, I mean. In the bedroom. But as early as the honeymoon, things changed. He had very specific likes and dislikes. I don't mean the normally adventurous things that sophisticated partners engage in—you know what I mean—but peculiar things. Props. Outfits. I know what you're thinking: I was naïve and inhibited, but I wasn't. I'm not. I can't say too much because he's still a partner in my father's firm, but he liked dressing up, and . . . I'll say only this: I should have realized he was *way* too insistent on my friends throwing me a lingerie shower; *way* too interested in my trousseau and Kathleen's shop. . . . But that's as far as I ever confide because he's well known in legal circles."

It is a set piece, sadly true, one that serves her conversationally in bars and on rare blind dates. She is silently rehearsing it as she packages the leftovers in deli containers and loads the dishwasher, wishing she hadn't suggested the mint chocolate chip, which is holding Richard up.

Actually, Richard's ice cream is melting as he urges Nash to be a good sport and to return to his far more comfortable hotel room.

"It's a lot of dough," Nash says. "Besides, what kind of lessons would it teach your spoiled sisters, which is all I'm trying to do here: to let the punishment fit the crime."

"Don't say that too loud," Richard warns. "Especially in front of Numbers One and Three."

But Number One has retired without even saying good night, and Number Three is out on a date. Nash is tempted to ask, "What about Number Two? Anything I should know about Lois?" But he doesn't. Richard appears to be ally material, but he waxes and wanes. The Dobbin honor evidently overrides loyalty to his fraternity of fellow males. Nash can wait. He is confidant that he'll hear Lois's story after Richard leaves. Poor Lois. He sees in her eyes that she has decades of heartache to confide and confess. She'll want to know if that letter she sent ever reached him, and he'll say, No, what letter? You sent a letter? He'll denounce the studio for not forwarding his mail, and she'll feel better. "What did it say?" he'll ask, and she'll say she can't remember. Nash will touch the hand that still wears the engagement ring, and ask, "Is there a story here?"

Richard is asking one more time if the joke is over, if he can drop Nash off somewhere.

Nash says no, he's quite comfortable, notwithstanding his bleeding face and stinging head.

"Am I crazy to leave you here?" Richard asks. "Will I have reason to regret this?"

"*I* haven't broken any laws," says Nash. "I'm not the one you need to police."

Richard sighs, takes Nash's empty bowl, and says, "I know that, Harv. Didn't mean to insult you." Nash offers his hand, and Richard shakes it.

"Good night, old man," says Nash.

⌒⌒⌒ After Richard leaves, Nash flips through the channels until he finds a coffee commercial he likes, a jingle that's been around for years, sung by a vocalist who must have earned, he calculates, a million in residuals. He helps himself to the granny afghan—Adele's handiwork, he guesses—and pulls it up to his chin. The time on the screen reads "8:37p ET." Excellent. His next dose of acetaminophen is due at quarter of nine, and he knows Lois won't forget.

Twelve

Kathleen has never seen Lorenz in anything but his two-toned brown uniform, so this—in a car, wearing a herringbone sports jacket over a V-necked sweater and wool trousers—feels different.

After twice circling the commercial blocks of Coolidge Corner in search of a parking space, he suggests they give up and have coffee back at his apartment.

Kathleen knows his address, having checked the Boston White Pages for signs of a joint listing, but she asks where he lives just the same.

"North End. Prince Street."

"I love the North End. You must not have to go anywhere else to shop."

"That's true," he says, but not wholeheartedly.

"Not true?"

He hesitates, then says, "My father does most of the shopping and all of the cooking."

Kathleen doesn't need clarification. It seems as familiar and inevitable as the shape of her own family tree: Lorenz lives with his elderly dad, who must be retired, who must putter around the shops of the North End during the day and cook for them by night.

"How old is he?" she asks.

"Seventy-seven."

"Healthy?"

"Knock wood," says Lorenz.

"Seventy-seven," she repeats.

After a pause he says, "I'm forty-nine, if you were wondering. Two old bachelors and a cat."

"Named?"

"Chicha."

Kathleen says the name fondly.

"Sixteen years old and blind in one eye. My father makes her fish soup."

"I'm forty-six," says Kathleen.

"Young." He grins.

"Will he be home?"

"Pop? Home but asleep. He turns in at eight and wakes up at five."

"Sweet," says Kathleen.

"Not sweet. He doesn't know how to be quiet in the morning. That's when he empties the dishwasher and listens to talk radio. I sleep with earplugs."

Kathleen says, "So I won't meet him?"

Lorenz meets her eyes briefly. "You will at some point."

"And when things calm down, I hope you'll get to meet Adele and Lois. Everyone's been a little crazed by the reappearance of the old flame."

Lorenz asks how the dinner went.

"Horrible. He invited himself to sleep over."

"No!"

"Yes! He thinks he should recuperate at our place."

"Recuperate from what?"

"I hit him with a casserole," she says.

Lorenz laughs, and Kathleen is relieved. She looks over to be sure it is a kind of indulgent laughter that she secretly believes the event warrants.

"I assume he wasn't badly hurt."

"It caught him on the side of the head, and he crumpled."

"And you hit him with a casserole because . . . ?"

Kathleen says, "You're the first person I've told this to, but he was flirting with me."

"Uh-oh," says Lorenz.

"Not regular flirting. This was the guy who ruined my sister's life, takes three decades to apologize, and on his way out the door, tells me I don't look a day over thirty."

"So you hit him?"

"I snapped." She checks the effect on Lorenz and says, "Which is not my usual behavior."

"I know!"

"Adele is furious. She won't even talk to him. My brother's mediating."

Lorenz asks if this Harvey is a good-looking guy.

"He's a little battered around the face right now, but Lois would say, Yes, very."

"*Lois* would?"

"Adele thinks she's always had a thing for Nash. She's acting really rattled."

"More than Adele?"

"Adele is . . . Adele pretends to be immune to most matters of the heart. She doesn't have a romantic bone in her body."

"Anymore."

Kathleen sighs and says, "That's true. She used to."

"Who *is* the big romantic in the family?" Lorenz asks coyly.

"That would be me," she says.

～ Mr. Sampedro is not asleep, but energetically scrubbing live crabs on the ridged sideboard of a big white enameled kitchen sink. The room is hospital white, with old-fashioned white metal cabinets; the marbled green linoleum looks as if it's been waxed with a space-age acrylic that Kathleen would like to know the name of.

"Papi," says Lorenz. "This is Kathleen Dobbin."

"How do you do," the old man mumbles.

"We came back for coffee."

The old man tears the legs off the body of a wet crab and drops them into a sauté pan. "Please go ahead."

"Can you join us?" asks Kathleen.

"I better finish this," he says in accented English.

Lorenz signals to Kathleen that something needs to be finessed. "Papi? We're going into the living room for a few minutes to talk, so you can finish up and join us." He leads Kathleen into the next room and to a seat on a plaid sofa. Lorenz waits for the running water to create background noise before he explains, "He didn't have his teeth in. This'll give him a chance to get them."

The water stops and a door closes.

Kathleen asks, "How long has he lived with you?"

"A couple of years. He stayed up in Lawrence after my mother died, but it wasn't a great situation for him, so I said, 'Let's give it a try. If it doesn't work out for either of us, we'll think of something else.' "

"So it's worked out? He likes the North End?"

"Sure. His first name's Antonio, so he fits right in: Tony Sampedro. No trouble there."

Kathleen looks around the living room, which is overfurnished with side-by-side black lounge chairs, a large TV, tinted family graduation photos, and two scarred maple coffee tables. "Where's the cat?" she asks.

"She's shy. I can bring her to meet you if you insist."

"No need to traumatize her," says Kathleen.

Mr. Sampedro joins them. Not only are his dentures in, but he is wearing a plaid shirt and a narrow tie in cobalt blue.

Kathleen says, "You didn't have to get dressed up on my account."

Mr. Sampedro takes her fingertips in his hand and bows slightly. "I don't like to greet lady guests in an apron."

"I'll make coffee," says Lorenz. "Regular or decaf?"

"Did you have supper, Miss?"

Kathleen says yes, she did. An early dinner.

"Because we could have my crabs," says his father.

"I think just coffee and those biscotti," says Lorenz.

"We could have cocktails," says Mr. Sampedro. "A banana-and-rum milkshake."

Lorenz says, "Let me check if we have what we need."

"We have everything," his father says. "I bought bananas today."

Kathleen says, "Sounds delightful."

"We have a Waring blender," says Mr. Sampedro.

"Can I help?" asks Kathleen.

"No, no. You stay and talk with me."

As soon as Lorenz leaves the room, Mr. Sampedro says, "He's a good boy. I have one son only and I couldn't ask for a better one."

"Papi! I can hear every word you're saying."

"He's not so great," Mr. Sampedro yells, then slaps his knee and guffaws.

"I don't think I've ever tasted a banana-rum milkshake," says Kathleen.

"I don't make it very often because I have hardening of the arteries, but when we have a special guest, I think it's only good manners to join her."

"I know what you mean," says Kathleen. "You have to treat yourself once in a while."

Mr. Sampedro smiles, and Kathleen senses another endorsement is bubbling up. "My son is lucky. He doesn't have to watch what he eats. He's very strong and very healthy."

Kathleen says politely, "He has to be fit for his job."

"That's right! It's an important job down there. A whole building depends on him."

"That's true. I know *I* do."

Mr. Sampedro asks, "Do you have children?"

"I was never married," says Kathleen.

"No babies?"

"No," says Kathleen. "Just a bunch of sisters."

"All pretty girls like you?" he asks.

Kathleen laughs. "And fading fast."

Whatever that means to Mr. Sampedro, he laughs too. "Do you like crabs?" he asks.

"Love 'em."

"I wasn't planning on buying them, but then I was walking by the fish market just when it was closing and I see them through the window and I knock on the glass and point and the man unlocks the door. He knows me. I'm a regular. I bought every one he had left."

"I saw you were cooking them in a tomato sauce."

Mr. Sampedro grins. "You smell that?"

Kathleen nods.

"It's a *sofrito*. I cook onion, tomatoes, garlic, some wine, in olive oil. No green peppers! I put the crabs into my sauce and we eat them with rice. They're cooking now."

"It smells delicious. I could smell it coming up the stairs."

"Lorenz," yells his father. "Stir the crabs. And turn down the gas."

"I did, Papi."

"How's the cocktails?"

"Coming right up."

Lorenz reappears, holding a tin Coca-Cola tray with three frothy drinks in parfait glasses. He places the tray on the nearest coffee table, presents the first glass and first cork coaster to Kathleen, and all three raise their glasses. "A celebration," says Lorenz. He glances at his father as if his presence is constricting his freedom of expression, but forges ahead anyway. "I had hoped this day would come," he says.

Kathleen touches her glass to his.

Mr. Sampedro adds, "Here's to our beautiful guest. I hope this is the first of many visits. Maybe next time she'll come earlier and eat with us."

"I'd like that," she says.

"You work in Lorenz's building, no?"

"I have a shop there."

"I know—" He snaps his fingers in Lorenz's face.

"Lingerie, Papi. Bras and girdles."

"That's right! I'll come see it and buy some presents. Do you have boxes?"

"Boxers?"

"Boxes. For the presents." He pantomimes the shape of something square.

"Oh! Of course. And wrapping paper and ribbon."

"It's a hop, skip, and a jump, you know. Lorenz comes home for lunch sometimes. It takes five minutes."

Kathleen smiles. Lorenz tells his father to move over, please, so he can sit next to his guest.

Squeezed between his father and Kathleen, Lorenz asks wryly, "Isn't this cozy?"

If there are hints being dropped, Mr. Sampedro ignores them. "He makes a good milkshake, doesn't he?" he asks Kathleen.

"Do I taste cinnamon?" she asks.

"Just a sprinkle," says Lorenz.

"Drink up," says his father. "It's good for you."

"You know what he's doing, don't you?" says Lorenz. "Remember in *Guys and Dolls* when Sky Masterson takes Sara to Havana and gets her drunk on Bacardi and milk? Well, this is my father's clever way of loosening up ladies who strike him as teetotalers."

"What?" says Mr. Sampedro. "I didn't hear what you said."

"I wasn't talking to you, Papi."

"I heard you say 'Habana.'"

"I did. I told Kathleen you were born there—hence the drink."

"That's right. But not my children. And my wife was European." He crosses himself quickly.

"Lorenz told me."

"Do you like to cook?" he asks.

"I love to. I cook for my family."

"She has no kids," Mr. Sampedro tells Lorenz.

"I know, Papi."

"Neither does he. My daughters all have kids. That's enough for me. Altogether they have nine. Six boys and three girls."

"I think you probably want to check the crabs," says Lorenz, adding in Spanish, "then go to bed."

Mr. Sampedro says, "I'm starting to feel a little tired. I'm seventy-five years old, and I need a lot of sleep."

Kathleen says, "I understand."

He thwacks Lorenz's chest happily with the back of his hand, then gets to his feet with an exaggerated groan. He turns to Kathleen. "I sleep like the dead. Once I'm in my room, I don't come out. I don't even get up to use the toilet. I sleep through anything."

"Good night, Papi," says Lorenz. "You're starting to get on my nerves."

"Lovely to meet you," says Kathleen.

"Likewise. And I know Lorenz will bring you back again. Maybe with your sisters. I'll make what I cook for special occasions—*lechón asado*." He looks to his son and snaps his fingers.

"Roast suckling pig."

"My butcher carries them for holidays."

"Christmas, I bet," says Kathleen.

"Before Christmas! You'll come sooner than that!"

Kathleen checks with Lorenz to be sure he isn't looking dismayed or overwhelmed. He finds her hand next to his on the couch and squeezes it.

"I accept," she tells Mr. Sampedro.

⟋ Lorenz has clicked off the three-way bulb next to the couch, and is grinning as he pours refills.

"What?" she asks.

"Remember that big sale you had?"

"Which one?"

"After Christmas. You were sitting on the floor, cross-legged, marking down panties and putting them into baskets labeled 'small,' 'medium,' and 'large.' You'd hold up each—all business—and either check the tag or guess the size, and toss it into the right basket. You had no idea how cute you looked, or the effect it had on me."

"I do remember that," says Kathleen. "And I might have had an idea of the effect it was having on you."

"So you were flirting with me?"

"I certainly was."

Lorenz throws his head back and laughs.

"Well, wait a minute: The reason you were there was personal—to return my Christmas check. Remember?"

"Definitely."

"January," she murmurs. "Has it been three whole months?"

"To me it seems the opposite: Has it been only three short months since that conversation? It seems that I've known you for a long time."

"What I meant," says Kathleen, "was that I should have reciprocated in some way. Three months of your bringing me cappuccino and I never said, 'Could you come to dinner next Friday night?' "

"Because we're in a delicate position. I'm *still* in a delicate position. I'm an employee of the building and you're a tenant."

Kathleen is listening, but not as easily as when there's a display case between them or a customer anecdote to recount. They've never been this physically close, hips and shoulders touching, and she is studying the details of his eyelashes and earlobes and freshly shaven cheeks.

"I went round and round on this," he continues. "I even talked to my father about it. I knew you felt obliged to give me a tip at Christmas, but I couldn't cash it. Then I'd say to myself, 'If you say something, it'll put her on the spot.' So then I'd be back where I started from, with your red envelope and the nice thing you wrote on the card. I changed my mind every twelve hours. 'Don't cash it, but don't make a federal case out of it,' seemed one option, but then I was afraid I'd screw up your books."

"What did your father tell you to do?"

Lorenz smiles.

"Go ahead," says Kathleen.

"He thought I should cash the check, but buy you something with it."

"Such as?"

"The usual—candy, flowers, a book of poetry. He thought it would make you weak in the knees."

Kathleen is feeling extremely weak in the knees. It isn't that she's gone unkissed in her forties, but it's been a long time since the wool of someone's sweater against her arm and the smell of male cologne has induced any effect in her at all. His voice and the shape of his mouth, and the swirls of dark hair across his knuckles . . . *Finally,* she thinks. *Finally. I didn't make this up.* She says faintly, "I guess it all worked out. I mean, I understood that your returning my check was a symbolic act."

There's only one bridge left to cross. Kathleen stares into his brown eyes and waits. Lorenz hooks a finger under her chin and brings her closer. His face is warm, and he tastes lusciously, tropically, of Bacardi and bananas.

"Kathy," he murmurs between kisses.

⟶ Lois is recapping the last thirty years, moving quickly over her marriage and divorce with the sexually confused patent attorney, then backward to her wildly mixed emotions on the night of March 11, 1967. "I was sick for Adele, but vain enough to imagine that it had something to do with me," she tells Nash, who is bored and working out a melody on the arm of the sofa. "But at the same time, it was probably because I was so young and so romantic—"

"Young?" he asks sharply. "How old were we?"

"Twenty-one. You were twenty-five. Adele was twenty-three."

"God: engaged to be married at twenty-five."

Lois slips off her gold sandals and folds her legs under her on the couch. "I doubt if you remember this," she says, "but you and Adele were practicing a ballroom step for the party, a slow dance, and I stood in for her when she went to take a phone call."

Nash looks over, blank.

"A week before the engagement party?" she prompts.

"It's coming back to me," he lies.

"We had the radio on, and they played 'You've Lost That Lovin' Feelin' ' by the Righteous Brothers?"

"In the living room of Dean Road?" he guesses.

"Yes! Dell was gone for the whole song."

"We started off at a polite distance but then, as the song played on, I held you a little too close?"

"That's *exactly* what happened. It started off totally innocently."

"As these things usually do," says Nash.

"And you knew the words, and you were singing them right into my hair, as if you were saying you'd lost that lovin' feelin' for Adele."

This sounds right to Nash. A lifetime of crooning lyrics into the temples of attractive girls in lieu of conversation gives the story a luster of truth. "I didn't kiss you, did I?" he asks.

"I was never really sure. I felt what I thought were your lips on the side of my head, but I wasn't positive."

Doubt it, he thinks. Although . . .

"I can ask you now, though: *Did* you kiss me when the music stopped?"

Nash thinks he might have. It wouldn't have been the first time

he landed a wistful kiss—usually interpreted as a brotherly endorsement and therefore not reported—near the barrette of a
buddy's fiancée. "I think," he says nobly, "it would be better for all
concerned if I just leave it at, 'No, it never happened.'"

"Even now? We can't discuss it openly?"

"A kiss doesn't have to mean a whole heck of a lot."

"I know that."

"I wasn't the most reliable guy. I may have been caught up in the
moment and—if I can be blunt—turned on by the music and by
pressing up against you."

"I wouldn't disagree with that."

"It doesn't mean I used good judgment. I was a creature of my
impulses."

"That describes me to a T," says Lois.

Nash pours himself another demitasse of cognac and offers to
refill Lois's glass. "You must have been expecting some word from
me after I took off," he ventures.

Lois holds her glass out. "I had a lot of boyfriends, so I wasn't
staying home waiting for the phone to ring. However, did I think of
you from time to time and wonder if I had anything to do with
your leaving Boston? Honestly? Yes."

Nash seizes on the topic of Lois's many beaus. "So, after dating
a lot of guys, you finally said yes to one?"

Lois says sharply, "What does that mean—'said yes to one'?"

"To the lawyer. I assume he proposed."

"Oh, that. Obviously."

Nash wags his finger at her. "You thought I meant sex, didn't
you? You were raising your hackles there for a second. I saw it."

Lois concedes the point with a smile. "I thought you were asking about my . . . dating habits."

"Wait: You're saying that in this day and age you'd consider that
an insult? Would you want me to think you sat out the sexual rev-
olution until you married at—what age was it?"

"Not that long ago."

"That's what you want the world to think? That you had no fun
until your wedding night?"

"I don't understand your point," she murmurs.

Nash has no point, except that he is touching on something fascinating to him, the collective virginity of the Dobbin sisters. Adele had been affectionate in a way that suggested certain future satisfactions, but she was waiting for them to become officially engaged before going all the way.

"I would have pegged you for the liberated one," he confides.

"Why?"

"Well," says Nash, twirling his glass by its stem, never having given Lois's comportment a moment's thought, "it's something hard to put into words: a look, an attitude."

"Really?" Lois raises her eyebrows.

"For example," Nash continues, "I doubt whether I would have even asked Kathleen to dance."

"Because?"

Nash, who now conjures the desirable Kathleen as an achingly adorable teenager, says sternly, "Too young. Still in high school."

"And shy."

"That, too," says Nash, who suddenly sees one of them—unclear who, but he hopes Kathleen—in a red-and-blue field hockey uniform, thighs chafed pink from cold weather.

"Could it have been my fault? Was I sending out signals?" asks Lois.

"Anything's possible," says Nash, "but it seems unlikely that someone would flirt with her sister's boyfriend."

"Then what was I doing there?" Lois pleads. "You and Adele were dancing, and I was watching. Why? Was I chaperoning? Was I looking for a chance to cut in? I've asked myself this for a lot of years."

"Maybe you were changing the records for us."

"No! You were dancing to the radio."

"Maybe you were giving us some pointers."

Lois smiles. "You remember—my dancing ability. But Adele was almost as good. You knew the box step but she was trying to teach you to waltz."

"You certainly have the details down," says Nash.

Lois opens her eyes wide. "Because, Harvey, a week later you broke your engagement. Everyone was trying to reconstruct what you'd done and said."

"I never actually *broke* the engagement," says Nash. "That happened by default."

"I always wondered: Was there a note left somewhere that never got read, or a letter mailed that we never received?"

Nash considers recasting his crime as just such a misunderstanding, a note nailed to the door that was tragically overlooked; a waylaid apology decomposing in the dead-letter office. But he doesn't bother. Lois might believe it, but the others never would. They'd cross-examine him on its contents, and he—no librettist—would have to supply the critical lines.

"You should have called," says Lois. "You could have asked for me and I could have broken the news for you."

"I know that. I should have asked to speak to your father, man to man. Christ, I know that better than anyone. And don't you think if I could turn back the clock that's exactly what I would do? Not only call, but come by days—hell, weeks—before the party and explain that I was losing my nerve?"

Lois shrugs. "Not really. It would have been out of character."

Nash is wounded by her answer. He thinks he's been a diplomat and a gentleman since arriving on the Dobbin doorstep, and that Lois has no basis for her low opinion. Well, good. Now he has a legitimate reason to shrink from Lois, who, despite her harsh assessment, is creeping closer on the couch.

"Okay," says Nash. "I admit it. I was a heel then and I'm a heel now. I don't know why I bother."

Lois thinks this over, then asks, "Bother to what?"

"To show up after all these years."

Lois touches his sleeve. "I thought it might have something to do with me."

Ordinarily, he'd encourage a woman in such a misapprehension: *You could tell what I was feeling? You picked that up from across the room without my saying one word? Wow. Are you here with anyone? Can I drive you home?*

But this is different. This is a house full of Dobbins, and he will be sleeping among them, setting his sights on some and disappointing others, negotiating around Richard's cautious goodwill. It is no sacrifice, though, to forgo an easy lay when the woman is not a temptation. Counterfeit tenderness clouds his gray eyes. "You're not altogether wrong," he begins. "You were one of the reasons I had to return. But to be absolutely honest, Adele was the first reason. She's the one I hurt the most."

"But—"

"And you understand that I couldn't say, 'Are you all right, Adele, after what I've done? Can you forgive me?' and in the same breath ask, 'Oh, and by the way, how's your sister Lois? Any chance *she'd* be glad to see me?' "

"I see what you're saying," says Lois.

"It's an untenable position. Then and now."

Lois pours herself her third shot of cognac. Nash wonders if Lois is a drinker, and immediately congratulates himself on this insight. Drinking makes perfect, unattractive sense. The unloved middle sister, a state employee, a divorcée with red hands and no touch on the keyboard.

Except, he notices, that she grimaces with her next swallow as if she's never tasted the stuff before.

"This is a very nice cognac you keep on hand," Nash tries.

Lois turns the bottle to read the label at arm's length.

He smiles, raises his glass in a toast, and remembers to wince from his injuries. "Who's this fellow Kathleen is seeing tonight?"

Lois, instantly tight-lipped, says, "I have no idea."

"My impression was, First date."

"Could be. You'll have to ask Adele."

"Because they're closer?"

"Adele and I are only two years apart, so there was more competition there than friendship growing up."

"And you're saying Adele and Kathleen have more of a mother-daughter relationship?"

"Why?"

Nash smiles. "I'm interested. I like to know how women think."

Lois cocks her head. "For your work?"

"Yes," says Nash. "Absolutely for my work."

"Psychologically speaking? Because women are the ones who buy the products that your jingles are trying to sell?"

"Correct."

"Kathleen does all our shopping and most of our cooking," Lois offers.

"And you? I understand that your field is unemployment. Does that mean that low unemployment is, in a sense, bad for business?"

The phone rings. Lois doesn't answer his question, but sits poised, listening.

"Shouldn't you get that?" he asks.

"Adele will get it. It's right by her bed."

The ringing stops. A minute passes before a door opens down the hall, and, if bare feet hitting hard wood can sound annoyed, these do. Adele appears at the door to the den, wearing the same no-nonsense navy blue fleece bathrobe from the afternoon, and the same determinedly neutral facial cast.

"Adele! Hello!" Nash cries.

"It's for him. He can take it at the telephone table."

"Me?" says Nash.

"Who knows you're here?" Lois asks.

"His accountant," says Adele.

Thirteen

The voice is professional and chilly. "I have one question only: Are you all right?"

"Cynthia?" says Nash.

"I'm not calling to make conversation," she says. "I'm calling as a concerned friend."

"Concerned how?"

"Over your disappearance. Which I think is an appropriate choice of words, considering last night."

Nash squeezes himself into the seat of the one-armed telephone table and whispers, "I was going to call as soon as things calmed down."

"No, you weren't."

"Cyn, listen: I had an accident."

Cynthia gasps.

"Mugged. In broad daylight."

"I knew it! I had a feeling!"

"Just a head injury and some facial lacerations."

"How?" Cynthia cries. "What happened?"

"I was assaulted in the lobby of their building."

" 'Their'? Whose building?"

"The Dobbins'," he says.

"Who did it?"

"An assailant."

"Obviously," says Cynthia. "Did they catch him?"

Nash says, "I couldn't give a description because it happened from behind—"

"Did you go to the emergency room?"

Actually, yes, Nash remembers. Where were they this afternoon—Cedar Sinai? Mount Sinai? Beth Sinai? He remembers and says proudly, "At Beth Israel. I was checked out and released. And we all came back here. I conked out this afternoon, and they woke me up for dinner. They're mortified, of course. And they feel responsible."

"Do you have health insurance?"

"Of course."

"Because you should have a CAT scan. A head injury is no joke."

"I think they gave me one."

"Who found you?"

"One of the sisters came home from work and she buzzed Adele, and they got me upstairs and put ice on the various swellings and lacerations."

A misstep, he senses, producing an unhappy silence. Finally Cynthia asks, "How many sisters?"

"Three."

"And they live together?"

Nash says, "That's correct."

"None of them can be married if they all live together."

He puts his lips against the phone's mouthpiece and cups his hand over his mouth. "I'll fill you in later. I can't really talk."

"Do you have my number?"

Nash hunches even lower over the phone. He whispers, "I do. *And* your fax. *And* your address."

"But?"

"No buts. I was hoping to come by soon. Tomorrow."

After a pause Cynthia says, "Nash?"

"What, doll?"

"I told Adele I was your financial adviser. I said you missed an appointment and that I was concerned because it wasn't like you not to show up."

Nash smiles at that gift. "A little white lie," he says. "No harm done."

"She said it was probably a mild case of amnesia, but I thought she was being sarcastic."

"I think that was Adele's idea of a joke."

"Seriously," she says. "I think there's something you're not telling me."

He considers the various possibilities, then says, "I'm so damned embarrassed, hitting the floor like an old geezer. And I haven't told you the worst: He took my wallet."

"No!"

"You know what a pain that is."

"What about your luggage?"

"At my hotel." *With the bellman.*

"What are you going to do?"

"I'll get by. I won't be driving here, and I try not to rely on credit cards. The cash was negligible."

"Still, it's horrible. It's a violation."

"Did I mention my black eye?" he asks cheerfully.

Cynthia makes a noise that may be either sympathy or self-reproach. "I'm usually the most level-headed woman I know," she says.

"Of course you are." He raises his voice and projects it down the hall. "Why do you think I chose you as my financial adviser?"

"I shouldn't have lied, but what could I say—'Hello? This is Nash's latest sexual conquest calling'?"

"You did the right thing. It was very clever of you. I mean that."

"Thank you."

"So what time tomorrow?"

"Tomorrow? Are you too sore to come by tonight?"

Nash's loins twinge as he conjures her naked form and his constituent role. "I'll see what plays out here," he says.

"If I can help, call. I have my internist's home number."

He makes his voice stern, clientlike. "I'll bring those papers and, um, those . . . canceled checks," he says. He lowers his voice to add, "And anything else you think you'll need."

Finally, she laughs.

"So? Do I get a second chance?"

"I'm breaking all my own rules," says Cynthia. "I'm acting like a teenager."

"Which I love," he murmurs.

"Seriously: I thought I was never going to see you again, so what was the harm of making one last phone call? What did I have to lose? I thought you were one of those men who talks his way into bed and is never heard from again."

"Poor Cyn. We're not all walking stereotypes. Some of us, believe it or not, get knocked down on our way to keeping a promise."

"You're saying you were headed here when you were mugged?"

What harm? he wonders. "God's honest truth," he says.

⟵⟶ "We've been discussing you," says Lois as Nash limps across the doorsill and lowers himself into the brocade lounge chair.

"What aspect of me?"

Lois looks at Adele. Adele says, "Your financial situation."

"Because you knew that was my C.P.A. calling?"

Adele looks to her sister and says, "Would you put on some water for tea, Lo? I'd do it, but I'm still sore."

Lois rises and leaves with a lingering, backward glance.

Adele doesn't speak until there is water running in the kitchen. "Here's what I'm offering," she says. "If you leave tonight, right now, I'll pay for a room at the Holiday Inn."

For a few seconds, Nash thinks Adele is talking about sex: She's gotten rid of Lois to arrange the world's most overdue assignation.

"Fascinating," he murmurs.

"Not *fascinating*," she hisses. "I want you out of here, and if I have to bribe you, I will."

He recovers to say, "Absolutely not. What kind of man would let you pay for his hotel room?"

"A man with a cash-flow problem," she says.

Nash does have a cash-flow problem, but that doesn't prevent his taking offense. After all, the desk clerk at the Copley Plaza had been reasonably civilized about the credit card embarrassment and in accepting the postdated, out-of-state check. "Is that what you think?" he demands. "Because my financial adviser called? I'm a wealthy man. I have unopened checks—residuals—piling up at home. This has nothing to do with cash flow or room charges. This is about making sense of what happened thirty years ago."

Adele leans closer and says, "But what you don't understand, Harvey, is that I'm no longer interested in making sense of you or anything pertaining to you."

"Can I tell you why? Because you hate to be seen as vulnerable. Today was a dramatic illustration of that. I saved your life and you do *not* want to factor that into your I-hate-Nash equation."

Adele asks, "How did your accountant know where to reach you?"

"I left the number with her service."

Lois returns without cups or teapot, and sits, all ears, as if slipping late into a lecture. "It's brewing," she offers when conversation stops. "I made a whole pot of Breathe Easy."

"Nash can't stay. He has to meet with his accountant."

"Tonight?"

Nash smiles. "That's your sister's version. I'm not so sure the question of my leaving has been settled."

Adele says flatly, "I've offered to pay for his hotel room if he leaves right now."

Lois cries, "I hate this! Why can't we just let bygones be bygones? We all have our reasons to be bitter, but I don't see why we can't act like civilized adults."

"Bitter toward me?" Nash asks. "What did I do to you?"

Lois keeps her eyes nervously on Adele as she answers. "You hurt my sister very badly. Which had emotional repercussions throughout our whole family."

"Lois thinks it's my fault that we're all old maids," Adele says.

Lois's normally ruddy face is splotchy and her voice shakes. "How dare you say that! I never said that in my life! I never said anything like that! I never called myself an old maid!"

Adele says, "It's poetic license, Lois. Don't be so touchy. We're three middle-aged, unmarried women."

"I was married. I'd still be married if I hadn't found certain things out!"

Nash decides that the novelty of the Dobbin sisters in their loungewear is wearing thin. He has satisfied his curiosity to the point of boredom, and poured cold water on his redheaded harem fantasy, especially now that Kathleen, his new favorite, is screwing someone at work. His checked sports jacket is draped over the couch, behind his hostesses. He pulls it free with a yank and puts it on, gravy stains on both lapels.

"Are you going?" asks Lois.

"Wouldn't you?" he asks. "Or would you stay here and play psychiatrist?"

"Lois will show you out," says Adele.

He straightens his shoulders and makes one last speech. "I only meant well. I wanted to make peace with you. I'm not a perfect person. I'm a flawed man, but at least I admit it." Ordinarily, in choreographing a dramatic exit, he would kiss the hand of the party being dumped, but facing the unyielding Adele and the unappealing Lois, he merely nods and retreats.

"Wait," Lois calls.

Nash keeps walking until he reaches the front door. She catches up with him and asks, "Where are you going tonight?"

"To a hotel."

"Which one?"

"*Not* the Copley Plaza."

Lois grasps his elbow with her two hands. "Are you well enough to leave?"

"I'll be fine."

"Are you angry?"

He answers, with all the parental condescension he can muster, "No, Lois. I'm not angry."

"Are you going to sue Kathleen for assault and battery?"

Nash hasn't thought of that. "I honestly don't know. I'll have to see how my recovery goes. Whether I scar, and whether I need plastic surgery."

"I want you to know," she whispers, "that you have one friend in this family. I think Adele and Kathleen have acted like crazy women and I don't want you to think we're all cut from the same cloth."

"I appreciate that," he says. "More than you know."

He has no choice: He leans over and places a soft good-bye kiss on Lois's wide brow, expecting she will close her eyes and accept it gratefully. Instead, Lois charges. She grabs his bruised face between her big hands and grinds her lips into his.

Fourteen

Nash, behind sunglasses, admires the pink garters hanging from the lacy black corset, and the adorable sheer bikini panties embroidered with the days of the week at the pubis—until he is galvanized by the sight of Kathleen Dobbin dressing a silver mannequin in the same window. Delighted, he raps on the glass, waves, then sweeps inside to declare the coincidence of the century: He, Nash Harvey, Boston babe in the woods, has, amazingly enough, stumbled upon temporary quarters in Harbor Arms, eighteen floors above this very spot.

Kathleen says, "I told you where my shop was."

"You absolutely did not. And frankly, I would have thought twice about inflicting myself on a Dobbin sister if I had known."

"This isn't a hotel," Kathleen argues. "People don't move in overnight. There's a whole procedure."

"I'm subletting," he says. "A lucky break. My accountant found it."

He's already wondering how to present this to Cynthia: *It's awkward, very. A sister of Adele's works downstairs in the ladies' specialty shop and I don't want to flaunt the fact that I've moved in with you so soon after I reached out to them. You understand, don't you? We'll simply take separate elevators and meet at the garage level.* He looks around the shop, which he finds heartbreakingly small. "Great space. I'd admired your window displays before I realized whose hands were buttoning up that nightie."

"Thank you," she says stiffly.

"How was your weekend?"

Kathleen blinks.

"Your date?" he prompts.

"I heard you."

Nash raises both hands in apology and surrender. "You're right. I'm too damn familiar—a product of too many years in casual California."

Kathleen lifts her chin an inch higher. "Haven't my sisters and I made it clear that we don't want to pursue a friendship with you?"

Nash smiles. "Not to a person."

"Well, Lois doesn't speak for the rest of us, especially not now. And if Richard appeared hospitable, then that was just a reflex. He's more gregarious than the rest of us." She crosses to the counter and puts price stickers on boxes containing—to his absorption and utter delight—a foam-rubber product called "False-C's."

"How much do those go for?" he asks happily.

"Why?"

"Just curious. People in advertising like to know products and prices."

"Twelve dollars."

"Do you sell a lot of these?"

"They're new."

"I hope," he says gravely, "that they do well for you."

Kathleen pounds the last sticker with a closed fist. "Is this what I have to look forward to? Daily visits and phony chats about products?"

"I'm not a stalker, Kathleen."

"But there's no avoiding you! We try, but you keep turning up."

Nash likes her suit. It's black with a short jacket and a silver squiggle of a pin that looks like modern art. "In that case," he says, making sure to stare dolefully, "I'll never darken your doorway again. And I trust you're sorry about my injuries even if you can't express it."

She says, "I thought we agreed it was an accident."

Nash flexes his eyebrows above his dark glasses. "Was that your formal apology? Because it doesn't sound very heartfelt." He raises his sunglasses to his forehead. "You'll be happy to see the discoloration under my eye is changing from purple to a nice dark yellow-green. It means it's healing."

"It's not that noticeable."

"Behind dark glasses maybe."

"Another day or two and you won't need them."

"Really? You have experience with shiners? Because I'm going to drop by in a couple of days and you can tell me whether I still look like Robert De Niro after the climactic fight scene in *Raging Bull*."

Unmoved, Kathleen asks, "Can I tell Richard that you forgive me for letting the casserole slip?"

Nash lowers his sunglasses back onto his handsome, straight nose and says, "Can I let you know?"

⟶ The neighbors have been complaining about the piano playing and the particularly annoying, repetitive nature of the noise. Cynthia thinks she can win over the complainants if she invites them for drinks, during which Nash will perform his jingle hits and give a brief talk on the history of musical advertising.

She is so much in love and so happy to announce obliquely their living arrangement that she thinks "An Evening with Nash" is a good idea. Bostonians are indulgent of genius, especially of the musical variety. She knows from many overheard conversations in elevators that there are music lovers and B.S.O. subscribers among her fellow residents. What comes through her walls sounding like short, sappy melodies will soon be understood as an art form and honorable livelihood. Complaints will metamorphose into dinner invitations when they see she is involved with a composer. Cynthia pictures Nash in tails, sitting at her gorgeous black Steinway & Sons grand piano, made in Hamburg, lecturing between tunes like the ghost of Leonard Bernstein enlightening children in Avery Fisher Hall.

She'd like to broaden the guest list to friends outside the building, a few clients, and a relative or two, but Nash says no—he is too modest to turn a public relations stratagem into a recital.

"There are people who want to meet you," she says.

He asks, rolling off her after intercourse and reaching for the remote, how she will introduce him at this shindig. Friend? Roommate? Client? Nothing cute, he hopes, or overly personal. Their relationship is special, but no one's business but their own.

Cynthia says coldly, " 'Friend,' of course. I wouldn't want to narrow your options."

Nash puts his arm around her and strokes her ample tricep. What had they agreed to? One step at a time, right? Hadn't he said an emphatic *No* to moving in after one night together, and hadn't she promised he wouldn't regret his decision? Hadn't they been honest in exploring the connotations of commitment? Don't get him wrong: He loves being here, loves the gourmet meals, and— why mince words?—the sex. But he's between two worlds right now—an old stifling life and a new uncharted one. Perhaps it would be better if he got his own place and they had an old-fashioned dating courtship?

"No," says Cynthia. "I want you here."

"Give me a kiss," he says.

Before he falls asleep they discuss the format—Cocktails? Tapas? Sit-down dinner? Desserts?—and decide on a buffet featuring products Nash has turned into jingles.

⌒ After Cynthia leaves the next morning, he calls California, ostensibly to see if Dina is keeping up with the mail.

"I sent it to the address you faxed," she says. "One looked like a check."

"From?"

"A.F.M."

"Good. I need that."

"Why don't you send change-of-address notices instead of me having to forward everything?"

Nash says things are fluid. He's subletting and doesn't know how long this address will be in effect, which leaves him dependent on the goodwill of the landlady to forward important mail. He walks the portable phone to the bedroom and lies down on top of the white damask duvet. "Have I asked how *you* are? How's the foot biz?"

"Do you know what a synclavier is?" Dina asks.

"I certainly do."

"Do you have one?"

"I intend to get one."

"It's state-of-the-art," she says.

"Who have you been talking to?" Nash asks.

After a pause she says, "A friend."

"A friend in the business?"

"A friend who's around music. A friend who has a friend who wrote 'I'd Like to Teach the World to Sing.' "

"Wow," says Nash.

"Where are you?" she asks.

"Boston."

"I know that. What's her name?"

"My landlady, you mean?"

"The last person who changed your sheets."

"Cynthia."

"And you've been together how long?"

"A week? Ten days?"

"House-sitting or cohabitating?"

Nash hesitates. "It's kind of a B-and-B situation."

"How many bedrooms?"

"Two. The views are phenomenal. I love the Atlantic."

"How'd you meet her?"

Nash says, "You sound belligerent."

"Wouldn't you be? Last time I heard you were flying across the country to mend fences or someone's broken heart, or find your roots, but now I hear you got waylaid."

Nash considers saying, If you mean Adele Dobbin, I found her easily. Just in time to save her life.

"Can you answer?" asks Dina.

"I did find Adele," he says sadly.

"Alive?"

"Of course alive. Why would you ask that?"

"The way you said it. I thought the rest of the story was, 'I got there too late. I found Adele's headstone in the cemetery where we used to go make out. They buried her last week.' "

"Not at all. I found her, and on some level it was enlightening."

"Meaning, 'She's fat and old and now I can cross her off my list'?"

"No."

"Then, 'She's married and happy. I didn't ruin her life and I can stop feeling guilty.' "

Nash switches ears and plucks absentmindedly at his chest hair. *Guilty* might give a name to the twinge he feels when he pictures Adele's life, her ochre kitchen and tender ribs. "How are the dogs?" he asks.

"Fine."

"Do they miss me?"

"No. What does your roommate do?"

"Manages people's money."

"How'd you meet her?"

"On a plane."

"The one you ran away on?"

"That's the only plane I've taken lately."

"How perfect: You met her on the plane five minutes after you left Orange County."

"She's a graduate of Harvard Business School," he says.

"Maybe she can fix your money troubles."

"I haven't availed myself of her services."

Dina laughs.

Nash says, "One of these days she's going to take a look at my returns, but this is her busiest—"

"How old is she?"

"Fifty."

"Old," says Dina.

"For a roommate?"

"Old for you to fuck," says Dina.

Nash says, "I won't dignify that, but I will tell you that I made the rounds of the local agencies."

"So?"

"Want to hear what I'm doing?"

"Not especially."

"I'm working on a unique instrumental with a vocal tag for a casino on an Indian reservation."

He hears a yawn, then a pallid, "Good for you."

"You don't sound terribly enthusiastic."

"You woke me up."

"You know, it wasn't easy to pick up the phone and call you because I didn't know what kind of shape you'd be in or whether we could have a civil conversation. And the longer I put it off, the harder it became."

"And finally you do call, *and* . . . ?"

"You tell me," says Nash. "What did I find when I called my old number and the woman who shared it?"

"That I want half of everything," says Dina.

⟨⟩ As soon as Nash's bruises fade, Cynthia gathers the names of the neighbors who wrote cranky, typed complaints to the board citing the noise clause. She finds high-quality ecru invitations embossed with G clefs and mails them with postage stamps of dead U.S. symphony conductors. "Regrets only," she writes at the bottom. No one calls.

The day before the event, fearing an empty living room, she invites Philip from the office and her two favorite doormen to what she calls a little musical get-together. "An impromptu salon," she amplifies, to meet—well, they *had* to have noticed the newly authorized handsome gentleman with the Burberry raincoat and sunglasses, hadn't they?

Felix declines because he has to work, but Lorenz asks if he may be so bold as to bring a date.

"Why, Lorenz! How wonderful. And you know, I suspected as much."

"I'll have to ask her first. Can I let you know—" He checks his watch. "She gets in at ten."

"I don't need a formal answer. Just show up at eight. Tie and jacket."

"What can I bring?"

"Nothing. Nada. Not a thing. Just you and your . . . friend."

"Kathleen."

Cynthia smiles at that, at the quaint, chambermaid quality of the name, and the melting-pot charm of a Lorenz and a Kathleen attending her chic affair. She drives to work feeling generous and democratic, and only moderately worried about Saturday night.

Fifteen

*E*verything's ready: the Orientals and kilims vacuumed, the black granite mantel buffed, the piano polished, the bridge chairs arranged in a half circle, the guest bathroom scrubbed and perfumed, the dimmer switches slid to atmospheric, the beans ground for the decaf. On a marble-topped pedestal table, there is imported champagne and fluted glasses. The Israeli oranges and California prunes of two advertising campaigns nest in Cynthia's beautiful rose-colored Sandwich glass bowl.

Cynthia is wearing new black velvet trousers and a black short-sleeved chenille sweater with a boat neck, accessorized by a long rope of grape-sized faux pearls. Her shoes are black patent leather with a Cuban heel and a thin gold bar across the instep. As for Nash, he and Cynthia reasoned that a Boston audience would respond favorably to both tradition and approachability. Accordingly, he wears a starched blue oxford shirt, cuffs rolled up, dark green gabardine trousers, and loafers made by a manufacturer of boat shoes. Cynthia thinks the preppy look on Nash is heaven.

It has not occurred to Cynthia that she may have invited future rivals for Nash's attentions until the first guest arrives, alone, in a Lycra spandex dress the color of raw frankfurters and green lizard high heels: the unexpectedly attractive, tall, platinum-big-haired Olive Boudreaux, whose dowdy name on the letter of complaint certainly did not conjure this beauty contestant. Her hands offer no clues: no obvious gold wedding band, but silver-and-brass-inlaid ethnic rings on many manicured fingers. Nash grins and shakes the new guest's hand for several long seconds. "Just you? No husband tonight?"

"No husband, period," she says.

"Would you like to choose a seat?" says Cynthia. "You have first choice."

"What's the hurry?" asks Nash. "Let's get your guest a drink. Champagne?"

Cynthia has a rigid outline for the evening, and champagne is scheduled after the question-and-answer period. Nash sees Cynthia hesitate and says, "Oh, why not? We've got plenty. That is, if Ms. Boudreaux—"

"Olive," corrects Olive.

The doorbell rings again, and it is Cynthia's unhappy job to leave Nash alone with Olive and answer it. It is the Glovers from across the hall, Susan and Charles, who don't work, who have sons at boarding school, who are tall and lean and are rumored to have trust funds. "We wondered if 'Evening with Nash' was some kind of tribute to Ogden Nash," Mrs. Glover asks as Cynthia shakes her hand. "A poetry reading or some such."

"It's a kind of poetry," says Cynthia. "Only this is words and music by Nash Harvey, the composer. Live and in person."

"Do I know his work?" asks Charles.

"Charles is an audiophile," his wife explains.

"Aficionado," Charles corrects. "Not that I know every living composer."

"Nash!" Cynthia calls. "The Glovers are here!"

Nash returns to the foyer with Olive, and shakes the hands of the severe, graying-blond neighbors. "So glad you could make it," he says.

"We almost didn't," says Susan.

"They thought it might be a poetry reading," explains Cynthia.

"No, parents' weekend," says Charles.

"Saint Paul's," says his wife.

"You skipped parents' weekend for *this*?" Nash asks. "I'm flattered."

"Ducked out early," says the husband. "We've been to so damn many that we hit the games and skip the assemblies."

"How many kids do you have?" asks Olive.

The Glovers look surprised that someone in the building wouldn't have heard about the academic and athletic accomplishments of their Jamie and Will. "Two boys."

"Do you know Olive Boudreaux?" asks Cynthia.

"I'm new," says Olive, who looks brassy next to Susan Glover's navy blue linen, her careless knot of hair, and her small gold hoops.

"This is my social debut in Harbor Arms," says Olive. "No one's invited me to anything before."

"How long have you lived here?" asks Susan Glover.

"Since the beginning of the year."

"Moved from . . . ?" Charles asks.

"Atlanta, Georgia."

"You know, I *thought* I heard the hint of a drawl," says Nash.

"What brought you to Boston?" asks Cynthia.

"A job."

"Which is?" asks Charles.

"Lexuses, Porsches, and Audis. I sell them."

The men's lips part and their pupils dilate. "For whom?" asks Charles.

"Flagg Lexus in Wakefield."

"You sell *cars*?" asks Susan Glover.

"I have an A-Six," says Charles.

"Silver with onyx leather?" says Olive. "I've seen it."

Susan says, "He loves cars. He subscribes to car magazines and watches car shows on television and goes into chat rooms about cars—and I mean this is a man who is utterly cerebral in every other area of his life."

Olive smiles and says to Mr. Glover, "You're not alone. We get doctors, lawyers, dentists, stockbrokers, bankers. Serious people who get a little silly over what they drive. I'm the same way."

"I'm from California," Nash volunteers. "Need I say more?"

"About what?" asks Mrs. Glover.

"Cars!"

"Models and makes we've never even seen on the East Coast,"

says Charles. "I was there over Christmas and I saw, one right after the other, an old Lamborghini Countach and a Bentley Turbo R."

"Unbelievable," says Olive.

Olive asks Nash where in California he lives, and Cynthia listens hard for what verb tense he will employ.

"South of L.A. Newport Beach."

"You sail?" asks Charles.

"No time," says Nash.

"Are the Brandts coming tonight by any chance?" asks Susan.

"I certainly invited them," says Cynthia. She checks her watch. "I could give them a call."

"Or just rap on the wall like they do," says Nash.

"I love going to a party in my own building and not having to worry about the weather or parking," says Olive, "or whether I've sprayed silicone on my shoes."

Nash brightens at *silicone*. "Did you say you're just below us?" he asks.

"I'm in Seventeen-H."

He lowers his voice and raises his eyebrows. "You wouldn't be the one banging the broom handle against your ceiling?"

"Tennis racquet," she says. "And I've got a nice gouge in the plaster to prove it."

As Nash is saying it would only be right if he spackled whatever damage he'd caused, there is another knock on the door. Cynthia doesn't want to stop monitoring Nash's conduct, but she excuses herself. She'll post Philip at the door when he arrives if he hasn't brought his less-than-charming law student boyfriend.

It is not Philip but Lorenz and his date, an attractive and sweet-looking redhead who Cynthia knows she knows. She is distracted by the date's vintage spring coat of yellow bouclé wool with big black novelty buttons.

"You know Kathleen Dobbin," says Lorenz, "from The Other Woman? Downstairs?"

"Of course! *That's* why you look familiar."

Cynthia is smiling and being gracious, but at the same time she is noting what this development says about Lorenz. He is dating someone not unlike Cynthia herself: not a teenager. Someone refined, self-employed, a likely college graduate, worldly if her shopwares and darling coat are any barometer. It is unsettling because Cynthia had wondered about Lorenz, about his marital status, his sexual orientation, his ethnicity; had thought about him for herself, fleetingly, on the nights she collected her takeout at what seemed to be the end of his shift. She shakes it off. Preposterous. Besides, she has Nash now.

Lorenz is helping Kathleen off with her coat, and they are exchanging fond smiles over nothing more than that. Cynthia asks, "Did you two meet on the job? Or do you know each other outside work?"

"We met here," Lorenz says.

"Of course, for months it was a very formal 'Good morning, Lorenz.' 'Good morning, Miss Dobbin,' " says Kathleen.

Cynthia's brain stalls at *Dobbin* at the same time the hostess imperative directs her to say, "Let me introduce you to everyone. You must know the Glovers? And Olive Boudreaux?"

"I own The Other Woman," Kathleen tells Mrs. Glover, then leans in to confide with just the right degree of humor and girl-friendship, "I'm the one who's been punching your Bra Club card all these months."

Mrs. Glover laughs, causing Mr. Glover to ask, "What, darling?"

"I'll tell you later," she says.

"Did the Brandts say they could make it?" Mrs. Glover asks again. "They love music. They go to everything."

"I saw the Brandts leave as we were arriving," Lorenz says.

"Oh," says Cynthia. She forces a smile and says, "*Please*. Come meet our guest of honor. Or should I say, the evening's entertainment."

When Kathleen gasps, Cynthia thinks she is just another appreciative guest reacting to the pitch of the cathedral ceiling and the gorgeous view of the harbor lights.

Nash glances over and says easily, "Hey, look who's here: Red!"

"You know each other?" asks Cynthia.

"Sure we do. So do you," says Nash. "She's Adele's sister."

"You're Adele Dobbin's sister?" asks Cynthia.

"Why does that name sound familiar?" asks Susan Glover.

"She's on television sometimes," says Lorenz. "She raises money for Channel Two."

"This is very awkward," says Kathleen. "I had no idea."

"You knew I was staying in the Arms," says Nash. "We discussed it that day in your shop."

"We didn't make the connection, though," Lorenz says quietly. "Not to Cynthia's party."

"A little ancient history," Nash explains to the others. "A long time ago I was as good as engaged to Kathleen's big sister."

"*And?*" asks Olive after no one responds.

"We broke up. We never actually made it official. We were kids, and this one here was a mere babe." He takes Lorenz's hand and pumps it. "You, my man. I knew you were coming but I never put two and two together."

"It's my fault," says Kathleen. "Lorenz knew you as 'Nash' and I always referred to you as 'Harvey.' "

"Is it 'Harvey' or is it 'Nash'?" asks Lorenz.

"Nash. Harvey was my childhood name."

"Childhood and beyond," says Kathleen.

Nash smiles and tries to engage Kathleen in a toast of forgiveness. " 'Longest adolescence on record,' I think is what you're getting at."

"How far back did you date her sister?" asks Olive.

"It ended in March of nineteen sixty-seven," says Kathleen.

"I was born that year!" says Olive. "June of sixty-seven."

"I assume your sister subsequently married?" asks Mrs. Glover. And to Olive: "She's so attractive."

"Let me answer that, Kathleen," says Nash. "No, she did not marry. Which is something I feel I bear responsibility for."

"Why?" asks Olive.

Nash sits down on the nearest bridge chair and hands his glass to Cynthia for safekeeping. "I'm sensing that I poisoned her view of men and I doubt whether she was able to trust anyone again."

Kathleen says, "I don't think my sister would like to be the subject of our cocktail conversation."

"You're absolutely right. Forgive me."

Lorenz is wearing a troubled look that says, I'm merely the doorman and you're the doorman's date, and I didn't know you'd be picking a fight with the guest of honor.

"Small-world department," says Mr. Glover.

"We have a 'GBH umbrella *and* a tote bag," says his wife. She turns to Cynthia and asks cheerfully, "Where did you and Nash meet?"

Cynthia smiles, her turn at last. "It was a flight from L.A. to Boston. We talked the whole way, and subsequently had dinner."

"That same night?" asks Mrs. Glover.

"I know how that sounds, but, after all, we'd just had a five-hour conversation, which is twice as long as most first dates."

"I think it's nice," says Mrs. Glover. "I never have interesting conversations on planes."

"Once in a while I do," says Olive, "but I think the whole dating-game thing on planes is overrated. Mostly I get seated next to old ladies who can't hear."

"And then she told you about an opening in her building?" asks Kathleen.

"Actually, an opening right here. Cynthia loves company, and I hate hotels." He turns to Olive and says, "You must have the same layout—two bedrooms, two and a half baths?"

There is a cocky knock on the door and then a male voice calling, "Anybody home?"

"It's Philip," says Cynthia. "My secretary. Don't discuss anything interesting while I'm gone."

Kathleen waits until Cynthia is out of range before saying, "Weren't *you* on the right plane at the right time."

"How so?"

"To meet someone who lets you move in after one cross-country conversation and one date."

"You could've been married with a couple of kids," says Olive.

"Or a psychopath," says Kathleen.

"Or a confidence man," says Lorenz.

"When all I am is a humble jingle composer without a place to hang my hat."

"What do you mean, 'jingle'?" says Olive.

"That's your line?" asks Mr. Glover.

"That's the noise I've been making over here: yours truly in the jingle-making process."

"This is Philip, everyone!" announces Cynthia. "Nash, Olive, Susan, Charles, Lorenz, and Miss Dobbin."

Philip is tall and dark, wearing a painted flamingo tie, and grinning. "Neighbors, right? So you've probably heard so many nice things about me."

"Not me," says Olive. "I just met everyone tonight. Except Lorenz, who I know from the front door."

"Miss Boudreaux sells luxury cars," says Nash, "and Miss Dobbin sells ladies' undergarments."

"Cool," says Philip.

"Actually, we have cars for every budget," says Olive.

"When I'm not tending to my family, I'm a literacy volunteer," says Mrs. Glover.

"Wonderful!" says Nash. "One of those thousand points of light."

"Shouldn't we get started?" says Cynthia.

⟶ Without preamble or introduction, Nash sits down at the piano and plays a medley: "I Love New York" segues into "Look for the Union Label," then "G.E., We Bring Good Things to Life," "I'm Chiquita Banana and I've Come to Say"; he ends with a jaunty, staccato "The Incredible Edible Egg." When the last note is played, he swivels around to face his small audience. "Familiar?" he asks.

"Very," says Mrs. Glover.

"Popular songs?"

"Commercials," she says.

"Did you write these?" asks Mr. Glover.

Nash says, "If only."

"How about a jingle sing-along?" Cynthia asks, activity Number Two according to plan. Nash surveys the audience: Kathleen curls her lip and avoids eye contact. Olive says, "Okay, but I can't carry a tune." Mrs. Glover checks with her husband, who says, "We only watch public television."

Nash says, "Let me start with something simple." His fingers flex and jump over the keys, producing a jingle that stumps everyone but Mr. Glover, who says tonelessly, "Plop, plop, fizz, fizz, oh, what a relief it is."

"That's an oldie," says Nash. "Charles and I are dating ourselves." He checks a slip of paper in his shirt pocket, plays a jingle from his crib sheet. "Anyone?" Olive and Cynthia supply an off-key rendition of "Sooner or later you'll own Generals."

"Excellent, ladies," says Nash. He hits the next notes playfully, fingers roiling. When no one else speaks up, Kathleen recites glumly, "We build excitement—Pontiac!"

"Bingo!" says Nash. "Ten for accuracy; zero for expression." He sits with his hands poised above the keyboard.

"Play one of yours," says Cynthia.

"Do," says Mrs. Glover.

He turns back to the keyboard, thinks, plays a few bars.

"Maybe if you sing it," says Cynthia.

Nash, in an unexpectedly thin and flat voice, croaks, "When the game's been lost or won, when the races have been run, when all's been said and done, you'll want Red Cat."

Kathleen is sitting at the end of the semicircle, feet pointed toward the door as if waiting to leave at the next annoyance. "Red Cat?" she repeats.

Nash explains, as he reprises the tune, "It's a microbrewed root beer made in Portland. I don't think the spot runs outside the Pacific Northwest." *Or at all.* "What I tried to do here was fuse the sounds we like to get with cola commercials—bouncy, effervescent—with the sounds that work for beer—big, full, powerful. I like to mix styles, and so do advertisers. That's why I was excited about doing root beer. It can be both fun in the sun and a little machismo."

"I assume you don't sing them yourself," says Kathleen.

Nash laughs. "Believe me, I've tried."

"Tell them why," says Cynthia.

Nash turns around fully, takes a deep breath and says, "Okay: Jingology One-oh-one: It's the singers who make the serious money, not the composers." Without looking back at the keyboard, his right hand crosses under his armpit and plays three familiar notes: Na-bis-co. "That's what we call a musical logo," says Nash, "and I'm here to tell you that the voice that sings those three famous syllables has probably made a million bucks in residuals, while the guy who wrote those same three notes was paid a one-time composing fee."

He hesitates, then decides to confide in his new friends. He plays his most famous, and therefore his most poignant financial failure: "*Leg-a-cy . . . it sets you free.*"

"You *wrote* that?" says Olive.

"I hear it every time I turn on the TV," says Lorenz.

"Well done," says Mr. Glover.

"The irony, of course," Nash says, "is that it damn well could have set me free, but I had to sign away my rights to the song. And when I wised up, and insisted on retaining rights, the agency stopped using me." He doesn't tell the rest of the story: how he made a pass at an assistant copywriter who went on to become the head copywriter. "Cruel business," he says.

"I would think there would still be some gratification in it," says Mrs. Glover. "To have sent a piece of music out into the world and to know it's endured, and it's still making the policyholders feel good about their company. It's not unlike the satisfactions of a volunteer job."

"It hurts whenever he hears the song," says Cynthia. "It's so unfair."

"Life's unfair," says Kathleen.

Sixteen

*I*t isn't the first time Lois has moved into Mrs. Chabot's establishment on Beacon Hill, walking distance from Unemployment, but she's never stayed this long. Mrs. Chabot likes Lois, considers her a model tenant and classy lady/career gal who's never smelled of liquor at the breakfast table, who scrubs the tub with Dutch Cleanser after every use, although it's not required, and carries a briefcase to work. Mrs. Chabot does not mind fielding the occasional phone call on her private line because Miss Dobbin's callers are as considerate as her tenant. "I hate to disturb you . . ." they begin. Or, "Would it be possible to speak to Lois Dobbin?"

This visit has been quieter than usual. Miss Dobbin looks a little washed out, or maybe it's the new hair color, or maybe the change of life. She's never in a jovial mood during her stays. She arrives looking sad or miffed, and seems to regain some good humor over the course of her two or three days, which is just the point at which she packs up and goes back home. Mrs. Chabot has never asked about the big rock on her left hand, and can only assume after all these years as "Miss," with no mention of a fiancé, and no visible bruises, that there's no fellow on the other end of it. She's known women who have worn engagement rings they inherited when their mothers died, and Mrs. Chabot gets the idea that Lois comes from money, which is why she doesn't mind her airs. Someday she'll ask, and the answer will be gracious. No one else notices that the orange juice she serves at breakfast is not from concentrate, or when the scones vary from plain to raisin. Mrs. Chabot lets Lois pay by personal check and has never had a problem.

⌒ It seems to Lois as if she's watching some sort of Jewish night on 'GBH—a documentary about Philip Roth, which is leading into *Goodbye, Columbus*. They have snagged the actor who played Ali MacGraw's brother, now a middle-aged doctor in New Jersey and still a big goofy jock, talking on tape about the importance of supporting public television. The volunteers answering the phones are introduced as members of Hillel at Harvard and Wellesley. Lois is evaluating Adele's appearance and, as much as she can tell on an eighteen-inch screen, her sister's frame of mind. Adele's dress is new—color uncertain in black and white; possibly navy or a chocolate brown; what their mother would have called "a frock," in a silk crepe, maybe a good rayon, with covered buttons. Adele looks happy, Lois thinks, but dismisses it as on-air poise and experience. Lois has volunteered in Studio A, has seen Adele smile on cue and ignite a fake inner glow as soon as the director's finger points her way. Sentence after sentence Adele beseeches, extols, and paints a bleak picture—no one dramatizes it better—of Life Without Public Television.

And now Adele is introducing 'GBH's new station manager, recently promoted from staff attorney, Martin Glazer, who, she says, is going to describe how much it costs to acquire shows produced at other affiliates and why financial support is so desperately needed. Lois watches Adele's face as she listens to him, and notices that her sister is not shuffling her index cards. She is listening as if Martin Glazer is fascinating, and he, in return, is addressing Adele with an eagerness that Lois recognizes, with a start, as puppy love. Lois looks for a wedding ring on Glazer's hand and sees none. Now he is saying that he grew up in Boston, on Dorchester's Blue Hill Avenue, and his family couldn't afford symphony tickets, but because of WGBH he got to hear some of the world's most famous orchestras and conductors.

"And the Boston Pops?" Adele reminds him.

"My grandmother's favorite," he says. "She used to send a birthday card to Arthur Fiedler every year."

"And your mother thinks she discovered Julia Child? Tell us about that."

And you know that how? Lois wonders.

"Well, you have to remember that Julia was a new commodity, and hardly formidable, this tall lady with a funny voice. My mother used to take notes—of course she's never followed a recipe in her life, but she kept a pad of paper and a pencil on a tray table in the living room expressly for this purpose."

Adele looks up and says, "How much time do we have? Can Marty tell us about his mother's letter to Julia?"

Marty?

Adele answers her own question. "Okay. No time. Next pledge break. It's a very sweet story about skimming soup. One eight hundred four nine two one one one is our number here. We'll be taking your calls throughout the movie. These charming and dare-I-say brilliant Harvard and Wellesley students can't wait to talk to you." She looks directly into the camera and says, "And now, the classic, almost folkloric *Goodbye, Columbus*."

Lois has been studying Martin Glazer the entire time he's filled her small screen. Around Adele's age, she thinks. No hair to speak of, just a salt-and-pepper ring around his male-pattern baldness. Dark suit, white shirt, tight in the neck, striped tie. His face is round and fleshy. His eyes look light—green or blue—and kind.

Lois snaps off the TV and does her abdominal crunches on Mrs. Chabot's hooked rug. In a sateen boudoir chair she skims the movie listings in the *Globe*, reads "Confidential Chat." At eight-thirty she runs a bath down the hall. As soon as her plastic bubble of champagne bath oil dissolves and sinks, she hears her name: It is Mrs. Chabot, saying, "Phone call! Your brother."

"I'm in the bath," Lois yells back. "Where is he?"

Mrs. Chabot answers, "He says he's at a phone booth. Can you get out for a minute?"

Lois puts on her big rose terry-cloth robe, goes to the extension in the hallway, picks it up, and says, "I've got it."

"Lo?" says Richard.

"How did you know where I was?"

He laughs. "You always end up there."

"I had to get away."

"Believe me, I know," says Richard.

"I was going to call you later."

"Whatever. Have you eaten dinner?"

"Hours ago."

"How long does it take you to dry off and get dressed and meet me at the Hampshire House?"

"I hate it there," says Lois.

"The Parker House?"

"Good. Oh, and Richard—I'm now a blonde," she says.

⌁ Marty Glazer's mother is still alive, and keeps one of her sets tuned to Marty's station all day. He doesn't live with her, but he calls every morning when he gets to work. Tomorrow she is going to inquire about the redheaded woman who asks for money in such a nice way—whether she's married, single, or by any chance Jewish. Tonight, alerted by her son she is all ears as he talks about his childhood (she doesn't like the part about their not being able to afford symphony tickets), but forgets and forgives when the Dobkin woman says, "Do we have time to hear about his mother's letter to Julia? It's a very sweet story about skimming soup . . ."

The girl is no youngster, but that's okay. They could adopt. Her visiting nurse went to China for a baby and got an adorable one. Mrs. Glazer drags a bridge chair over to the set for closer examination. The redhead is touching the sleeve of Marty's suit jacket to interrupt him with an announcement of a dollar figure. They look happy. She turns up the sound. Maybe she'll call in a pledge and say, "That's my son on television. I'm not kidding. I'm Marty Glazer's mother. Could you put him on?" Her boy can't take his eyes off this girl. Maybe she'll call Leota to make sure she's watching and to second her own, very clear impression: that this girl in the claret dress wants Marty to take her on a date.

⌁ In the time it takes Lois to walk from the door of the Parker House to her brother's table, Richard doesn't recover from the shock of how terrible she looks as a blonde. He stands and kisses her cheek.

"Do you like it?" Lois asks.

"Sit," says Richard. "I ordered you a glass of white wine."

Lois touches her hair, rakes it back from the temple with her fingers. "You hate it," she states calmly.

"It's just . . . people dye their hair red to get your natural color."

To his dismay, Lois's voice shakes when she answers. "We're not three redheaded sisters rolled into one. I'm sick to death of that. I want people to be able to distinguish between us. You never had to worry about that."

"Lo, it's fine. If you like it that's what's important."

"You don't get tarred with the same brush: the three spinsters."

"Who said that?"

"Adele!"

"It doesn't sound like a word she'd use."

"She used it! She *reveled* in it. She smiled when she spit it out! I'm no spinster. 'Spinsters' don't marry. Spinsters can't be women who are popular and—I'm going to say this because we're both adults—not dead yet." Lois doesn't know how to whisper. The man at the next table looks over. "I can't conduct a social life from Stearns Road, and that's the problem."

"Because?"

"Because I have too many chaperones there. I can't invite someone for dinner, light some candles, put on some music—"

"And who'd cook for this tête-à-tête, Lo?"

"I can cook a meal for company! I certainly can follow a recipe. Or defrost something of Kathleen's."

Richard asks if she has kitchen privileges at the bed-and-breakfast.

"Unfortunately not."

"So you're not exactly throwing dinner parties every night."

"But my life is my own! I come home from work and if I want to go out, I just go. No questions asked."

"Where do you go?" he asks.

Lois waves a hand with each lie: "Restaurants. Theater. Parties. I just go. I don't have to tell Kathleen by nine A.M. to buy one less lamb chop."

"Hey," says Richard. "You don't have to justify that to me. You don't see me apologizing for not living there."

Lois nods once, twice, as if entering into a black-sheep pact with her brother. She holds up her glass, then stops in midgesture. "Richard," she says. "I just had the most incredible idea."

A waitress brings a salad bowl of pretzel mix, and Richard thanks her by name: Kelly. Kelly asks if he'd like a refill and he says, "A little later. My sister might like something to eat, though."

All of the sisters know this "my-sister-and-I" routine, the announcement to an object of possible desire that he is in the company of family. Kathleen—the one most easily mistaken for a date—has perfected her role as Richard's wry accomplice. She'll confide in the woman being wooed, "He's trying to tell you that he's single and I'm to be ignored."

Lois says without consulting the menu that she'll have the shrimp cocktail, and Richard says, "Nothing for me this minute."

Lois repeats that she has an amazing idea: She and Richard should get an apartment together.

"Absolutely not," he says.

"Because?"

"Because guys my age don't live with their sisters unless they're eunuchs."

"I wouldn't interfere. You could come and go as you please and I wouldn't care what you did or with whom. Besides, I'd look after certain things you don't care about."

"Such as?"

"Bookkeeping. Changing the linens. Watering the plants."

"I like things the way they are," says Richard.

"Which is how?"

"On my own. Living in Newton."

"With this Nora woman?"

"It's her apartment, but she's not there that much—"

"Where is she?"

"At her girlfriend's."

The connotation doesn't register. Lois asks if Richard met her on the job.

"Yes, but not in the usual way; not serving her any papers. She's a colleague. Came over from Franklin County last year."

"Are you seeing her?"

Richard laughs. "You're so dense, Lo. She's not interested in men. She likes girls. Women."

"Oh," says Lois. "That doesn't shock me. I'm no stick-in-the-mud."

"We're friends."

"Okay. I get it."

Richard thumbs the condensation on his glass and smiles.

"What? Is there someone else in the wings?"

Richard grins and pops a few peanuts. "The lesbian thing aside? I think she likes me."

"Nora?"

"I'm trying to find out."

"So she's not a real lesbian?"

"She lived with a guy once."

Lois says, "There's so many nice single women around, Richard, without this complication. Can't you find one who prefers men all the time?"

He shrugs and says, "I like her. She's great."

"You like the unavailable ones, the uphill fights."

"It may not be as uphill as you think," he says, and raises his eyebrows.

Kelly brings Lois's shrimp cocktail and a bottle of Tabasco. Lois says to Richard, "You're eyeing mine already. Why don't you order one yourself."

"Should I?" he asks Kelly.

"Up to you," says the waitress.

"I'm not sharing," says Lois.

"I'd go for it," says the waitress.

"My treat," says Lois.

"Absolutely not," says Richard. "Besides you're making me look like the poor relation in front of this very charming young lady who serves shrimp cocktail all day to yuppies in Armani suits with big wads of cash."

"Platinum credit cards," says Kelly. "But I'm not impressed by guys who are impressed with themselves."

"He'll have one," says Lois, "and I'll have another glass of the house white."

"I'm Richard Dobbin," he says.

∽ All six rows of Hillel volunteers are staring at the monitor, where Richard Benjamin is lying on top of Ali MacGraw. No phones are ringing with pledges. "How are we doing?" Marty Glazer asks Adele.

"Too soon to know. Ninety-odd calls so far, which is low. We'll see how we do during the movie."

"I found the movie pretty faithful to the novella," says Marty. "Or maybe I'm merging the two in my memory."

"I never saw the movie," says Adele. "And I'm embarrassed to say I never read the book."

"I saw it in college." He smiles. "With Barbara Dinoff, if I'm not mistaken."

"Old girlfriend?"

"Blind date."

"And you remember her name?"

"I knew her from afar, and my sister engineered the fix-up." He grinned. "To no avail. That was all there was to it: *Goodbye, Columbus,* good-bye, Marty."

"I'm sorry," says Adele.

Marty shrugs.

"Did you call her, or did you just assume she didn't want to see you again?"

"I called. She had a quiz the next day."

"Ouch," says Adele.

"Terrible time, my twenties."

"Mine, too," says Adele.

Marty smiles and tilts his head. "I find that hard to believe."

Adele doesn't amplify. She has written a new rule and here is its first test: no more relaying the hard-luck broken-engagement story to any man, and no more evoking the name of Harvey Nash. "Oh, you know," she says. "I think we feel more confident now. I was a self-conscious kid, and relatively tongue-tied. At this age, I feel like I can carry on a conversation with almost anyone. I think it gets easier." She glances over to the movie on the screen. "What am I missing?" she asks.

He wants to put his arm around her shoulder and explain the plot as if they are staring at a distant shore and he is helping her locate the dot that is their cottage. But he can't. He is the station manager; she reports to him. He's attended seminars and knows he should not propose renting *Goodbye, Columbus* at a later date, and watching it without phones ringing or calculators whirring. Instead, he allows himself to move an inch closer so he can narrate the mid-movie action. "Her old man is a plumbing contractor, and he's taken his son into the business."

Adele checks the studio clock. "Less than five minutes . . . I'll reintroduce you, then I'll say something like, 'Tell us about the letter your mother wrote to Julia Child.' You'll have about thirty seconds."

Marty looks newly worried. "If I don't get in the part about the kosher salt, she'll never forgive me," he says.

"What about kosher salt?"

"My mother thinks that regular salt has cornstarch in it and makes the soup cloudy. So you have to use the kosher."

"Is that true?"

"I never researched the question," says Marty.

Adele smiles. "Then I think we can give you another ten seconds. And don't be nervous. Just pretend we're chatting at the copy machine, just the two of us, with no one else listening." Marty swallows hard. It draws Adele's gaze to his Adam's apple, where she notices that the knot of his tie is askew. She hands him her index cards, and, in the interest of good television, straightens it.

⟵⟶ Cynthia is washing glasses in the kitchen, and has declined Nash's insincere offer to dry and put away. He doesn't notice that she is angry—snatching plates aggressively from tabletops, banging the stainless into the dishwasher's utensil basket, soaping crystal petulantly. In bed alone, he is studying *TV Guide* while flipping channels with the remote control. A familiar voice causes him to look up. "New members, old members, lapsed members," the woman's voice is saying. "We want to hear from all of you . . . *right* now."

It is the televised, dressed-up Adele, looking damn good. He takes another pillow from Cynthia's side of the bed and props himself higher against the headboard. The dress she's wearing shows off her waistline, and even if she has small tits, she's got curves. Who knew Adele would look this good on TV, better than she does in real life? He revises that with a charitable thought: What dame'd look good after choking on a steak and breaking a rib and hanging around in her bathrobe, scowling the entire time? Here she's looking happy, confident, less like a bitter and pissed-off old maid. Good makeup job. He knows this phenomenon, having seen enough middle-aged actresses looking haggard in the supermarket, then a week later on a talk show looking pretty sensational. Now Adele's talking to some suit, a wimpy guy with no hair. Overeager, Nash thinks. Adele's lips match the maroon of her dress, and Nash likes the effect against her pale skin. So does this guy, obviously; it'll be fun to tease her later about her new admirer. Now that flat-chested Ali MacGraw is on the screen. And here's Jack Klugman. *Love Story*, he guesses. He had some buddies who were extras in the hockey-rink scene, pretending to be Harvard fans. Maybe if he'd stuck around, he'd have been an extra, too. Maybe even talked his way into some composing or arranging. Francis Lai got rich on that sappy score.

Cynthia strides into the room, dish towel in hand, and blocks his view of the television. "I've reached a decision," she says.

After a minute, Nash says, "I'm listening."

"What are you watching so intently?"

"I just tuned in, but I think it's *Love Story*."

"Really?" says Cynthia coldly. "What's that about? You and Olive Boudreaux?"

Nash doesn't startle; doesn't even reduce the volume, but smiles indulgently. "Sweetie—"

"I want you to leave tomorrow," says Cynthia.

Seventeen

*I*f only Nash hadn't cleaned out their joint household account on the way to the airport, Dina wouldn't be traveling north on the 405 to meet with a partner in the firm that coined the word *palimony*. The $1,779 Nash helped himself to was generated entirely by Reflexology Unlimited, earmarked for car payments, which promptly bounced and cost her forty bucks in penalties. As she told the paralegal on the phone, she is not going after Nash to get rich but for the principle, and to punish and annoy him. He has no money that she knows of, except for the checks that dribble in. Yes, it's possible he has assets hidden away but she doubts it. Yes, he has property; his parents left him a house in Boston that has been on the market for three years due to lead paint and radon. Everything sells eventually, doesn't it?

But this wasn't about greed. Someone should make an example of him. For womankind. For his future girlfriends. Thief! He left a balance of one goddamn dollar in their account, and charged his airline ticket to their Visa. It's hard to catch him in lies and even harder to embarrass him, but right now, stuck in traffic in her marred scarlet Miata, feeling nauseated as she inhales exhaust and sees a smog cloud in the distance, she wants his head.

In Government Center, Nash is stationed at the main entrance of the Massachusetts Division of Employment Security. He is wearing a camel-colored pullover sweater that looks like cash-mere; the edge of one starched shirt cuff reveals a discreetly mono-grammed NJH II. He doesn't recognize the blond Lois even though she is exactly the person he is waiting for—not until she stands res-olutely in front of him and taps his shoulder with her *Boston Globe*.

His bruises have faded, but his tan has not. "Last time I saw you, you were black and blue," she says in what she hopes is non-chalant fashion. He smells of something luscious and masculine, an expensive West Coast cologne, she guesses.

Nash grins. "That's right: You've never seen the uninjured, healthy, healed Nash Harvey until now." He fingers one blond ten-dril at her ear. Gruesome hair color, he thinks. She should sue the salon.

So handsome, she thinks.

"Except you knew me in my youth," he continues. "Back when we were teenagers dancing to the Everly Brothers."

"The Righteous Brothers."

Nash asks if he can buy her a cup of coffee.

"I'm supposed to be in at eight-thirty," says Lois.

"Then how about your office?"

"For what?"

He lowers his voice and asks, "Couldn't I pass for someone who needs the services of an employment specialist?"

Lois doesn't answer, thinking, No one who looks like you and dresses in cashmere has ever set foot in my office.

Nash crouches a bit to peer into her face diagnostically. He gives her elbow a friendly shake. "You seem a little dazed," he says. "Is it me or is it other things?"

Lois hopes the coworkers rushing past are noticing her in the company of this unusually handsome and well-dressed man, star-ing into her eyes and touching the sleeve of her raincoat. "I'm just surprised you remembered where I worked and that you found me," she says.

"What's so hard? You said 'Unemployment' and I looked it up in the phone book: 'Massachusetts, Commonwealth of.' "

She checks her watch to buy a few seconds and to make herself appear unruffled. Gladly she will entertain him in her office; all day if he wants to. "Still, I'm impressed," she says. "And flattered."

Nash motions: You lead the way, and she does, into the building, across a large open room past lines of people—the unemployed, he guesses. Her office is a cubicle with a dying ivy on top of an army-drab filing cabinet. She puts her coat on a wooden hanger and hooks it over the top of a partition. Nash takes the interview chair. "There's something about you today that reminds me of spring flowers," he begins.

Lois looks down at her outfit, a suit of pastel blue and a silky blouse of pale yellow. "This? I packed in a hurry. One of these days I'm going to have to go back and get the rest of my things."

"Or go on a big shopping spree."

"No time," says Lois. "I'm not the kind of woman who shops on her lunch hour."

Nash says, "I believe that. You're probably the kind of woman who goes to New York once a season and does it right."

"I should," says Lois. "Kathleen goes every season on buying trips."

"You could go with her, share a hotel room, and have her take you to some designers' showrooms," Nash says. "That's what I'd do if I had a sister in the rag trade."

Lois confides that she hasn't talked to Kathleen in a long time because she, Lois Dobbin, has finally flown the coop. She waits for Nash to ask her to elaborate on her well-reasoned separation from her spoilsport sisters—but he doesn't.

"They're probably mad at me for moving out," she tries again.

"Or maybe Kathleen's just tied up with the new fellow."

Lois's right hand moves to her hair, where she coaxes a few off-shoots into their intended waves.

"The doorman," Nash prompts. "Lorenz. Nice guy. He works at Harbor Arms. Everyone's crazy about him."

This is what she's missed and why Kathleen hasn't called: a romance. "How do you know this?" she asks.

"I told you! My accountant has a condo there and an extra bedroom."

"I see," says Lois.

He pinches one cuff militarily, then another. "Must be true what they say about a man in uniform."

"I didn't know he was a literal doorman. I thought he helped manage the building."

"He does! Nothing gets by Lorenz."

"He's a security guard, then?"

Nash smiles. "You don't look thrilled with this information."

"Why wouldn't I be? If he's a nice guy." She turns to her In box and takes an interoffice envelope, unwinding its string with too much concentration.

Nash looks around the office. "You're what? The chief head-hunter here?"

"Not exactly."

"You find jobs for people, though, right?"

"Not me personally. We pay unemployment benefits and adjudicate certain disputes, and we try to match people up with openings."

"I have to be my own headhunter. Until I'm known on this coast, I'm doing the jingle writer's equivalent of pounding the pavement. Some days, 'doorman' sounds appealing." He salutes with a crisp chop to an imaginary brim. "Yes, ma'am. Good day, ma'am. I have a package for you, sir. Let me get that for you, sir." He grins. "I could do that, don't you think? Bow and scrape and hail taxis?"

Lois takes a pen from a WGBH mug. "Are you looking for employment, Nash?"

"I'm looking for clients, same as ever."

"Are you not getting enough work?"

"There's never enough work," he says. "That's the music business."

"I meant, are you not getting enough work here to cover your expenses?"

Nash scratches his cheek thoughtfully and tests the spot on his cheekbone that has only recently healed. "I think I'd characterize it as a geography problem—I'm on the East Coast while my un-cashed checks are piling up on the West."

"Didn't you plan for that before you left? For someone to deposit the checks for you, or at least to forward them?"

"I was stupid," he says. "I didn't know how long I'd be away."

"What's your best guess?" she says. "Another few days? A week? A month?"

"I'd say . . . open-ended. But look, I'm not passing the hat. Some days my check's on the wrong coast, and some days there's no money in the mailbox at all. That's the jingle business."

Lois clears her throat into her fist in ladylike fashion before asking, "May I ask what you're living on?"

"Savings. Interest on my investments. Early pension from the union."

"And your housing is covered, right? You're staying with your accountant?"

"That was temporary." He reaches for her newspaper. "May I? I need to find another place."

Lois puts her hand on the *Globe*. "Let me ask you something. I assume you have a return ticket to Los Angeles. If you have no money on hand, yet you have the means to get home, and presumably a buck to get to the airport by subway, why stay here and suffer?"

Nash wonders, Which looks worse—poverty or infidelity? "I don't know if I mentioned this, but the driving force behind my trip was my situation at home. I needed to put space between me and someone who wanted more from me than I could give. It certainly wasn't for professional reasons." He forces a hollow laugh. "I'm finding that out: the *very* last reason."

"How old?" Lois asks.

"Me?"

"Her. The woman you were involved with?"

Nash leans back against the chair and smiles. "Not 'What's her name?' 'Occupation?' 'Height and weight?' "

Nash's smile is teasing, possibly even flirtatious, giving Lois hope about why he came. She places her pen across a yellow legal pad as if everything uttered from now on is off the record. "You'll have to excuse me," she says. "I hear a lot of sob stories from that chair. It's always the other guy's fault. I'm the bad cop most of the time."

"No, no. It's a fine question. She's around your age."

"Can I ask what happened?"

"It ended before I gave up on it," he says. "I don't know if you've been through that same experience: You keep trying and you keep beating the same dead horse, unwilling to pull the plug until someone finally looks you squarely in the eye and says, 'Face it. It's not working. And it probably never will.' "

"What's her name?"

"Dina."

"Was Dina devastated?"

Nash sits up straighter, as if he's been tossed a thoughtful and interesting question. "Devastated? I hope not. Angry? Of course."

"How long ago was this?" asks Lois.

"Christmas."

"That's a hard time of year," says Lois. "I know because I left my husband right after Thanksgiving and next thing I knew it was Christmas and I was back at home with my old stocking hanging from the mantel between Adele's and Kathleen's. A very sad symbol, I thought."

"Back in the bosom of the family, dangling limply between two unhappy sisters?"

"Precisely. Plus this was the end of a marriage, not just a romance. Then I had the trauma of a potentially humiliating divorce."

"He was weird, right? A transvestite? So you had no choice. I'd look at it this way: You wouldn't be such a strong and independent woman now—dyeing your hair blond on the spur of the moment— if you hadn't had to declare your independence once before."

"Moving out," Lois reminds him. "Welcoming the privacy."

"Did you get your own place?"

Lois smiles. "Lois's hideaway. Not far from here. A bed-and-breakfast on Grove Street."

"May I ask what you pay for a night's lodgings?"

Lois waits a beat, then says in as pragmatic a fashion as she can, "Seventy-five dollars with a continental breakfast: best bargain around."

"Any vacancies?" he asks.

Lois can't believe what he is suggesting; can barely disguise how her heart and lungs are squeezed by the possibility that she and Nash might live under the same roof. "I think so," she manages to say. "It's kind of a well-kept secret."

Nash winks. "No one keeps a secret better than I do."

"Do you mean right away? Today?"

"I'm homeless," he says, making it sound like a charming over-statement. "I might as well see if there's a bed there with my name on it."

Lois scribbles three lines on a corner of her yellow pad, and tears it off.

"Would she take an out-of-state check?" he asks.

"I'm sure she would."

Nash reads the landlady's name aloud, and Lois corrects him.

"Should I say you sent me?"

"No need," says Lois. Her mind has raced ahead to future tryst-ing. Best to let Mrs. Chabot think she introduced them at her breakfast table and mentored the monkey business herself. "She'll like the looks of you. Not everyone who shows up on her doorstep is presentable."

"A woman of discriminating taste, then."

Lois laughs. "She's not the blue-haired Beacon Hill dowager you might be picturing."

"No? Younger?"

"Does it matter? She has a vacancy, the price is right, and it's walking distance to everything."

"Irrelevant," says Nash. "I don't even know why I asked."

⌒ Mrs. Chabot has never seen such an elegantly handsome man on her doorstep, or a valise made entirely of leather. He asks for a room with a queen-sized bed and a television, and she assigns him to the one double that has a name: the Mallard Room, after the family in *Make Way for Ducklings*. The new guest signs her cloth-bound ledger and asks, "May I?"

"May you what?"

"Flip through the pages?"

"Why?"

He smiles. "Do you know when the last time was I signed some-thing like this to register for a room? Not a credit card slip or a printed form, but a *book*? I feel like I've entered a time warp."

"I take credit cards."

"I'd heard this was a charming place, but I didn't realize how charming. It's right out of—what was that film? *The Thomas Crown Affair*."

"Oh, my," says his new landlady. "They took the pictures for that up the hill in Louisburg Square."

"Charming," he repeats.

"Newport Beach, California," she reads from his entry.

"Do you know it?"

Mrs. Chabot says she's never been to California. She and her late husband had saved for Disneyland, but then when the other one opened, they only had to go as far as Orlando, Florida. It was Christmastime, and the lines were awful, but it was so beautiful—the parades and the Christmas trees as tall as telephone poles—that she wouldn't go any other time.

"And may I ask when you lost your husband?"

Mrs. Chabot bats the question away as if it's a matter of little import and no tenderness.

"Recently?"

"Ten, eleven years."

"I'm so sorry. It must be hard running a bed-and-breakfast by yourself, worrying about changing every light bulb and fixing every leak."

She shrugs. "I have a handyman. He's on disability so I pay him under the table."

Nash picks up his valise and motions that Mrs. Chabot should lead the way. "I'm no Mister Fixit," he says, "but while I'm here, feel free to ask me to hang a picture or move a piece of furniture."

"Really?"

"If I'm here, why not?"

Nash follows her up the front carpeted stairway, then the length of a narrow, dark second floor for the ascent by back stairs to the third story. "Woodwork!" he exclaims. "Colored water in lovely decanters. . . . Is that a Maxfield Parrish? A tub on legs! Claw feet!"

"You folks from California—you always like old stuff. You think everything's an antique."

Cracks in the beige walls of the converted attic have been patched but not repainted. Mrs. Chabot stops in front of a door bearing a badly painted 300. "I usually put gentlemen guests up here because of the color scheme," she says. The room is square with walls and trim a dull gold, and window shades that his mother had in all the bedrooms in Brighton. The floors are bare except for a furry brown bathroom rug, a purported match to the crisply new and ugly comforter patterned with duck decoys. "Perfect," Nash exclaims.

"I change the linens every Saturday, and you get a new bath towel and facecloth every day. If I forget, remind me."

"I'm enchanted! And what're those buildings?"

"Mass. General."

"Of course! The famous M.G.H."

"You get used to the ambulances." She points to the ceiling. "There's smoke detectors in every room."

"I don't smoke."

"No, I meant we meet code. There's a fire extinguisher in the hallway, and a plunger by the toilet."

"How nice that there's a table and chair I can work at," he says. "A matchbook under one leg will get rid of the tilt." He asks if the room is remote enough and soundproof enough to accommodate a synthesizer. Mrs. Chabot—confusing it with a former medical-student boarder's white-noise machine—shrugs and says, "As long as it fits, and it's not a fire hazard, I don't care what you plug in."

"Great!"

"Breakfast's at seven-thirty weekdays, and eight on weekends. Continental."

"My triglycerides are a little high . . ." he tells her.

"I got margarine in a tub," she says.

The lawyer is a woman, fiftyish, lean and snappish, not remotely attractive. Good, Dina thinks; Nash won't like her and vice versa.

They discuss property, leases, joint accounts, expectations, intentions, wills, and services rendered. "Did your acquaintances hold you as husband and wife?" the lawyer asks.

"Hold?"

"Regard you as. Consider you to be. Think you were."

"Some," says Dina. "I wore a wedding band." She displays her left hand, which hasn't fully tanned over the evidence.

"Did he purchase the ring with his own funds?"

"I picked it out."

"But who paid for it?"

Dina hesitates, then says, "Me."

"But he sanctioned it? You wore it and he understood its significance?"

Dina looks out the window of the conference room. A man in purple spandex is reading headlines through the glass of a newspaper dispenser. "I considered it an engagement ring," she says. "It had a marquis diamond set into it. After a while, when we didn't set a date, I just considered it . . . us. Old marrieds without the ceremony."

"No," says the lawyer. "You held it to be a wedding ring."

"Okay," says Dina.

"Did Mr. Harvey wear a ring?"

The man in purple is stretching his hamstrings. Dina turns back to the lawyer. "Never."

"No matter," says the lawyer. "Married men often don't wear wedding rings. My husband doesn't."

Another married woman, Dina thinks; another man who followed through.

"No children, correct?"

"We tried," says Dina. "I mean, seriously tried. Then he changed his mind."

The lawyer looks up.

"I wasn't getting pregnant so we saw an infertility specialist."

"And he was a party to it?"

"Sure! It was his sperm all the way."

"And you represented Mr. Harvey to your doctor as what?"

"My husband."

"Excellent," says the lawyer.

"He got cold feet, though. We stopped trying."

"Stopped having relations?"

"No, stopped taking the shots. He got nervous when that woman in Iowa had septuplets."

The lawyer harrumphs.

"Nash wasn't crazy about the idea," says Dina. "He thought he was too old to have a baby. But a lot of men aren't so keen at the beginning. Until they have them. I've seen that happen—the man's not sure, then the baby's born and he falls madly in love with it."

"What interests me here," says the lawyer, "is Mr. Harvey being an active and willing participant in the infertility process."

"That's a fact," says Dina. "The name on my chart was Dina Dorsey-Harvey and when the receptionist called my name in the waiting room, she said, 'Mrs. Harvey.' "

"How many visits? Approximately?"

"A lot," says Dina. "Like, every month, then every week."

"For how long?"

"At least a year. First I was on Clomid, then they gave me Pergonal."

"Excellent," says the lawyer. She has forms ready in a manila folder with Dina's name typed on it. "Our questionnaire. You'll take it home and use it as a worksheet."

Dina reads aloud from the form, " 'Assets.' 'Property.' 'Personal possessions.' 'Inheritance prospects'—ha. 'Business situation'—ha. 'Relative education'—exaggerated. 'Behavior.' " Dina looks up. "Behavior?"

"In this context," says the lawyer, "sexual behavior. Has your spouse ever been unfaithful?"

"To me?"

"Most certainly to you."

"I'm pretty sure he has," says Dina, "but I've been a little bit in denial."

"Until now," says the lawyer.

"Is it good or bad—I mean is cheating on me good for my case?"

"The more evidence of bad behavior we can document, the better our position. They call this 'equitable apportionment,' and conduct is one of the factors taken into consideration."

Dina checks the back of the form.

"Questions?" says the lawyer.

"I was looking for the questions about me, the place where they ask about *my* conduct," Dina explains.

The lawyer frowns. "Were you unfaithful to Mr. Harvey during the period we're holding you to be husband and wife?"

Dina takes a sip of water from the plastic cup. "Like, say that he moved out in the morning. Are you asking about the period of time we were together? In other words, did I cheat on him from the day we met until the day he left? Or even the next day?"

"Correct."

"Never!" vows Dina.

Eighteen

Mrs. Chabot, intercepting Lois on the front porch, whispers urgently, "We got a gentleman from California, and I mean that—'gentleman.' I put him up on the third floor. I didn't want you two to share a bath. It's not a good way to meet someone."

Lois feigns mild, polite interest. "Young?" she asks. "Old?"

"A nice age. Fifty? I put him on the third floor."

"You told me."

Mrs. Chabot confides the real reason for her excitement. "Did I tell you he's a movie star?"

Lois stops, her hand on the doorknob.

"I put two and two together: He's from California, was playing it a little cozy as to what exactly he did—and he looks like he just stepped out of *People* magazine."

"Handsome, you mean?"

"A sexpot," says Mrs. Chabot. "And if an old lady like me notices, he's got it to spare."

"Wouldn't a movie star stay at a bigger hotel?"

Mrs. Chabot has thought this through and has the answer. "He could be hiding out here. Ducking the press."

Lois asks the name of the new famous boarder.

"Oh. Something short—a made-up name. I'll have to get it off the book."

"Don't bother. You can introduce us at some point."

Mrs. Chabot studies Lois for a few seconds, then pats her back. "Make yourself up a bit, hon," she says.

⟶ Nash is shaving in the gents' bathroom (powder blue and black plastic tiles), experiencing something close to regret for having escorted Olive Boudreaux back to her apartment—"safely back," is how he explained it to the heretofore obliging Cynthia. He is unaccustomed to introspection, so the face in the mirror doesn't look back any more thoughtfully or guiltily than usual. In fact, reflecting on Olive has put a smile on his lips. He is shaving with a blade that needs replacing and has suffered two nicks in the difficult area around the cleft in his chin. All his women have liked the cleft. Sooner or later, when the sex gets a bit more adventurous, all his partners dab something in there—whipped cream was popular for a while—and lick it out. Cynthia would have done that soon; she didn't worry about fat grams like everyone else. She was okay, Cynthia: invites him to move in like a long-lost brother. Well, hardly a brother. She liked to have sex every night. And he obliged, even though he'd never have looked at her twice on the West Coast. But maybe that meant something; maybe it was proof he was acting his age. Cynthia was everything that his previous girlfriends were not: plump, smart, olive-skinned, ambitious, educated, and postmenopausal. And he loved her apartment, its view, her running tab with the gourmet grocery store in the lobby.

And now there was a price to pay for ogling Olive: this dump of a boardinghouse. No elevator, no air-conditioning, no complimentary shampoo or shoeshine cloth, no hair dryer, and—unheard of—no telephone. His pillow seems to be filled with chunks of foam rubber, and his bed sags like a hammock. There's a smell he doesn't like, an institutional wintergreen he associates with the bathrooms from his catechism days, and rough, brown paper towels. The night before, he was sleeping under Cynthia's big white duvet looking out at the Atlantic Ocean. And best of all, he had the place to himself the whole day—and her Steinway B. Maybe he could apologize profusely to Cynthia, his best shot, and if that didn't work, lie low for a few days. Only then would he call Olive. He suspected she was one of those women who'd sleep with a guy

because she wanted to, without having to be in love. He'd definitely picked up signals from Olive—what else did a business card
mean when it's slipped into your shirt pocket? That was the problem with Cynthia. With all women. They couldn't just enjoy the
sex act. He remembers the Dobbin sisters, first Adele, then Kathleen, and finally, unhappily, Lois, his new ally. No way. No fucking
way. Too flat-chested and chapped-looking, like a coach at a girls'
school. Like a lesbo. That brought him back, almost fondly, to big-
bosomed Cynthia, her feather pillows, and her good red wine.
What would be a respectful waiting period? Twenty-four hours?
Wake her up with a phone call tomorrow morning and say, "I'm
miserable. Tell me what I have to do to come back?" Cynthia has
principles and a master's degree, but she's lonely. Love-starved.
And she believed in me, she must have, to throw a party and serve
French champagne.

Which brings back Olive Boudreaux, tall and built, studying
him above the fluted glass, fingernails a slutty brownish red. Green
eyes? Turquoise blue? Her hair—why not?—is silver-blond. Her
breasts straining against that stretchy pink dress. He wipes the dots
of shaving cream off with a towel and reaches into his pants. He
closes his eyes. Olive's face appears at his waist, smiling a smile
that says, I couldn't stop thinking about you. I'm not wearing
panties. I'm a real blonde. This is my favorite activity, and the
pleasure is all mine. "That's great, baby," he whispers. "You're the
best." With his free hand, he latches the door.

⌐ Too bad she hadn't thought to have a fruit basket sent, one
with cheese and crackers, wine and wineglasses, even a slice of pâté.
She'd write a card that said, "Welcome to Beacon Hill from a fellow . . . outcast?" No, the wrong inference. "Fellow . . . runaway."
I've left home because my sisters oppressed me. You left home in
search of . . . Above her, the toilet flushes. Has to be him, she thinks,
and smiles, the nagging question of his whereabouts answered. She
runs a bath down the hall, and chooses her green-apple soap and
grapefruit body lotion. She undresses in her room, refreshes her lipstick, and goes to the bath in her rose terry-cloth robe, barefooted.
Tonight or tomorrow night, she thinks, I'll do my toes to match.

⌒ Nash falls asleep after he finishes in the bathroom. He doesn't mean to; he's keeping an ear out for Lois so that he can ask her to recommend a restaurant nearby. Unquestionably, she'll invite herself along, and he'll fight her for the check and she'll say, No, let me. You can get it next time. The money problem and the work problem make him sit up in bed, then reach under his sweater for his roll of Tums.

Jobs and money. He'd better let Dina know how to get ahold of him in case any of his demos make the cut, or if there're any checks to forward.

He doesn't know how long he can live without a phone. He'd noticed one on the floor below—had exclaimed to the landlady over the quaintness of its rotary dial—but Jesus Christ, what a pain to go through an operator and announce your credit card number to whoever's eavesdropping in a joint like this. He gets up, combs his hair, and goes down one flight. The phone sits in a niche in the wall. No chair and no phone book. He dials, smiles absently at the prospect of a friendly chat with a good-natured operator, but the voice is male, all business. He hates that.

Nash states his problem—no Touch-Tone—and murmurs his credit card number. In Newport Beach, Dina's studio phone rings. He gets her overblown Reflexology Unlimited greeting, so that by the time the beep comes, he is impatient. "Dina," he says. "It's me. I'm still in Boston, at a B-and-B called"—he reads from Lois's scrap of paper—'The Lucky Duck.' Here's the number. The front desk can take a message. Will you call me if I get any checks? And did I hear from anyone in New York? I've got stuff out that I'm waiting to hear on." He recites the phone number and the address, says he doesn't know the zip code but she could get that easily enough—Boston. "Okay, kid," he closes. "Hope all's well with you."

At the last second, Dina picks up to bark, "I'm not your goddamn secretary."

A door opens behind him, followed by a postbath waft of steamy, perfumed air. He turns around. It is Lois in a bathrobe, looking pinker than usual, as if she has bathed in boiling water.

"Nash!" she gasps.

"Who's that?" asks Dina.

Nash says into the phone, "I'm at a public phone. Another guest of the hotel."

"Who knows you, obviously."

"It's small," he says. He holds an index finger up to signal to Lois: *Don't speak.* Lois stops obligingly.

"How long have you been there?" Dina asks.

"A day."

"You make friends fast," she says. "Especially if they have a vagina."

Nash chuckles nervously. If Lois weren't standing at his shoulder he would deny any such history or inclination, and throw in an insult of this fellow guest for good measure. "I think that's beneath you, Deenie," he replies.

Lois pantomimes, *Let me go get dressed. That's my room over there. I'll be back in two shakes.* Nash smiles and nods.

"How long will you be there?" Dina asks.

"It depends."

"On what?"

"My finances. What MIDI equipment I can rent here. If I can get a phone installed."

"Poor Nash. A roomful of junk at home, and now you have to rent stuff there. I guess you're thinking you never should have left."

Nash doesn't answer right away. He sighs and says, "Aren't you with a client?"

"Have you maxed out on your credit cards yet?"

"To answer," Nash says with quiet, injured dignity, "implies that that's your concern."

"It is," says Dina. "Big time. Starting with one thousand, seven hundred and seventy-nine dollars you helped yourself to on your way out of town."

Nash switches ears, and tests his left cheekbone for tenderness. "Is that what's got you so crazed? Me withdrawing money from our joint account?"

"It was my money. My deposit. I only had your name on there for emergencies."

"This *was* an emergency," he says.

"This was a *burglary*," she shouts. "You stole my money. I bounced two checks because of that."

"Sweetie," he tries. "I'm sorry about that. But, I swear, I didn't think of the money being yours or mine. I was catching a plane and I needed cash—"

"You stole two thousand bucks!"

"I will definitely make good on every cent," says Nash. "We'll work that out. I've been thinking that I want to come home soon." He lowers his voice to whisper, "I miss you, Deenie."

Dina is now addressing someone else, someone he pictures lying on the reflexology table, repeating and ridiculing what he just confided.

"Who's that?" asks Nash. "Who's there?"

"No one you know."

"It's not very professional, airing your personal problems in front of a client."

"It's a friend," says Dina. "Someone who's collecting your best lines."

"Someone I know?"

"I doubt that."

"Male or female?"

"I gotta run. I'm being rude," says Dina. A male voice in the background calls to her. Nash hears Dina's hand muffling the receiver, but nothing after that.

"Are you there? Can I write a check on our joint account without it bouncing?"

"For how much?"

"I still have to pay what I owe before I leave. If you saw the sweet old lady who runs this place, and the sad, faded—"

"I'm not interested," says Dina. "Just write the fucking check and don't compose a commercial about it."

There is a tap on his shoulder: Lois in black, with dangly, beaded earrings, dressed for a date with a Beat poet or a jazz musician. Nash raises his eyebrows, faking artistic appreciation.

"Whenever you're ready," she mouths.

⌒⊃ Ten and a half years at 'GBH, and until today, no one has had grounds to tease Adele about a man or a suspected crush. She knows why they are almost giddy: She and the station manager are single, whereas most flirtations that blossom under the station's roof are extramarital or messy in some other way—unsuspected homosexuality, a one-night fling with a visiting BBC producer, a quickie in a control booth.

Now no one is home at Stearns Road to discuss the day's disappointment, namely that Marty twice came into Development on business but did not speak to or acknowledge her. Scott and Michael noticed, just as they had noticed his frank on-air admiration, and hummed various corny songs when she'd arrived this morning.

Kathleen is staying downtown for dinner, which Adele understands to mean she is spending time with Lorenz. And then she thinks: Richard, perfect—an expert on work-related mating rituals. Surely he will have advice, and surely he'll welcome her confidence.

She misses him. And she knows he is worried about her. The expression on his face when she choked and as she was being saved was one of such panic and grief that she felt as if her baby brother had declared his love publicly at Maison Robert.

⌒ He is in his car, traveling west on Storrow Drive, but says he is happy to swing by. "What'd you have in mind?" he asks.

"Just wanted to see you."

"Has to be about Lois."

"It's not."

"Harvey Nash?"

"Patooey," says Adele, and they both laugh.

"Kathleen and the doorman?"

"No," says Adele. "That's taking care of itself."

"Isn't it great?" says Richard. "I've checked him out half a dozen times since I heard about it. I mean, if your sister's going to take up with a complete stranger, why not a doorman in a public place? I walk in, tip my hat, buy a newspaper at Fredo's or a gift at The Other Woman, and walk out. He's awfully pleasant."

"I haven't met him," says Adele. "Kathleen's keeping him under wraps."

"Do what I do—swing by the store. You can't miss him."

"Unlike you, I work at a desk," says Adele, "which limits my freedom to spy on my sisters during the day."

There is static on Richard's end. When his voice comes through it, he is talking about Lois.

"What about her?" asks Adele.

"I said I take it you know she's at The Lucky Duck again."

"I know. I checked with the landlady to be sure she was alive."

"In fact, I just called over there before I left the office."

"And?"

"She was out." He doesn't add the rest of what he elicited from the chatty Mrs. Chabot: having dinner with the new boarder, a man from California; a movie star on holiday, she suspects.

"Where are you now?" Adele asks.

"Comm. Ave. at B.U. Want me to pick something up?"

She asks if he can come by the apartment first.

"What's on the docket?" he asks.

Adele wonders how much she should tell Richard. He'd be a little too happy to hear there was the possibility of a romance, and he'd feel sorry for her for years if it turned out to be all a big misunderstanding.

"Professional or personal?"

"I'd have to say . . . both."

"A man, obviously. Either someone you want to encourage, or someone you want to sue?"

Adele laughs. "Not sue. Quite the opposite."

"Opposite of 'sue.' Hmmm. I think that would be 'have sex with.' "

Adele laughs. "Can you say that on a car phone?"

"Are you kidding? You can have phone sex on a car phone."

"I wouldn't know," says Adele.

"Me neither. I read about it in *Newsweek*."

Adele laughs. "You must be here now. Can I hang up?"

"I'm on your street and I see a spot," says Richard.

⌒ Adele presses the "play" button and points at the screen. "That's him," she says.

Richard watches and nods, occasionally emitting sounds that express comprehension and insight. Within a minute he announces,

"He's smitten. Trust me. See that—" He pauses, then rewinds. "While you're talking to the camera, he's looking at you." He peers closer. "Are those people on the phones wearing yarmulkes?"

"They're from Hillel. Now take a look at this."

It is Marty talking on a volunteer's phone. "Read his lips," Adele instructs. "See if he isn't saying 'Adele Dobbin.' "

They watch carefully, rewind, watch again. "Could very well be," he says. "Obviously, it's some viewer asking, 'Who's the red-headed bombshell?' "

Adele shakes her head. "It's his mother."

"He told you that?"

"No. He told me, 'My mother is completely thrilled that we talked about her in the same breath as Julia Child.' But it wasn't until I got home and watched the tape—"

"And why did you tape yourself in the first place?"

"I do sometimes. To see how a certain tactic works." She smiles. "Or how a certain dress looks."

"I like it, by the way."

"Thanks. Brand-new. Kathleen came with me and made me buy it."

"Good for her. So we need to know: What is the question to the answer 'Adele Dobbin'?"

"Whatever it was, he looks annoyed, don't you think?"

"He was caught red-handed! You don't want your mother seeing you in action. It's like having her drive you on a date. Besides, if she called him in the middle of a pledge break, you can bet she calls him regularly. *Too* regularly: hourly."

Adele reports on today's unsettling behavior: that this same man who looks so devoted on-air avoided her at work.

"Could've been your imagination."

"It wasn't. Twice I saw him duck into an office when he saw me coming."

"Simple: Somebody razzed him about having a crush on you and he clammed up."

"You think so?"

"Of course! He advertised on TV—enough so his mother weighed in—so he's playing it close to the vest for a while."

Adele takes this information with her to the kitchen, and comes back with two bottles of beer and two glasses. "So I'm supposed to take the hint and not speak either?"

"It's hard to explain. He's looking for a sign from you, but at the same time, he doesn't want anyone else to see it. I mean, he's the boss, right? It's tricky."

"It hasn't been a problem up till now," says Adele. "Just the opposite."

"Of course: romance in the cafeteria. It's what makes the world go round."

"People were starting to notice," says Adele. "Scott and Michael had started to tease me—and that was before this spectacle."

Richard nods toward the tape. "How long has this been going on? Weeks? Months?"

"Months," says Adele.

"Not married, I assume?"

Adele smiles. "Only to his mother."

"How perfect—drawn to a girl who's married to her sisters."

Adele makes a face. "Although the sisters seem to be going through a divorce."

"Isn't that good? If things work out for Kathleen?"

"Of course," Adele says quickly.

"It's just that you haven't met him yet, so how seriously could you be rooting for Lorenz the doorman?"

"Pretty seriously," she murmurs.

"Good girl."

Adele asks, "Now what? What's my next step?"

"You wait."

"For what?"

"To run into him when no one else is around. Like in the elevator."

"And I say . . . ?"

Richard leans back against the sofa and closes his eyes. "You could say . . . 'Marty, I need some help in reeling in a big corporate sponsor.' Pick one—there must be dozens that actually fit that profile. Then you say, 'So if I set up a lunch for next Friday, whatever, would you join us?' "

Adele shakes her head. "It's too . . . I don't know—"

"Manipulative?"

"Unethical. Using a client to advance my personal life. Too silly. Plus we use talent to reel them in, not the suits."

Richard snaps his fingers. "I know: Cozy up to his secretary, and next time he's working late—"

"That's the worst—'cozy up to his secretary.' I can see you doing that, sitting on the edge of a secretary's desk, fingering her knick-knacks, but it's ridiculous—"

Richard takes the remote control and snaps on the tape again. After a minute he declares, "He's gonna call you. I can see that. He wishes he lived in the neighborhood so he could memorize your schedule and run into you accidentally on purpose—"

"Like high school."

Richard grins. "Haven't I taught you that much: Men don't change after high school."

"So that means what? Call him about a homework assignment? Hope he asks me to the Senior Fling?"

"No. You and I leave the premises and go out for either Indian food or sushi. If he doesn't reach you, he'll call back."

"Or we could get takeout. Both those places deliver now."

Richard puts his arm around Adele's shoulder and squeezes. "I don't remember you sitting around in high school waiting for boys to call. I hope you don't start now."

Adele stands and collects the two bottles and two glasses. "In that case," she says, "sushi."

⟋ After they are seated, after Adele has finished her California roll and her Brookline roll, and as Richard is still working on a deluxe sushi platter as big as a steering wheel, Adele asks who he's buying gifts for at The Other Woman.

"Can I have the rest of your ginger?" he asks.

Adele nods and Richard helps himself. "You said that you sometimes buy gifts at Kathleen's when you spy on Lorenz," she prompts.

"I'm surprised Kathleen didn't go running home to report on their size and color."

"Don't be silly. First of all, we're not that interested in your so-cial—"

"Ha!"

"And secondly, Kathleen is not going to be feeding me the details of your love life while withholding details of her own."

Richard stops chewing and says solemnly, "I don't like the way that sounds, Dell."

Adele raises her chin an inch higher and asks, "How does it sound?"

"Angry. Like you're sore at Kathleen. And a little bitter."

"You don't understand. I love Kathleen." Her voice breaks slightly on her sister's name.

It reminds him, in an awful rush, that the last time they dined out together he had failed to come to her aid. "Dell," he says. "Honey. What's the matter?"

She holds up her hand: Don't. I'm fine. It's nothing.

"You're upset. Is it about Kathleen, or you, or this Glazer guy. Or me?"

Adele finds a crumpled tissue in her jacket pocket, and says, "Finish your sushi."

Richard leans over the table. "Nora. Her name's Nora. I'm staying at her place for the time being and every so often I bring her home a little thank-you gift. Kathleen picks it out. Nothing sexy. Flannel."

Adele adds beer to her glass but doesn't drink and doesn't answer.

"You think I'm kidding? I'm not. We have an almost pure friendship."

"What does 'almost pure' mean? Unconsummated?"

"Exactly."

"How odd," says Adele.

Richard surveys what pieces are left on his platter and eats something big and beige. "Mmmm," he says. "Giant clam." He pours himself more beer from their large bottle and says, "There's a key piece of information you're forgetting about Nora, which, understandably, got lost in the trauma of—you know—lunch with Harvey."

"Remind me."

"Nora has a track record as a lesbian," Richard says solemnly, "but not an unbroken one."

"Richard," Adele begins, then sighs.

"I know, I know: Lois says the same thing—"

"Lois?"

"I took her out for a drink on Friday night, and we got on the subject of my love life, and she expressed the same ambivalence over Nora's . . . ambivalence."

"She's right. For once Lois is right."

"Now, now." Richard's expression brightens at the prospect of delivering gossip. "She's a blonde! Did you know that?"

"Nora?"

"Lois!"

"Does it look good?"

"It does *not* look good."

"Does she think it looks good?"

"She must. She said she tried on a blond wig at Filene's before she made the decision, and that convinced her."

"It's sad," says Adele. "That's what it is: sad. Going blond at fifty-one."

"How about running away from home at fifty-one? That strikes me as even sadder."

"She'll be back," says Adele.

"Did you want to give me shit about Nora? You're welcome to if that would make you feel better."

Adele smiles sadly. "You're the dearest boy," she says.

Nineteen

Lorenz's father is not cooperating with efforts to lure him out of the apartment. He says "No thank you" to an invitation from his daughter in Plymouth, and "No!" less graciously to a weekend in Atlantic City with his brother-in-law.

"Papi," Lorenz finally says. "Look, I'd like to have the place to myself for one night, okay? Dinner through breakfast? A little privacy."

They are at the kitchen sink, father washing, son drying. Mr. Sampedro evidences no vicarious macho pleasure. "I don't like it," he says.

"Don't like what?"

"What you're thinking about."

"Which is what?"

"A private party. The two of you—"

"I thought you liked Kathleen."

"Don't be a wise guy! You know what I mean."

"It's not like that. I'm not plotting anything. Kathleen's in on this too."

Mr. Sampedro stops thrashing his hands in the gray water and barks, "Don't tell me lies."

"We're not kids. We discuss these things like mature adults." He pauses. "And we think it's time."

Mr. Sampedro has never heard of such a thing. He knows

women don't discuss sex as if they're making plans to see a show; they let you or they don't let you. Unless it's a honeymoon, they don't circle a date on a calendar.

"You'd rather we go to a motel? Because we certainly can do that—get a nice unit on Revere Beach Boulevard. Maybe even one with heat."

Mr. Sampedro shuffles to the stove, takes the front burners back to the sink with him, and dusts them with Ajax. He mutters in Spanish about burnt-on spills, not his doing, then spits out, "Revere? That's your idea of a nice place to take a girl?"

"I was teasing you. You're acting like I'm your teenage virgin daughter. What happened to your big speech when we decided to try this arrangement? 'Ignore me! Invite your friends over. Pretend I'm not here!' "

"You're the one who can't ignore me. I *want* to be ignored."

"I'm forty-nine years old. We're not kids, and we're not cheating on anyone. Don't make us sneak into a motel."

Mr. Sampedro puts on big blue rubber gloves, then turns the water to scalding. "Take her to the Four Seasons or the Ritz Hotel, by the swans. You can afford a night there."

"I don't have to show off for her. Besides, she'd give me a hard time and would want to split the bill."

Mr. Sampedro recoils. "Don't you let her! How much can it be for a big night out—a hundred and fifty bucks?"

"Double that, minimum, plus room tax, breakfast. Coffee's five dollars from room service."

Mr. Sampedro thinks this over. "You make good money. You can spend it."

"I'll do that for an anniversary, but I want a routine. I want to take her out to dinner or a movie, then I want to be alone with her." He tries to take a dripping burner from his father, who won't let go, saying it will leave smudges on his towel. "Are you worried that if things move forward, I'll want you to move out?" Lorenz asks.

Mr. Sampedro is not worried because, one floor below, the widow of Amato Nocera is moving to a place for old people in Randolph that brings you the big meal of the day. She's freeing up a one-bedroom, spotless, with a self-cleaning oven and Levolor blinds. "I'm not worried about nothing!" he shouts. "Leave me alone. I'll go to Anita's when I feel like it."

Lorenz reaches over and turns the water off. "What's the real problem? Are your feelings hurt because I'm farming you out for a couple of days?"

His father says angrily, "I didn't raise you to bring girls home to your bed. This is no place for that! We got no nice pillows! Under the pillowcases they're all stained. And the shower curtain needs replacing. It's got mildew on the edges."

Lorenz laughs and wraps one arm around his father's resistant shoulders for a squeeze. "That's it? You're house-proud?"

"She won't like it. She won't come back."

"And you want her to? Is that what I'm hearing? You like my girlfriend?"

"You're too old for a girlfriend! You should get married before it's too late."

"One step at a time. I'm just trying to negotiate the big one."

"Joker!" Mr. Sampedro raises his wet glove and fakes a chop.

"I'm teasing you. She's not going to be inspecting the apartment."

"Have you seen her house?"

"The lobby."

"It probably looks like where you work, with a revolver door and marble on the floors."

"She thinks her building has no character." He transfers his towel to his father's shoulder. "Let me finish up here. And tomorrow I'll buy new pillows and I'll toss out all the ones stained with our drool."

Cornered, Mr. Sampedro fakes a hospitable smile. "What about this: You bring her here. I'll cook something special—I can make Italian food—and then I'll go to bed the minute we're done. I won't even clean up till the morning. You can smooch in the parlor till it's time for her to go home, and then you can drive her."

"No. You'll go to Anita's. I'll put you on the bus here, and she'll pick you up in Plymouth."

"When?"

"Monday night. I have Tuesday off, and Kathleen doesn't open till ten." Lorenz smiles. "One night. It's the best plan, and it's easier than getting rid of her sisters."

Scowling, Mr. Sampedro shakes more Ajax on the burners.

"You think I'm going to blow it, and you'll never see her again? Is that it? I'll offend her?"

"She's a nice lady," he growls. "Not some neighborhood girl with an itch."

"She likes me," says Lorenz. "A lot."

⟨⟩ Kathleen doesn't pack an overnight bag at home, because she has all that she needs for her date among her wares at The Other Woman. Lorenz has never ogled any particular undergarment or category of undergarments, so she uses her own judgment and chooses a silvery nightgown, silk charmeuse, fitted and ankle-length, something she could go dancing in if only big bands still played at night clubs. In the back room, she is steaming its creases, admiring its French seams, when the shop bell rings.

"Be right there!" she calls.

A woman's voice answers, "Ms. Dobbin?"

She sets the steamer down and unplugs it. It is Cynthia John in an orange sweatshirt and flowing, flowered palazzo pants, drinking coffee from a Fredo's travel mug. Unbidden, Cynthia pinches a fold of sweatshirt and says, "This is purely for comfort. I'm working at home today. *Finally.*"

Kathleen understands it is a cue. "Finally?" she repeats.

"I couldn't work at home while he tinkered with the same stupid few notes like a broken record."

"Do you mean Nash?"

"You heard him at the party! He was trying to give the impression that all we were about was work. That he rented studio space from me by day and used the guest room by night."

"But that wasn't true?"

Cynthia says, "He slept in my bed, Kathleen. With me, his so-called roommate. I'm old enough to remember when that wasn't done, so I hope you know I'm not bragging."

Kathleen looks away to welcome two women who chat their way through the door, carrying Newbury Street bags that identify them as serious shoppers, and tumblers of fruit salad that testify to a pass through Quincy Market. Both have subtle and professional blond streaks in their sleek hair, wonderful blazers, and early tans. Kathleen says with true regret, "I'm so sorry, but I don't allow food in here."

Cynthia raises her coffee mug and says smartly, "This is water."

"We'll finish and come back," says the younger woman. "I see all kinds of new goodies."

"I have some fabulous new washable silks," Kathleen calls after them.

They stop.

"Kimonos, short and packable. And tees from Fazzoletto."

"Two minutes!" says one.

"Or sooner," says the other.

When the door closes behind them, Cynthia asks, "And who might they be, the delirious shoppers?"

"The Perlmutters. The daughter's engaged and the mother believes in trousseaus."

"Unfortunately," says Cynthia, "I'll be back to utilitarian underwear and flannel nightgowns. Too bad the teddies aren't returnable."

"They are if they haven't been worn and the tags are attached."

"Oh, they've been *worn*! Very much worn. Worn and then fished out from between the bedclothes in the morning!"

Kathleen would like Cynthia to leave, especially now that the Perlmutters are hovering outside, pointing animatedly with plastic forks at the matching bandeaux and tap pants in the window.

"Do you have to get back to work?" Kathleen asks.

Cynthia stares at Kathleen making red felt-tip notations on price tags hanging from the very silk goods just touted. "Are you marking those down? With those women out there salivating and waving their credit cards?"

"I was going to anyway. I've got bathing suits in the back and I need the room."

"Wait a half hour," says Cynthia. "Jeesh."

The Perlmutters return. Cynthia says, "I was just saying that I agree: These silk tees are incredible. I have them in a couple of colors. On two little birds like you they'd be long enough to sleep in."

"We're shopping for *her*," says the mother. She smiles. "For her trousseau."

Cynthia says, "Now, there's a word I haven't heard since nineteen sixty."

The daughter moves to the circular rack and pushes padded hangers back and forth.

"Men love silk," adds Cynthia. "My ex did. Although he liked things a little trashier and scantier. Which she carries if you know where to look."

"Cynthia lives in the building," says Kathleen.

"And I'm interning here," says Cynthia.

The women excuse themselves to finger a camisole on a silver mannequin.

"I was kidding! I'm in finance. Which waits for no man." She sighs but doesn't move.

Mrs. Perlmutter says, "It must be nice to work at home and not have to worry about heels and hose and . . . dry cleaning."

"This?" says Cynthia, stretching the side seam of her palazzo pants out at the hip. "This is depression. I'm in the throes of a breakup, which has hit me like a ton of bricks."

"I'm sorry," says the mother.

"I came here to talk to Kathleen because she knows the louse in question."

"In his youth," says Kathleen.

"He was engaged to her sister, who I would love to sit down with someday." She takes a mannerly sip from her mug. "But that'll take time, I'm sure. And distance."

The Perlmutters exchange glances. The daughter says, "We can come back. Really. We don't want to intrude."

"Don't be silly," says Kathleen. "It's a store. I want you to intrude."

"I have to apologize for being so pathetic today," says Cynthia. "I'm going to come back at a more convenient time." She turns to the Perlmutters. "I don't even recognize myself. Ask Kathleen: I have an M.B.A. and I have my own business." She pats her hips. "I don't have pockets or I'd give you one of my cards."

"We should run," says the daughter.

"Do you work?" Cynthia asks.

"I'm taking the summer off before the wedding," says the bride-to-be.

"It's a full-time undertaking for both of us," says her mother.

"Then it should be a spectacular event," says Cynthia. "If I don't see you before that, have a beautiful wedding and a wonderful life. I mean that, for both of you."

"And we hope things work out for you," says the daughter.

"Sweet," says Cynthia. Before the door closes behind them, she turns back to Kathleen. "What I really came to ask you about is Olive Boudreaux."

Kathleen wants to shove the big, immovable, hideously attired Cynthia out the door and beg the Perlmutters to stay. She finds her voice and hisses, "You just kicked my best customers out of my store."

"Oh," says Cynthia. She looks over her shoulder. "Well, they'll be back. Women like that shop full-time."

"This is how I make my living. I buy expensive things wholesale and, if I'm lucky, I sell them retail. I'm not here to discuss tenants with other tenants."

Cynthia brightens. "You mean Olive?"

"Whom I barely know."

"Has Lorenz ever said anything to you that would indicate—"

Kathleen stops her with a raised hand. "I don't know her except as an occasional customer. You can ask Lorenz whatever you like, but he has a policy of not gossiping about the residents. I'm sorry things didn't work out with Harvey—"

"I kicked him out! I was being strong and true to myself and loving myself and having self-respect and all that shit, and now I'm having second thoughts."

Kathleen decides she needs help. Cynthia hasn't taken one hint; hasn't apologized for homesteading in the store or hindering commerce. Accordingly, she waves to Lorenz across the lace café curtains, and in thirty seconds he is there. He tips his hat to Cynthia, then turns to Kathleen. "Miss Dobbin? You called?"

"Yoo-hoo, Lorenz: This is me, the hostess of the party you brought Kathleen to. You can knock off the act, unless I've got it all wrong."

"No," says Lorenz. "You haven't."

"Is it the class thing? She owns the shop and you guard the castle?"

"It's the privacy thing," says Kathleen. "We don't think everyone in Harbor Arms has to know our business."

Lorenz asks Cynthia if she's taking a sick day.

"Tell him," says Cynthia. "It's fine if he knows."

Kathleen says, "Harvey left."

Cynthia relocates to the striped stool that serves the bra bar. "I threw him out! Do you believe it? I, who haven't had a date since Dukakis was governor. *I* threw *him* out because he flirted with Olive Boudreaux. I was hurt. Furious, actually. I let that rule the day."

Kathleen has rarely heard so honest an advertisement for a disastrous social life. She is stuck with lugubrious and inappropriate Cynthia, clashing with the salmon-and-olive-striped satin stool, rambling and confessing. The famously empathic Kathleen feels nothing for Cynthia's plight. She'd taken Harvey Nash in—she who owns waterfront real estate; she who usually had a *Wall Street Journal* tucked between her arm and her rib cage—had made a foolish decision based on an airplane flirtation, and is now looking for sympathy and sisterhood.

"I wish I could rewind the whole stupid evening and do it over with no Olive Boudreaux, no jealousy, no *opportunity* for jealousy. No big scene."

"It's probably for the best," says Kathleen.

"What is?"

"That Nash showed his true colors relatively early in the affair."

"You know what shocks me? How I'm taking this. Like a teenager."

"You were in love with him," says Lorenz.

She turns to Kathleen. "I know you think I'm pitiful and that I had to be a dope to fall in love with him in the first place, but he's not the same man who walked out on your sister. I knew what I was getting into. He confided it all—Adele, the girlfriend in California with the emotionally disturbed kids, his addiction to temptation. But he'd been working on that, and he'd been honest with me. 'It's

not pretty,' he said. 'It's not a flattering portrait.' 'I'm a complicated man. I don't make women happy.' "

"That's for sure," says Kathleen.

"I'm going back upstairs," she says. "I know I've been laugh-
able, but I'm going to pull myself together."

"It's fine," says Kathleen.

"You're nice to say that," says Cynthia, "considering your history with him. Not that I'm putting myself in the same boat with
Adele, because I don't think that was ever consummated."

Kathleen catches Lorenz's eye and they smile. "I think you're
right," she says. "We Dobbin sisters are slow."

Cynthia says, "Sorry about the rich ladies."

"They'll come back," says Kathleen. "The wedding's not till
September."

"I'm going on a shopping spree here," says Cynthia. "Not
today—don't worry. But soon. I'm going to spend as much as the
Perlmutters would have so you won't feel cheated."

"That's not necessary," says Kathleen. "Especially since you
told me you'd gone overboard . . . you know . . . the teddies."

Cynthia shouts, "Look at her blush! It's adorable."

"I agree," says Lorenz.

"You know what? I'm taking you two to dinner, absolutely."

"Sorry," says Kathleen. "We can't."

"Are you working?"

Lorenz says, "I have the night off, but we have plans."

"Together?"

He nods. Kathleen says, "Kind of firm plans."

"Tickets?"

They both say, "No, but—"

"I want to treat you to a fabulous dinner. I mean it. Someplace
great. To apologize and to celebrate."

"Celebrate what?" says Kathleen.

"You two. Love at Harbor Arms that's not ruining anyone else's
life in the process."

"It's not the least bit necessary," says Kathleen, "especially if it's
because of the Perlmutters."

"It's for me," says Cynthia. She repeats: "Someplace really special, Biba or Hamersley's or Aujourd'hui. We could eat early so you could get on with your plans."

Lorenz says to Kathleen, "Y'know how many times I've put people in taxis and said to the driver, 'Biba,' or 'Hamersley's Bistro' or 'Aujourd'hui'? Hundreds of times."

"I'd love it!" says Cynthia. "Just what the doctor ordered. Otherwise I'm going to be eating a Lean Cuisine stuffed pepper and feeling sorry for myself."

"I suppose if it was early . . ." says Lorenz.

"Five-thirty!" says Cynthia.

"I'm here till six," says Kathleen.

"Nothing will change," says Lorenz. "We'll pick up our plans from there."

"I hope so," says Kathleen. She smiles. "I like to think I'm flexible."

"And patient," says Lorenz.

"I'll go upstairs and use my powers of persuasion with the maître d's in question," says Cynthia.

"I was going to go home first and shower," says Kathleen. "I guess I could close up a little early."

"Six-thirty? Seven?" asks Cynthia.

"I can make six," says Kathleen. "I'll close up at four."

"Aren't we spontaneous?" says Cynthia. "Aren't we just like three characters in a Fitzgerald novel moving from tragedy to dinner to—what?—a drunken party at someone's estate with Chinese lanterns?"

"I suppose we are," says Kathleen.

Twenty

As Nash explains to Lois across State House place mats: He is entering his monk's phase. The Duck House is the perfect place for a guy to renounce his creature comforts and worldly goods for a couple of days. With no television and barely a phone, he'll meditate and lie low. Also, absolutely no socializing with the opposite sex. He is Brother Nash until further notice. Why? Because he has inadvertently hurt several good women, and though he doubts he can change his spots overnight, he's going on hiatus.

Lois smooths the black jersey sleeves of her dress and confides that she sought exactly the same thing when her marriage broke up—a cloistered existence and celibacy, which may have contributed to her rush to move back in with her sisters.

"I don't want to pry, but is it really a case of what you see is what you get over there?"

"As far as . . . ?"

"Their love lives."

"I suspect it is." She raises her eyebrows. "Unfortunately for them."

"Here's what I can't figure out: How do they get along, as in, What's their outlet? Aren't they—I don't know how to say this any less crudely—love-starved?"

Lois murmurs, "One wonders."

"I'm asking because I don't have any sisters and I missed the

boat on communes and coed dorms. I don't know how women respond when they haven't had a date in a decade."

"That's not literally true."

"I'm not talking about dinner and a movie. I mean lovers."

Lois counts on her fingers. "First of all, I wasn't home every
night to monitor my sisters' social lives, and don't forget I was
married for almost a year. Second of all, they could have been con-
ducting serious relationships discreetly. Third of all . . ."

Nash's attention has wandered. Someone new is on tonight:
"Babette" her tag says. No beauty. Nice eyes but a bump in her
nose. No tits whatsoever, but unexpectedly good legs—smooth
and shiny as if they've been waxed. He wonders if Babette will
think Lois is his date. Or his wife. Maybe she'd be interested
enough to ask the other girls and they'd say, "He's single. The coast
is clear. He's a composer, you know." Nash catches her eye and
grinds his two fists end on end. Immediately, Babette brings a multi-
colored pepper mill to the table.

"Say when," she says.

"Don't stop."

The waitress smiles ruefully.

"You wouldn't leave it here, would you? And come back for it
tomorrow?"

"You'll be just fine," says Babette. "Ma'am?"

Lois declines with a raised hand. "Do you know her?" she asks
after Babette leaves.

Nash confides that during his sojourn at Harbor Arms, he
dropped by in the morning, read the paper here, nursed a cup of
coffee—free refills—and sometimes had an early lunch. This gal
was new, though.

"And where did you usually have dinner?"

"At home. My roommate cooked."

"Do you mean Cynthia?"

"Cynthia John. My accountant."

He can see from the set of her eyes that Lois is drafting a sticky
follow-up question that will require a creative answer.

Finally she asks, "It's unusual for a woman to invite a client into
her home, don't you think? You could have been a serial killer."

He smiles. "But I wasn't, was I? I was quite harmless."

"Is that what Cynthia would say?"

"Cynthia . . . right now—you're right. She would say 'toxic.' "

"Because she thought you and she had a personal relationship, correct? In addition to your professional one?"

Nash leans back against the booth and exhales loudly.

"Too hard a question?"

"I'm trying to gauge what I can say in front of you."

"Because you think I'm spying for my sisters?"

"Because I came back to Boston so I could take a good hard look at myself, starting with your sister. I thought we'd shoot the breeze, reminisce a little, then something I said almost killed her, quite literally. I'm trying not to deliver any more verbal letter bombs."

"In other words, you need her blessing to move on. You'll never make a relationship work without that. That's why things didn't work with Cynthia."

Nash hasn't given Adele much thought at all in the intervening thirty years, so he doubts whether she's the one responsible for his protracted bachelorhood. But maybe Lois is right. Maybe there's guilt beneath the surface, goading him, driving him, stunting him. Maybe he's more sensitive than he knew; maybe it *is* Adele's fault. "Adele's blessing?" he asks. "Or will any Dobbin do?"

Lois waits; stalls, he thinks, when she raises an index finger to signal that she couldn't possibly answer with an atom of food yet unchewed. "Can I ask why Cynthia kicked you out, as long as we're being forthright?"

"I'll tell you: A young woman flirts with me at a party and, whammo, my head gets turned."

"Were you flirting back?"

"To be honest? I was. I walked her home from the party—"

"Stranding Cynthia?"

"Not exactly. The party was at Cynthia's. I walked Olive back to her apartment."

"Why?"

Because she was a knockout and she slipped me her card when Cynthia wasn't looking and I couldn't see any panty line and I got the idea . . . He says sorrowfully, "Because I'm weak, and I'm addicted to temptation. Cynthia happened to be correct. I was walking Olive back to her apartment because I was attracted to her and I was thinking with my . . . you-know-what, wasn't I?" he asks.

"All men do," says Lois. "How long were you gone?"

"Ten minutes? Fifteen? We had a nightcap. Half hour, tops."

"And Cynthia was angry?"

"Furious. And now I'm out on my ass."

"Were you in love with her?"

The question strikes Nash as absurdly sentimental. Where do women get these ideas? "We met on a plane," he says. "We hit it off. We had dinner. I needed a place to stay, she has a big heart, and she thought I had an honest face."

"No," says Lois. "I'm sorry. She thought you had a *handsome* face. 'Honest' is a reason you hire someone, not why you take him home. My guess is that Cynthia fell in love with you before the plane landed at Logan."

"Do you think so? A woman can fall in love with a man in, well, let's count—a five-hour flight, then drinks at her place, then dinner here . . . Seven, eight hours?"

"Basic chemistry," Lois explains. "It can happen like *that*." She snaps her fingers and her silver bangles clang.

Nash taps his index finger against his forehead. "You know what I think? Something got out of whack up here thirty years ago when I welshed on Adele. I don't want to bore you, psychoanalyzing myself, but I think there's a pattern: If I get close to someone and I'm even *contemplating* commitment, I run away because I'm afraid of hurting her as badly as I hurt Adele." He nods with conviction, takes a sip of wine and rolls it around in his mouth. "Ahh. I love an assertive Bordeaux with my meatloaf."

"I prefer red wine with everything," says Lois. "Even with fish. The scrod, by the way, is excellent."

"I wasn't changing the subject. I was trying to inject a little humor into my X-rated autobiography."

"I'm sorry. Of course you were. I date so many men who are wine snobs, who actually *say* things like that, that I heard it as a statement of fact."

"Tell me you don't go out on second dates with these stiffs."

"No," says Lois. "Absolutely not." Seconds pass before she adds, "A sense of humor is chief among the qualities I admire in . . . anyone."

He winks. "But especially in a man?"

Lois lowers her voice. "You know what people say when you list the qualities you'd like in a male friend? 'You're too fussy.' Meaning, When you've been divorced and are no longer twenty-five years old, can you afford to be fussy?"

"By 'people' do you mean 'sisters'?"

Lois puts her fork down. "It's remarkable."

"What is?"

"The way you pick up on every signal, every nuance, relating to my family."

He grins. "I am a student of the Dobbins. A Dobbins scholar. Half of them hate me and the other half . . . feed me."

"This? This is nothing, meatloaf special and wine by the glass. When you're back on your feet financially, I'll let you reciprocate."

He should have thought of that: the inevitable thank-you dinner, another night in public with Lois and her curlicued blond bob. He smiles gratuitously. "*Or,* if that door is closed, if I'm still lying low, I'll pay you back in full."

"But you'll still be taking meals, won't you? Monks eat. We could go to a vegetarian restaurant."

His attention is drawn to the cash register, where Jennifer, his favorite waitress, has just arrived and is pinning her embroidered handkerchief inside the pocket above her left breast. Because she went to high school on an island in Maine and is studying elementary ed, he is sure she has not had implants. Lois is talking about something that happened at the Division of Employment Security, some wet-behind-the-ears commissioner who killed a benefits program that was not only humane but . . .

Nash swirls his wine, tries to think of some way to get this Dobbin dame laid short of doing it himself. "Let me see," he muses. "Who do I know?"

"For what?"

"For you!"

Lois blinks.

"You know: 'D.W.F. seeks man between fifty and—what? sixty-five?—for dining, movies, plays, good times, et cetera. Must have marked sense of humor.' "

Lois says, "I hope you're joking."

Nash leans closer. "No, listen: I think I may be on to something. I didn't know what was bubbling up until I said it—which is not unlike the creative process. Your fingers take on a life of their own, and next thing you know your right hand has a melody."

"A personal ad? Do you know what that brings? Hundreds of letters from weirdos and prison inmates."

"So? After you screen them, you can send the overflow Adele's way." He grins and pats her hand, which has closed around a balled napkin. "I'm teasing you! Your sister is the last woman on earth who would find a guy through a personal ad."

"No," says Lois. "*I* am."

He wags his finger. "Unh-uh. Don't say that. What do you have to lose?"

"Time," says Lois. "Self-respect. Personal safety."

"Seriously? You never read them for fun, and once in a while see one that grabs you?"

"I may scan them from time to time, but that's as far as I could ever take it."

"Really? You were never tempted to pick up the phone? I've done it. Not the ones that require sitting down and writing letters, but since I've been here, I read the ones in the Sunday *Globe.* There's a nine-hundred number you call."

Lois says, "And is this where you say, 'Loosen up, Lois. You're a snob and a fussbudget'?"

"No, frankly, I'm thinking of all of you: Adele, Lois, Kathleen—three great women who never found the right man. Maybe it's worth some examination. Maybe no man can measure up to the family standards."

"That's not true. And it's unfair. You haven't married anyone. What about *your* standards? And what about Kathleen? She's relaxed the famous family standards, wouldn't you say: a doorman? A Hispanic doorman?"

"Worse than me!" says Nash. "Worse than a college-dropout musician from Brighton, son of a mail carrier."

"I didn't mean that the way it sounded. I'm not a racist. I just meant, he's not the person our parents might have chosen for her."

"But we're not like our parents, right? What matters to us is that he's a very decent guy who seems to be ga-ga over your sister, and vice versa."

"*Is* he decent? I've never exchanged two words with him except 'Good morning' or 'Good day' in the line of duty."

"I like him very much—"

"Based on?"

"Conversations. Observation. I've always found him polite and helpful. Cynthia was crazy about him. Invited him to her parties, in fact, which must tell you something."

"Such as?"

"That he fits in. That he's comfortable socializing with people outside his own sphere. Kathleen isn't the only one who saw past the braid and the epaulets." He grins slyly. "And who knows? Maybe he has a friend."

There is a forkful of scrod on its way to Lois's mouth, but she returns it to her plate.

"For *you*," Nash continues. "What do you have to lose? You did it by the book the first time, married one of those college graduates who, I assume, had the right pedigree. And look how that turned out—a Victoria's Secret customer." He laughs appreciatively, but stops to admire Jennifer, who is making her way from table to table, with a pot of regular in one hand and an orange-cuffed pot of decaf in the other.

Following his eyes, Lois tries to relay a cautionary tale about a friend who signed up with a dating service for Ivy League graduates, well, Ivy League and Seven *Sisters*, of course, and the first man she contacted was not even divorced! Nash tunes her out, then jumps back in to cut her off. "Do you want me to ask Lorenz myself? I'm probably going to see him in the next couple of days."

Lois, peering into her big black pocketbook, brings out a compact and a lipstick but doesn't open either. "Please don't. I'm lying low, too, Nash. I'm certainly not seeking out dates with people I don't know." She opens and untwists her lipstick, and with mirror poised says, "I guess you could say I'm not looking for any more trophies for my mantel, either."

"It does take energy," agrees Nash. "And who the hell needs to be worrying at our age about viruses and diseases? God, I remember when the worst thing you could get was gonorrhea."

Lois says, "True."

"Obviously, we're in sync," he continues. "Regrouping and staying out of trouble."

"We're in a good place for that," says Lois.

Nash looks around The Gold Dome. He's grown fond of the place; big portions served by young waitresses in tight uniforms and saddle shoes. He loves the schoolgirl look, the ankle-sock dress code, required, apparently, even on the coldest nights. "Wasn't sure if you'd like it," he says.

⟶ Lois says nothing for most of the ten-minute walk to Grove Street. Now she knows that Harvey Nash's occupancy at The Lucky Duck is meaningless, and she feels the fool. Lately she's been thinking about her marriage. Cullen didn't want the divorce. He'd insisted that he loved her, that the pleasure he derived from silky fabric against his own skin was a benign and not extraordinary condition, affecting but not harmful to their marriage. He was without question heterosexual. She knew that. She could testify with her hand on ten Bibles to that, couldn't she? Was their conjugal life a lie—had she forgotten they had to make love on their honeymoon with the TV volume turned up so their cries wouldn't be heard in the next suite?

He'd written her after she'd moved back home, asking was it such a huge price to pay? Lots of women lived with this. And whom did it harm? He thought he could confide in her. Don't prove him wrong. The volume of mail had to be explained to her sisters. "Did he hit you?" they asked. "Is it another woman?" And then he'd sent the book, which effectively solved the riddle. Hadn't he realized that the sisters opened their mail without self-consciousness in the foyer, hardly expecting anything in a Dobbin, McLendon, Katzenbach and Jessep mailer to be *The Man in the Red Velvet Dress*?

Tonight, every man and woman they pass on the street between

The Gold Dome and The Lucky Duck is part of a couple. Surely some of these men have secrets more debilitating than ownership of bras and slips? Some must be criminals and adulterers, yet these women stay. Cullen was truthful, at least. When she walked in on him that first time, fastening not anything of hers but a turquoise satin garter belt with cheap black lace bias tape as trim, he didn't lie. And for as many months as it took to file the papers, she had refused to listen to his explanations or read the books, as if she were so popular and marriageable that she didn't have to salvage what they had.

Men could do worse things. Cullen had courted her and proposed to her and married her in a beautiful garden wedding at the DeCordova Museum, conducted by a justice of the Massachusetts Supreme Judicial Court. Adele had been her maid of honor, and her father had been Cullen's best man, which everyone in the firm thought was a lovely gesture. They didn't depart from any tradition. She'd worn white. The judge had been rather reserved until he announced parenthetically that Cullen's moot court argument in law school had been so brilliant that he had remembered it to this day. Lois now thinks, Brilliant and kind and heterosexual wasn't good enough for me. I needed perfection. No compromises; no room for individual expression. If only she had kept her job when they married, he might have had the time and space to come home at lunch and indulge his needs in private, and she never would have burst in on him, and never would have been put at such a disadvantage by the truth. Maybe if she'd been so horrified and so unforgiving she wasn't such a woman of the world. Sometimes she thinks about writing to Cullen. Fetishes, she now understands from her reading on the Internet, don't have to destroy a marriage. It takes understanding and tolerance on the part of the wife, who is encouraged to pray, to enter chat rooms and discuss the five stages of grief with women in the same boat.

It may even look to the passersby that this man is her date, confiding in her, fine-tuning details of the next outing. But he is not. Nash is counseling her in the ways of meeting men so he can feel less guilty about seducing every woman except her. What kind of man while on a date—and few would argue that dinner between unrelated, eligible people is *not* a date—would volunteer to match-make and screen personal ads as if he's never had one millisecond's romantic inclination toward her himself? His monk's phase! Brother Harvey! Who did he think he was dealing with, Mrs. Chabot? Harvey Nash is just another unemployed fast-talker hus-tling for benefits. And Lois Dobbin, who makes her living sizing people up and rejecting their appeals, is the wrong woman to in-sult.

She hitches the shoulder strap of her big black pocketbook more securely on her shoulder so she can walk with a self-assured stride. Look at what the streets of Boston showcase: couples. But not Lois Dobbin. She had her chance, but she took care of that with one scream, one hastily packed suitcase, and two deaf ears.

Has she considered a younger man? Nash asks. Not a kid, and definitely not a guy in the market for the mother of his child. Watch out for those guys. That guy is looking for a uterus. Hmmm, maybe older is better—fifty to seventy. But beware, in that range, of crazy grown children—not crazy literally, but jeal-ous, spoiled brats who worry about the money and always take their mother's side. She should show him the ad first before she places it; better yet, let him write it! He knows what buttons to push. He's a guy! Insist on a photograph; anyone who doesn't com-ply is too old or too ugly. And while he's at it? One more piece of advice, Lo, not immaterial? Your hair.

Twenty-one

Nothing better to do on a Monday night than star in a little drama of his own design, Richard figures. And what could be easier for Senior Deputy Sheriff Dobbin to ascertain than whether Marty Glazer is working late? After dropping Adele off at home, he drives to 'GBH to devote the postdinner hour to the cause, happily. Security's better than it used to be, but still he doesn't even have to flash his badge to get the guard to confirm, "Mr. Glazer hasn't left yet."

Richard knows exactly what he needs to project—his unthreatening, lanky, boyish, winning self. A loving brother waiting. A ride. At 8:42 P.M., Glazer, or at least the guy Richard studied on Adele's VCR, comes through the front door of the station in a banker's suit, raincoat over one shoulder, stuffed briefcase tilting him leeward. Short. Pleasant and approachable enough. No movie star.

Richard does *hopeful* as the door opens, then *crestfallen* as it shuts. Marty stops and asks this disappointed, well-dressed fellow, "May I help you?"

"No, thanks," says Richard. "I'm waiting for someone. I thought this might be her. Leaving."

"Sorry."

"Must've got our signals crossed." He waits a few seconds, oozes devotion from every pore before saying, "Adele Dobbin. I thought I was picking her up, but maybe I got the time wrong."

Richard won't swear to it, but, in the dim light of the entryway, he thinks the guy looks a bit shaken by his invoking Adele. Now Glazer sets his briefcase down and looks at his watch. "I don't think anyone's up in Development. In fact, I'm sure of it."

"Gee," says Richard. "You don't think I should be worried, do you?" He presses his lips together, frowns. Takes a few steps back on the sidewalk to look up at what could be Adele's window. "You're right. I don't see a light. She wouldn't have left through another door, would she?"

"She usually leaves between five-thirty and six. And actually, that's our American Experience unit." He offers his hand. "I'm Martin Glazer."

"Oh! Right right right. The big guy. Nice to meet you. Richard Dobbin, the brother."

"That's right—the state trooper."

"Sheriff's Department."

"As billed," says Marty, and points to Richard's car and its "Suffolk County Sheriff's Department" seal.

"Just got off," says Richard.

"Long day," says Marty.

"You, too," says Richard.

"Loose ends," says Marty. "Loose ends and spread sheets." He jerks his thumb back toward the door. "Do you want to call upstairs?"

"I'll use my car phone. Try her at home." Richard smiles. "You have sisters?"

"One," says Marty.

"So you know." He retreats a few steps, walking backward, grinning in good-natured brotherly fashion, then asks, "Need a lift?"

"No thanks," says Marty.

"Got your car?"

"I walk. I live right over on Memorial Drive."

Richard dangles his keys at shoulder level. "Ever ridden in a cruiser?"

Marty hesitates.

"It's on my way. And if it wasn't? I'd want to give my sister's boss a ride anyway. Win points."

Marty doesn't contradict him; doesn't reassure Richard that Adele, of all people, needs no leg up in the good-relations department. So Richard himself offers, "Not that she needs help, I would imagine."

"You're right," says Marty.

"I mean, I watch her on TV; never miss a fund-raising weekend or the auction, and I have to ask, with all due modesty, is she good or what? I'm a little prejudiced, of course, but I think she's the best you've got."

"All true," says Marty.

"Get in," says Richard. "I could have had you home by now."

"If you're sure—"

"I insist. And this way, you'll find out if she made it home safely." He disengages the cell phone, presses one button, doesn't press the "send" button. He pretends to wait, count the rings, then brightens. "Kathleen? It's me. Is Adele home? . . . Taking a bath? No! Don't bother her. I'm calling from the station, and I think I might have screwed up. . . . No? She didn't work late? . . . Okay. Whew. I must've got the days mixed up." He pauses. "You can say that again." He winks at Marty and hangs up. "Taking a bath," he repeats. "This says to me"—he looks at his watch—"at *this* hour, *this* early: She had a rough day."

Marty doesn't respond; gives the buckling of his seat belt his full attention.

"You married?" Richard asks.

"Divorced."

"What happened? If you don't mind my asking."

Marty does appear to mind. "Ancient history," he snaps.

Richard does a U-turn in front of the station and heads toward the river. "What number Mem. Drive?"

"Ten-ten," says Marty.

Richard whistles appreciatively.

"You know it?"

"I've had business there; had to repossess some artwork. Big stuff. Wall-sized."

"Whose?"

Richard smiles. "The artist? Or the deadbeat owner?"

"The latter."

"Can't remember. Gray hair, ponytail, yappy dog."

"Interesting," Marty murmurs.

"I do it every day," says Richard. "You wouldn't believe what I see."

"Sounds dangerous," says Marty.

"Our uniformed guys do more of the lowlife stuff. I more or less take the white-collar crowd. The doctors and dentists and executives who need finessing rather than strong-arming. Sometimes it's going to a beautiful house in a wealthy neighborhood and letting someone walk out with a little bit of dignity left, no handcuffs, and get into an unmarked car so he's not humiliated in front of his neighbors." Richard checks for audience reaction, but his passenger is staring straight ahead into the traffic.

"On the other hand," Richard continues, "I couldn't do what you do—run a station; deal with a big staff, the creative crazies; get up in front of a camera and ask for money."

"I don't do much of that," says Marty. "Thank goodness."

"I thought you did," says Richard. He feigns mild perplexity. "I saw you the other night—was it last Saturday?—and I thought you looked pretty damn happy up there, rubbing shoulders with the professional fund-raisers."

"Did I?"

"Sure. And I know Adele thought you did a great job."

Marty stares out the passenger window at Harvard houses, Harvard brick walls. "It sounds as if you were watching quite closely."

"I can't help it. And you know why? I have a lot of sisters, but if I had to put my hand on a Bible and testify as to which one—"

"Don't get in the right-hand lane yet," says Marty.

"I know this must sound hokey, spending a Saturday night watching my sister do the same thing she's been doing for a dozen years. Which reminds me, Marty—if you don't mind the first-name basis—call me hyperobservant, an occupational hazard, but during one of the pledge breaks? You went to a phone and I wasn't paying all that much attention, but I read lips pretty well and I think you may have said 'Adele Dobbin' to whoever you were talking to. And because I serve a lot of restraining orders, I thought,

'Holy shit! Did this guy just announce to some potential stalker that this damn attractive woman is named Adele Dobbin?' "

Marty mumbles, "Our on-air fund-raisers introduce themselves every few minutes."

"I know they do—"

"As far as I know, it's never gotten anyone into trouble."

"Hey," says Richard. "Now I've embarrassed myself. And probably you. You have to excuse it as the paranoid ramblings of a guy who sees a lot of awful stuff, and doesn't want his sister taking any chances."

"Understandably."

"Because you have a sister! I had hoped at some point to run into you, so it's amazing that I did so soon. Because here's another question, Marty: I picked up on a little something myself. I'm a good reader of faces—I have to be in my line of work. I ring doorbells and wives say, 'He hasn't lived here in months,' and I have to know when they're lying."

Marty waits.

"And you know what I saw when I was watching, Marty? Which I know you'll keep in complete confidence. But I know my sister, and I don't often see a look on her face like I saw on TV the other night. And I don't think it had anything to do with the tally on the pledge board."

Marty freezes and offers nothing; asks for no amplification; doesn't ask the name of the rare look on Adele's face.

"Maybe I shouldn't have opened my big mouth," Richard tries, and is not contradicted.

I've blown it, he thinks; no question. Major diplomatic blunder. Something's bothering this Glazer guy. Can't even bring himself to ask what any kid in junior high would want to know: Does she like me back?

"Anywhere along here is fine," says Marty, fifty yards before Ten-ten Memorial Drive.

"Let me pull up."

"Thank you," says Marty.

Richard puts the car into park with a jolt. After a short silence he says, "Guess you have no reaction to any of this."

Marty has his left hand on his briefcase, and his right on the door handle. He waits, exhales a labored breath. "I *was* saying her name when I was on the phone, but it was just a little old lady asking, and completely benign."

"By the name of?"

Marty opens the car door, gets out. Just before closing it, he leans in to say, as if it were his thanks, "Pearl Glickman Glazer."

⟍⟋ He can't find a comfortable position, even with the orthopedic pillows. His left knee feels funny; not a pain, exactly, but as if the kneecap is slightly askew. He takes two coated ibuprofen, 200 milligrams each, with seltzer. Why hadn't he asked the brother up for a drink, a Coke, a beer. Why hadn't he just walked home, as always. Yet . . .

It was interesting to see this male version of Adele's physical properties: tall, long fingers, faded freckles, auburn-haired; the same eye color, if one could tell at night—not brown, not green. A dry lawn. Now he's embarrassed himself, waxing poetic. He thinks it was a setup. The brother wanted to feel him out. Adele didn't need a ride home. Her brother didn't live with her, or chauffeur her around.

But he was smooth. Adele has a modicum of that charm, without the cockiness, and happily for the station, her highest wattage shines on-air. Viewers love Adele and write in to say so. He has a file of such letters, which he has perused more than once. Had she ever seen her fan mail? he'd asked her. Did his predecessor send her cc's? "Some," Adele had said. She had smiled sardonically and added, "The ones that wouldn't inspire me to ask for a raise."

He'd made copies himself after his secretary had gone home for the day, and put them on Adele's desk. "FYI, Marty" was all his note said. The truth was, he'd kept the Post-it note she'd returned with it. "But did they enclose checks?" she wrote with characteristic modesty and job devotion, and signed it only "A."

But what a pickle he'd made at work today! He hadn't realized until his mother called—Jesus, of all the humiliating moments, of all the clichés—that he was handing out valentines on live TV. So goddamn embarrassing.

His secretary hadn't said anything except, "Nice job. You were very natural." When he'd frowned, she had added, "I know you were nervous beforehand, but it went great."

"I don't know the totals yet," he'd grumbled.

"Do you want me to check with Development?" she'd asked. Marty thought he'd heard an acknowledgment of an office romance.

This is why he is single, he thinks. He's terrible at this. He can get promoted to station manager but he can't do anything else right. Maybe it's for the better. Soon enough she'd find out he has inhalers in his desk drawer and epinephrine in his night table. He has acid reflux, bad gas, and lactose intolerance, new. He thinks his penis is unremarkable, and maybe Adele has seen better. What a jerk, refusing to come clean with the brother. Now Richard could say, "I saw that guy in action, watched the two of you raising money. Is he as much of a jerk as he struck me on TV?"

It is past ten, too late to call anyone. The Boston phone book has no listing for Richard Dobbin. Of course it wouldn't—a sheriff wouldn't have his number published. He stares at "Dobbin, Lois," on Stearns Road. What a shmuck, to have a crisis at an hour when he can't fix it. What can happen between now and tomorrow when Adele is at her desk? Richard might poison the well. Adele could call in sick. Adele could quit! He'd seen her in Development and barely acknowledged her. Coward! Shmuck!

He might be able to fix it. Maybe his mother was right: Maybe Adele likes him; maybe he did look handsome on television. He was so happy Saturday night. They'd sent the Hillel kids home with their thanks and their 'GBH water bottles, and acted as if it were the job of the station manager and assistant director of development to lock up. They were the last to leave. She'd called a cab, and he'd waited with her on the curb, wondering what he could do to prolong the evening. When the taxi arrived, he wanted to give the guy ten dollars to disappear. But how could he? She'd made the call; it was not his place to cancel it. He opened the door for her, and as she passed him to step into the back seat, she—a mind reader, a miracle—kissed him lightly on the lips.

What a shmuck he was not to have put his arms around her and kissed her as if he'd meant it. But he was not a master of the grand gesture. *Here buddy, here's a ten. This lady's going with me.* It never occurred to him to slip in beside her and ride with her to Brookline like a spontaneous leading man would. To find a bar still open and have a nightcap like normal people do. He knows how he must have looked when she kissed him: astonished. He'd felt torn and hopeful, standing on the curb, watching the white taxi pull away, and inept. Had he responded at all? Had she known how pleased he was? He'd almost called her that night, too, but it was late when he got home and she lived with her sisters. He didn't know if she had a phone by her bed. And how would he ever ascertain such a thing? *Adele, do you have a phone by your bed? Why? Because I didn't want to disturb anyone.*

Sexual harassment! He couldn't ask that. That was like asking if there was someone in her bed.

Was there? Did he really know anything about her? What did a peck on the lips mean between colleagues of long standing? Why hadn't he called on Sunday, at ten A.M.? At noon? At eight o'clock, after *60 Minutes*? What was wrong with him? How late can you call a coworker, an employee, who's kissed you?

What time was it now?

Twenty-two

People never ask, but they do wonder: Is it possible for relatively well-adjusted and attractive women to have passed into middle age without having found a path across the great divide into sexual activity?

Almost. Adele, for example: Her scorecard shows one time with one man, a deflowering engineered by the intact Adele herself in a hotel room in Chicago—sexual congress with a proper (well-mannered, well-spoken, well-educated) stranger, fourteen years ago last Christmas.

She had decided in advance, a plot suggested by novels and movies, and by the rumors that fly about after affiliates' conventions, that one can step out of one's life while out of town, ignore one's own moral compass, meet someone amenable and discreet, and have a fling—without dating, falling in love, or ever seeing the sexual partner again. Like a man would. Like a character in an Erica Jong novel would, repeatedly. No family to meet; no family standards to uphold; no (insurmountable) regrets.

So on the second night of an affiliates' convention (first night being a banquet hosted by the John D. and Catherine T. MacArthur Foundation, with remarks by Judy Woodruff) the thirty-nine-year-old Adele bathed, shaved, darkened her eyelashes, reddened her lips, put on a peacock-blue wool crepe dress over a special bridal-white lace bra and bikini underpants, and went to the bar one hotel over.

As soon as he sat down two barstools away, then asked her permission to move one seat closer, Adele knew he was exactly right for the job: young, eager, apologetically on the prowl. His eyebrows and mustache were blond, his cheeks ruddy, his jacket corduroy. There was a Slavic tilt to his eyes and cheekbones. The Modern Language Association badge on his chest announced, "Ted Jelavich, U. of Illinois, Urbana-Champaign."

Adele kept her mission to herself for the first two glasses of wine; needed only to smile at his clunky lines and say yes to dinner. She could see him growing hopeful; sensed that he'd come to the bar to get lucky in the manner of an academic on holiday. His field was English, seventeenth century. Confidentially? He was interviewing with—oh, what the heck—Yale, Tulane, Rutgers, and U.C.–Santa Barbara. Adele nodded and asked questions, all the while making meaningful eye contact; when they moved on to a steak house and were toasting over their menus, she murmured, "To tonight."

Ted repeated her words and clinked her glass. Adele, by now tipsy, leaned in and asked the coy question she'd fashioned in advance, "Would you believe that someone my age could still be a virgin?"

As soon as Ted grasped that he'd been elected, his demeanor changed. He wanted a role in, and credit for, this seduction. "I find you incredibly attractive," he soon proclaimed.

"I'm thirty-nine," Adele had offered. "You look about twenty-five."

"Twenty-eight. What could be better?" he murmured.

"How so?"

"An older woman, the mythology: *Tea and Sympathy? Candida. The Graduate?*"

"Except," said Adele, "in this case—"

"In this case, I walked into the bar and saw you sitting at the end of the row, looking a little wistful, a little sad in the half-light of the Tiffany shade, twisting the stem of your wineglass. It wasn't that you were telegraphing any coded message, just the opposite, but now that I know what I know . . ."

He continued the needless campaign over dinner, staring dreamily while she conversed, then snapped himself out of his fake reverie with, "I'm sorry. You were saying? Your eyes are extraordinary." He found her hand wherever she hid it. She was sure that the waiter, the busboy, the cabdriver, the doorman were in on the countdown: One more course, now just the check, now just our coats, and now, amazingly enough, I'm going back to the hotel to get laid. I just rolled into town! I fell into it!

He kissed her passionately in the taxi, his sturdy Czech or Serbian or Estonian barrel chest clamping her to his trench coat, crinkling his badge.

"Would you like to come up to my room for a nightcap?" he whispered at the elevator.

"I assumed that was the plan."

"I'm a gentleman," he said. "If you meant what you said back there, this isn't something you do lightly."

"Or ever."

"Would you mind if I took a quick shower?" he asked when they got to his room.

Adele waited quietly at the foot of his queen-sized bed. It was not thrilling or romantic, but at thirty-nine it was time, not necessary but recommended, like a baseline EKG or a mammogram. He sounded happy in there, sloshing confidently, now the shower door creaking, now the hair dryer roaring. She didn't remove any clothes, or slip off her shoes, or skim his convention materials, or proofread his C.V., or eat the mint on his pillow, or change her mind.

He exited the bathroom, still damp, wearing only his eyeglasses and a white towel around his waist. Beneath the thin terry cloth, a mass the size of a jelly doughnut shifted.

He sat down beside her. "How *are* you?" he asked.

"Fine."

"Are you ready?"

"For . . . ?"

He stood up and faced her in front of the TV/armoire. "This!" The towel came off with a flourish and a triumphant smile, as if doves would fly forth. Adele blinked, then stared while the new Ted, star of his own instructional video, lectured.

Pedagogically speaking, he was ideal—proud of what he had

and how it obeyed him. "Have you seen one of these before? Of course you have. You're not a nun. Watch what happens as I respond. Now I'm going to kiss you. See what I do. Now you do it. Right there is the best. Ahhh. Two hands. Do you remember how it started off, flaccid, but as the blood flow increases it enlarges and becomes turgid. What would you estimate? Thirty-five percent bigger than what you first saw? Forty? Are you glad you chose me? Those are just veins. That's normal, too. This clear emission? This is not semen, but something men produce in preparation for ejaculation." He was a sexual pedant, a verbal exhibitionist. "This is the glans. This is the head. This is an exquisitely sensitive area. I'm probably about average—maybe a half inch bigger—in case you were wondering.

"You know what's nice for the man?" he continued. "To see the woman naked. Start with the top button. Not too fast. That's good. Slow is good. Now the arms. Upsa-daisy. Now the slip. Can I do that? Those are pretty. Leave them on for a while. God. Let me help. Isn't this liberating? Even interesting? Are you feeling anything? Isn't this nice?".

She said she knew her own anatomy; yes, she did have a pocket mirror in her purse but didn't feel the need to use it right now.

"You wouldn't want to kiss it, would you, at this stage? You haven't touched it much. Before I put on the prophylactic? Or before *you* put it on? It's nice to incorporate that into the lovemaking.

"Are you ready?" he asked, his voice finally strained.

"I guess so," said Adele.

"Now we'll lie down. I'll get on top. This is the missionary position. Am I too heavy?"

He stopped the play-by-play once he'd worked his fully engorged teaching tool into Adele, after a brief soliloquy about the overvalued currency that some cultures assigned to the breaking of a woman's hymen. He didn't talk as he climbed the scale to a loud climax. When it was over, he offered her a chance to investigate the semen pooled in the tip of his rose-colored condom.

He said he could do it again in a little while if she was interested. He was at her disposal. He said he felt this evening would appear in a poem because he'd been profoundly moved by the experience.

This wasn't like other M.L.A.'s, and she wasn't like other women. This was extraordinary. How could he thank her? He'd never forget this night. Would *she*? It was a rare privilege for him. For any man. Virgins were generally freshmen, and while several in his Introduction to Reading and Writing had tried to enlist him for this very lesson, he had an ironclad rule against sleeping with undergraduates.

About the poem: No one would recognize her. He might have to keep the hair of the woman in the poem vermilion, because auburn pubic hair and ivory skin and the lightly freckled chest and arms were images he couldn't easily forgo. But that was hardly something to worry about. He wouldn't use her name. "Susan" didn't resonate for him anyway. Too common. He'd think of something—Maggie, maybe. Or Allegra. If the poem was accepted anywhere, he would alert her.

"Was it all that you had hoped for?" he asked. "You weren't disappointed, were you? The first time is a physical and an emotional experience, but not necessarily an erotic one. Would tomorrow after my last appointment, Rutgers, be convenient? It doesn't even have to be dinner, if you wanted to use me purely as mentor rather than date. Anything. Feel free. I know this is important to you, isn't it? Approaching the big four-oh?"

"Next month."

"No wonder. A passage. I'm so honored. Even if nothing comes out of the meeting, professionally, then it all will have been worth it."

"Thank you," Adele said.

"No, thank *you*. And may I presume to give you a small piece of advice? Don't regret this. You did the right thing, opening yourself to this experience."

"We'll see."

"I'm worried that it wasn't satisfying for you. I was concentrating too much on the anatomical component without giving enough thought to your pleasure. I could take care of that right now. If you relax, it probably wouldn't take long."

"It was fine."

"Are you glad? Was it all that you had hoped it would be? Can I have a hug?"

Adele said, "I'll get dressed in the bathroom and call it a night. No need to walk me back; no need to get out of bed."

"I most certainly *will* get out of bed and give you a proper farewell," he said, springing to his feet, immodest as an undiapered toddler. At the door, Assistant Professor Jelavich pressed his lips to her right hand. "Adieu, sweet and slightly sad lady."

"I'm not sad in the least," said Adele.

⟝‿⟞ Antiseptic on one hand, messy on the other, is laboratory sex without affection or desire. This many years later, Adele thinks of Ted Jelavich more often than she'd like to, not wistfully but inevitably, her sole context for intercourse and male anatomy in action. Some days she thinks she is lucky to have come away with the job accomplished tidily by a volunteer gigolo, because she didn't want him then, and she doesn't want him now.

Adele has the apartment to herself tonight. Tomorrow is the weekly meeting between Development and Promotion, which Marty usually attends. To her annoyance, she is experiencing what could only be described as man trouble. Unseemly and unworthy. She concedes that she may be due for a policy change because it's been difficult in this world to never have married. Occasionally, when asked, she lies. "Divorced," she'll say to a stranger at a wedding reception to avoid a certain conversational airlessness. Of late and on occasion, she has replied, "Widowed." Everyone blames Harvey Nash, but Adele on this night blames herself. She could have encouraged some men who came calling; could have gone on second dates with otherwise respectable candidates who didn't appeal to her for superficial reasons, such as height or table manners or dandruff on lapels. At twenty, twenty-five, possibly even thirty she wouldn't have gone out with Marty Glazer; wouldn't have crossed paths with him for reasons of geography and sociology. And now, at fifty-three, she is looking around her apartment, wondering what chore she can undertake to keep her mind off the fact that she and Marty had flirted, stood out on the curb shoulder to shoulder, remarked on the full moon, and would have—if they hadn't been in the figurative shadow of the station, and weren't a lawyer and the daughter of a lawyer worried about every footnote—kissed in earnest. Gone somewhere together. Erased Ted Jelavich as a record holder, or at least superseded him.

She could do work. She could read—the memoir she's started is a seven-day book and not renewable. She could iron while she watched—what night is it?—*Live from the Kennedy Center*. She could return phone calls or write a thank-you note or hem a dress. She could clean house, which would please Kathleen when she came home later, especially if she tackles Lois's eyesore of a deserted room.

She begins by hanging up Lois's clothes, which leads to a pairing of her shoes on her shoe tree, a disposal of dry-cleaner polyurethane bags, and a vacuuming of Lois's wall-to-wall. She straightens the perfume vials and bottles of lotion on the mirrored surface of the vanity table. Lastly, she strips the bed and remakes it with what she thinks of as Richard's sheets. Lois had painted her walls, against everyone's objections, a corned-beef rose with white woodwork for a surprisingly pleasant effect. If Lois remains at the boardinghouse, Adele thinks, or if Kathleen marries Lorenz, she'll gain a guest room. Or two. The concept of living alone takes her by surprise, and she sits down on Lois's vanity chair to imagine life without sister-roommates. Tonight, it is just right. Could she swing the rent on her own? She dusts mementos, including a small silver picture frame in the shape of a heart—Lois and Cullen, coming back up the aisle as husband and wife—and slips only that one into the top drawer of the vanity, which belonged to their mother and which gives off a trace of her sachet. Adele takes a last look at poor Cullen. She was fond of him; any one of them might have found Cullen suitable before the revelation. Kathleen passes Cullen occasionally on Congress Street, and reports that he nods briskly, but can't meet her eyes.

It is only on her way back to the kitchen for glass wax that Adele spots Kathleen's note, secured to the refrigerator with their only racy magnet—a tanned male torso wearing polka-dot boxers slipping down pale buttocks, a trade-show giveaway that offends only Richard. "I'll be staying chez Lorenz tonight," it says.

Why am I surprised? Adele thinks. Of course it would lead to this. Well, good for her. Sex with love. She suspects Kathleen has passed the rest of them by because she went to college in the 1970s, when men were allowed in the dorms; even before that, she was the first Dobbin to stay out all night after her senior prom. What was the boy's name? Lived on Tappan. Went to Hamilton, or was it Colgate? Brian? Brad? Kathleen said they'd gone to Crane Beach like everyone else in the entire graduating class, and after two other daughters her parents should know this is B.H.S. tradition, for God's sake.

It is the way of the world, and has been for decades: Kathleen will be staying at Lorenz's apartment, sleeping in Lorenz's bed, having sex with him and enjoying it. Lois will be sipping drinks in a bar, smoking cigarettes and looking for company. After all this time, the Dobbin girls are getting brave or getting foolish— except for me, Adele thinks. I'm fifty-three years old. What could I do that would be out of character, something that would have shocked Mother? Everything and nothing. There are no house rules anymore. The Dobbin sisters are orphans now, and not minding it. Breaking rules. Some of them. Richard Dobbin is sleeping on a couch in a bisexual coworker's apartment, probably walking around in polka-dot boxer shorts, happy as a clam, while on the other hand, Marty Glazer, dressed in suit and tie and starched collar, can't handle having a cup of coffee with her by the station microwave. What could *I* handle? she wonders. What could I write in a note left casually on the refrigerator for all comers to read? "Staying at ——'s tonight. P.S. I lost my virginity years ago (no one you know), so this isn't the milestone you think it is."

Adele goes to her own room. The night is not young. The night is over. She could set the soda bottles right now and get into bed with the thin memoir, due in two days. Or she could make a phone call. Bring it to a head. Not apologize for waking him. Ask, "Did I do something to offend you, Marty? I had the distinct feeling you were avoiding me at the office today."

It's late. One doesn't make phone calls at this hour. One doesn't call boys at all, even to ask the homework assignment. You don't go out with sons of parents we don't know. The boy always comes to the door when he picks you up. Never let a boy in when you're home alone, and never go to his house unless his parents are there. Don't talk on the phone if there's an electrical storm. Don't go out with wet hair. Don't let a boy touch your knee.

I'll read, Adele thinks.

But then the author of the memoir describes in detail what she did at fifteen, willingly, exuberantly, expertly, with the scholarship college boy who tutored her in her three failing subjects. Adele is amazed that someone still alive, someone whose "About the Author" says she is married with two young daughters, would confide these activities to anyone but her therapist, let alone brag about them in a book. She puts the memoir down. She finds that the confessions have, nonetheless, dumped something chemical or hormonal into her bloodstream, something potent and very nice. She picks up the slim volume again and finds her place.

⟜ After dinner—and by dessert, Kathleen and Lorenz can't bear another word, good or bad, about Nash—Cynthia drives them to the North End. She has invited them up to her condo for a nightcap, complaining, "It's barely eight-thirty," then guessing what their pressing engagement is. "I'm betting that someone lent you his apartment for the night, and you don't want to waste a second. Do you both have housebound roommates or something?"

"I live with my sisters, but Lorenz has his own place," says Kathleen.

Lorenz, in the front passenger seat, flashes her a look that signals *It's almost over.* "Left at the next corner," he says, "then left again."

"Espresso," Cynthia reads from a neon sign. " 'We invented chocolate-chip cannoli.' . . . Anyone?"

"Some other time," says Lorenz.

Kathleen leans forward and touches Cynthia's shoulder. "Dinner was delicious."

"It was, wasn't it? I love that place! I love the woodwork, and the floors, and the whole look of it."

"My lamb was out of this world," says Lorenz.

"And my crème brûlée," says Kathleen.

"My father makes a great flan," says Lorenz.

"He's from Havana," says Kathleen.

"Is he home now?" asks Cynthia.

Lorenz laughs.

"What?"

"It took a whole campaign to get him out of the house for one night."

"Why?"

When Lorenz doesn't answer, Kathleen says, "He didn't think it was proper for us to be there unsupervised."

"You two? At your age?"

Lorenz says quietly, "He thinks there're two kinds of girls in this world, and Kathleen's a nice girl, period. Regardless of how old we are."

Cynthia slaps her steering wheel. "You know what? I should give you a key to my place. I'm never there during the day, am I, Lorenz? I leave around eight and I don't get home till six at the earliest. You wouldn't even have to give me advance notice. I'd knock before I opened the door. I mean it. I'd get a kick out of helping you two."

"Why?" asks Kathleen.

"Because I would. I'd like there to be a little luxury in your lives, and a gorgeous view, and a Jacuzzi. *Somebody* ought to get some pleasure out of it, because it sure ain't going to be me. I'm back to where I started—a big empty apartment."

"Which sounds like heaven to some of us," says Kathleen.

"Here," says Lorenz. "The green triple-decker with the barrels out front." Cynthia shifts into park and sighs. "You can have it, the big apartment and the big empty bed." She studies Lorenz's house through the windshield, then adds, "Quite literally, I meant that—it's yours any time you want to use it."

Lorenz says, "Thank you, but—"

"But what? How do you know you won't want it on a spur-of-the-moment basis? You take a lunch hour, right? If this is your first night together, you don't know what this might unleash. Ever heard of a quickie?"

Kathleen laughs.

"See?" says Cynthia. "She's no prude."

⁓ When Kathleen touches Lorenz's penis—finally!—it is easier than she thought possible, a meeting and greeting, a quick rub through his trousers as they kiss their way up the stairs past Mrs. Nocera's apartment. Lorenz's hands travel down Kathleen's raincoat to her bottom—this still before he's unlocked the apartment door—and she, Kathleen Dobbin, presses against Lorenz with the confidence that comes from having negotiated the evening's agenda in advance. Lorenz kicks the door closed with his foot, and this time slides his hands under the layers, and encounters—where he expected silk or cotton—not much. "May I see?"

Kathleen raises her skirt. The kitchen is dark except for a fluorescent bulb on the stove.

"My room," he murmurs. "Let's go."

"Wait a sec," says Kathleen. She unbuckles his belt. Lorenz straightens his spine and sucks in his fuzzy middle. "Don't worry. I do this for a living." She undoes his trousers and peeks in. "Briefs! I had to know."

Lorenz's eyes are closed. And now she is kissing him, and he is tugging at the knot of his tie with one hand and leading her by the other to his room and his double bed. His room is wallpapered in pink-and-gray apple blossoms. "Some bachelor pad. Flowers and fruit trees," he says. "Makes you wonder, huh?"

"Not for one second," says Kathleen.

Lorenz locks the door and pulls down the bedspread neatly, in stages, then the blue sheet and white thermal blanket.

"Pretty," says Kathleen.

"New—Bed, Bath and Beyond." He asks if she would like to wash up, use the bathroom. Anything?

She tells him she's forgotten to bring her things; her overnight bag with her beautiful silk charmeuse nightgown is spread out on her bed at home, left behind in the rush.

"I'll see it next time, won't I?"

"I forgot everything—my toothbrush, my clothes for tomorrow. And Lorenz? I'd bought some condoms, just in case."

"Just in case what?"

"You didn't buy any."

He is smiling, unbuttoning his shirt at the same time he liberates his shirttails.

"What's funny?"

"I've been carrying them around with me for a couple of months now."

"Since?"

"Do you want the exact date?"

"I meant, 'With me in mind?' "

"Night and day." He points to the door. "I put out clean towels. My toothbrush is red. The toothpaste is in the medicine cabinet. Don't use the Poli-Grip. Don't take too long."

"You don't mind sharing your toothbrush?"

Lorenz takes her face in his hands. "What would I mind? Your germs?"

"Good point," says Kathleen. "I'll be right back."

Lorenz gets undressed quickly, gets into bed, pulls up the sheet, plumps the pillows next to him, experiments with the three-way bulb's settings and chooses the brightest.

Kathleen returns wearing his oatmeal-colored terry-cloth robe, holding her clothes, her underwear, and her shoes. "Couldn't find the belt," she says.

Lorenz stares and finally says, "There *is* no belt. I mean, there was, but it disappeared."

"And who needs it anyway?"

"Lock the door," says Lorenz.

"You don't want to use the bathroom or anything?"

"Later."

"Got everything?"

He opens his night table drawer and closes it again. "Right here."

"Should we set the alarm?" says Kathleen.

"For what?"

She moves closer to the bed. "So I can leave before your father gets home."

"Unh-uh. He promised. He gets into South Station at eleven."

He slips his arms inside the open robe and pulls her to him.

Kathleen looks down and sighs. It's all come together, and she's floating in its center: His cheek is pressed against her belly fondly, his warm hands are stroking her expertly, and his patient, gallant, bobbing penis, half-liberated, half-draped by new linens, is wholly thrilling.

Twenty-three

"*D*id somebody get up on the wrong side of the bed?" Nash coos from the sideboard as he pours his coffee and pokes the scones. Lois, at the round oak table, stares at his black silk kimonoed back.

"Can I warm yours up?" he asks.

"No thank you."

"Cream is where?"

"Milk. In front of you."

Nash carries his mug to the table and drags a chair closer to hers. "So it's continental breakfast here at The Lucky Duck, sans landlady?"

"Correct."

"Same menu every day?"

"No. She alternates with muffins." Lois tugs at one of her starched white cuffs and touches her father's onyx cuff link. "And we dress for it. Bathrobes are not considered proper attire for the public rooms."

Nash rattles one corner of her newspaper. "Is that all, because you seem a little . . . funny this morning."

Without further encouragement, Lois lets loose: "Did you stop to think that it might have been a hurtful thing to say to me, about my hair color? What am I supposed to do about it? Snap my fingers and make it go away?"

Nash puts his mug down and gives her shoulders a quick squeeze. "I'm sorry, Lo. I didn't say I didn't like it. It's just that I loved the original color. Now I feel awful. I stepped over the line last night because we were confiding in each other and I got a little carried away in the adviser department." He chuckles. "Believe me, I'm no beauty consultant. And you know, when I see it by the light of day, it's quite Marilyn Monroe-ish."

"Stop it," she says.

"I mean it. It's her color."

"Which you won't have to look at much longer."

He looks at his watch. "You head out at what time?"

"I meant, I can't stay here forever. I'm weighing my options."

"In what areas?"

She reaches down to the floor for her pocketbook and briefcase. "Why exactly would I be confiding any of that to you?"

"Because you trust my instincts."

"No, I do not."

"I meant my social instincts, since we were discussing sources of future relationships. I was just trying to help."

"I have a brother for that."

"Of course you do. A great guy. With excellent instincts of his own."

"Don't be so patronizing," says Lois.

"I wasn't! I like Richard. Very much. I would think he'd be an excellent sounding board for you. For all of you."

"Maybe," she says. "Maybe for Kathleen. And of course he's got Adele on a pedestal."

"Understandably," Nash murmurs. "Being the oldest, and a household name, and now with your parents gone . . ."

"It's true. She gave me my wedding. And she was my maid of honor." Lois holds out her left hand.

"I noticed. A showstopper."

"Did you know it was my engagement ring?"

"I assumed as much."

"You didn't think it was some sad piece of expensive jewelry I had given myself as a present to cover up the fact that I had no wedding ring on my hand?"

"Not for one second."

Lois pinches an invisible fiber presumably caught in a prong. "What did you make of the fact that I still wear it?"

Nash shrugs; butters a piece of scone and asks, before popping it into his mouth, "Do you know what happened to the diamond I gave Adele, by the way?"

It elicits her first smile of the day. "Of course I do: She gave your engagement ring to the retarded messenger for the firm who wanted to propose to the girl who cleaned the latrines. It was a perfect fit."

Nash can't remember what the diamond looked like or how much it cost, but he's never heard anything less sentimental. "I was a poor kid on scholarship. I had to work hard for that ring," he protests.

"You told Adele it was your grandmother's, and it had great sentimental value."

Now Nash remembers. He'd bought it on layaway from a jewelry store near Park Street Station. He can see the store window in his mind's eye—rings tagged with prices written in India ink. Preowned, obviously. Estate jewelry, but cheap. It must have been *some*body's grandmother's, he'd figured at the time. "Is that the custom? The girl gets to keep the ring if the wedding doesn't come off?"

"Correct. The wronged party." She looks at her own hand again.

"Am I picking up on some of that old feeling for your ex? Pre, pre—and how to put this in the public rooms?—before he donned his gay apparel?"

Lois whispers furiously, "That is an exceedingly private matter which I only confided to you in a moment of utter personal trust."

"Sorry!"

Lois stands up. "Don't apologize. You've helped me. Ironically. I'm able to see things a little more clearly after a few conversations with someone like you."

"No small matter," says Nash.

"And you should start looking at your own life—such as who you want to spend the rest of it with, and get a grip. Maybe even get some help."

Nash looks up.

"The rest of your life," she repeats. "Like normal people do. Like people who aren't sex addicts."

Nash wipes his mouth carefully and returns the napkin to his lap. "What made you say that? What prompted that kind of sweeping indictment, or should I say diagnosis?"

Lois says primly, "Nothing."

～ Cynthia saw it too: a Los Angeles psychotherapist hawking *The Sum of His Parts: Men, Power, and Sexual Addiction* on the *Today* show. How fascinating, Cynthia thinks, and how pertinent. A crippling disease, the doctor asserts. A compulsion that carries a tremendous social stigma. Can ruin one's life if left untreated. And for the partners of sex addicts? *Please know this:* What you've been living with is *not* about you.

"Aren't these guys just jerks with no self-control?" asks Katie Couric.

"It's a condition not unlike alcoholism," says the doctor. "My book offers a catharsis to the anger, confusion, and even personal embarrassment many victims feel."

"Wait," says Katie. "Who's the victim here? The sex addict or his girlfriends?"

"Everyone: the family, the partners, the sufferer . . ."

Katie makes one of her famous faces, and the crew laughs off-camera.

～ At the ten A.M. meeting, Marty takes a seat next to Adele, not his usual place at the head of the table. She is cool. Everything about her is—her white blouse, her straight navy blue skirt, and the diamond solitaires in her earlobes. Her two coworkers from Development are blank masks. Keep us out of this, they seem to be saying.

"Doughnut?" asks Marty, starting the plate around the table without taking one.

"No thank you," Adele says.

"Did everyone get my memo?" he asks.

"Yes," say the others.

"Which one?" says Adele.

"Yesterday's."

"Concerning?"

"The old Cousteaus."

"What about them?" asks Adele.

"The cost. Do we want to spend that much?"

"He's dead," says Adele. "Who cares about Cousteau? People just want Sunken Treasures of the *Titanic*."

"Adele?" Marty clears his throat. "Did you get my E-mail this morning?"

"I came in late." And here she meets his eyes. "Since I stayed so late on Saturday, I figured I had some comp time coming."

His face reddens. He opens a file folder and shuffles its contents.

Adele adds, "I would have mentioned it yesterday but I only saw you in passing."

Marty flinches. Finally he says, "Adele? Could I speak to you for a minute? In private?"

She hesitates, then stands.

"Take your time," says Scott.

"We're fine," says Michael.

In the hall, Marty opens the door to the stairwell. "You embarrassed me in there," he says as she passes. "We have to go back into that meeting eventually. It's going to be awkward."

"They're my friends," she says. "You embarrassed me yesterday in front of them by looking right through me."

"That's what I'm trying to fix. I mean, it's Tuesday. It's not a month later, or a week; I'm one, maybe two days late. I decided to E-mail you—"

"To say what?"

"More or less: 'Are you free for dinner this evening or any evening this week?' "

Adele replies, "No, I am not."

"Just like that? Without a moment's reflection?"

"That's my answer. Sorry."

But she doesn't look sorry. She reverses direction and ascends one step. "Shall we go back into the meeting now?"

"I didn't know—" he begins, but the door above them opens and a skinny production assistant with maroon hair clanks down the stairs in lethal-looking platform shoes. "Hold on to the banister," says Marty.

The girl stares, too new to recognize a quasi-order. "I'm not going to fall," she snaps.

They wait for her to pass. "I'm not having good rapport with my women employees today," says Marty.

"No manners—someone should tell her she's snarling at her boss."

He smiles weakly. "Which I would *never* tolerate."

When she doesn't answer, Marty asks, "I'm apologizing. I was rude, I was cowardly, I was worrying too much about the politics—"

"Politics!"

"Let me finish. Technically, I'm your boss—do I need to spell this out?—and I was afraid that I had pasted my heart on my sleeve and acted like a jackass, on-air, no less."

The word "heart" has an unexpected effect on Adele, but her vexed expression doesn't change.

"I'm sorry," he says. "I guess I misunderstood."

What has Adele learned lately about dignity being less important than love? Not enough. Her stiff upper lip wants to remain rigid, but possible relief nips at the corners. She can see herself sitting opposite Marty at dinner with this long-standing attachment finally accredited, and gaining the freedom to do whatever next thing they are so moved to do. But all she allows is a brisk, dismissive, "I'll read your E-mail after the meeting."

⌒ Richard calls her midday. He wants to know what's happened on the all-important Tuesday following the barren, silent, disappointing Monday.

"Why?" she asks.

"*Why?* Jesus Christ. You have to ask me why I want to know what happened and if you might possibly be feeling better today than you did last night?"

"I'm not."

Richard waits. "Nothing got said today?"

"I didn't say that."

"You talked to him?"

"We had a meeting, the usual Tuesday one—"

"But no personal conversation, I mean?"

"It evolved into that."

"Did he acknowledge anything?"

"Such as?"

Richard yelps, "Such as he's sorry he acted like a jerk! That he's an emotional midget and should let you in on how he feels."

"How do you know how he feels?"

"I'm a guy! I fleshed out the whole scenario for you—"

"I'm not going anywhere. If he wants to try me again, I might reconsider."

" 'If he wants to try me again . . .' Try *what* again?"

She says, not without pride, "He asked me to have dinner with him tonight—but with no notice."

When Richard doesn't answer (*How can a sister of mine have so little aptitude for courtship or coquetry?*), Adele cites chapter and verse: "It's common courtesy, Richard. You do not ask someone for a date on the same day. It's insulting. I have more pride than that. And you know it."

⟅⟆ At four o'clock, she simply leaves. Runs off like a free woman, and would appreciate the symbolism of her own act if she weren't so goddamn sick of being free. Fellow passengers on the subway smile the way they do when they see her familiar face and trademark haircut and perfect posture. *Isn't that . . . ? Don't I know you from . . . ? Aren't you the woman who . . . ?*

The man in the fare booth at Park Street shakes his head at "Harbor Arms."

"On Atlantic Ave.?"

"Aquarium. Green Line to Blue Line to Aquarium stop. Ask when you get there."

"I know where it is above ground," she says impatiently.

"Then walk it," he says. "Keep your girlish figure, if I'm allowed to say that."

She does walk, toward the water, detouring slightly to take the familiar streets near her father's old firm. Finally she spots Kathleen's building, then the uniformed man with a whistle in his mouth. Cream-and-brown uniform, shiny shoes, not only hailing taxis but taking charge. She sees him do a thrilling thing: In the middle of Atlantic Avenue, he stops traffic with a balletic pumping of his hand so that a car nosing out of his garage can make a U-turn. The driver salutes him. My sister's boyfriend, she thinks. My sister's lover.

"Ma'am?" he asks as he hops back onto the sidewalk.

Adele keeps walking toward the revolving door.

"Let me," says Lorenz, whose name tag reads, inexplicably, "Felix."

Then they are inside, two abreast in his eagerness to guide and sign her in. She says, "You're not Lorenz?"

"It's his day off. Can I help you?"

"I came to visit Kathleen Dobbin."

Felix bends slightly at the knees to match her height, and points across the lobby.

"I know where I'm going," says Adele. "I'm her sister."

"Hey!" says Felix. "Nice to meet you. I knew she had a bunch of sisters. Now I see the resemblance."

"I'm late," says Adele. "Excuse me."

Kathleen is wearing what she went out in the night before, a green peplum jacket over a swingy skirt. Short; not Adele's favorite outfit, a little loud, a little too much yellow in the green. Is she a tad disheveled, too? Kathleen glances up with an automatic smile; looks startled, then alarmed.

Adele says, "Nothing's wrong. I escaped, that's all."

Kathleen comes around the counter to kiss her. "No one died, then?"

"Not that I know of."

"You just . . . left?"

"I didn't feel like working, and I didn't feel like going home."

"You got my note, right?"

"I did."

"So it's not like you've been worried?"

"I wasn't."

"Were you shocked?"

"I'm not Mother," says Adele. "My being here has nothing to do with your date." She takes off her raincoat and throws it on the striped stool. "Maybe I came to see if you wanted to have dinner. I thought it was time I met Lorenz."

"He's off today. But soon . . ." Kathleen stares at her sister's chest.

"What?" asks Adele.

"What are you wearing?"

Adele looks down. "This. What you see—my white silk blouse and my linen skirt."

"I meant your bra."

Adele pulls the neckline away from her chest and looks inside. "It's white and it's comfortable. Some of them hurt my rib cage. Besides, it's one of yours. How bad can it be?"

"With those seams? We can do better." She goes back behind the counter and reaches into the glass case. "Look at this row. Have you ever seen anything so delicious?" She holds one up to her own chest, cups it over her own breasts. "Under the white silk, delicate with just a hint of something sexy? Here, try these two. Thirty-fours and thirty-sixes in each. Yell when you're ready."

"For what?"

"For me to check. Go."

Obediently, Adele takes the bras and crosses to the dressing room.

After a minute she hears, "Need an opinion?"

"No." Not an opinion, not a new bra, not a soupçon of lace beneath her nearly opaque blouse, not anything.

"I love the Calvin Klein," Kathleen calls.

Adele glances at the manufacturer's tag. She doesn't do anything but unfasten the covered buttons on her blouse and meet her own eyes in the mirror. Something's terribly wrong with me, she thinks. Maybe there always was. Calvin Klein can't fix it. Richard and Kathleen can't fix it. I certainly can't.

She sits down on the padded bench and leans back against the cool peach wall.

"Hon? Ready?"

She touches the bras in her lap. She'll tell Kathleen she likes this one. She'll buy it. She'll buy both styles. She'll even wear them, though she doubts she needs seamless lace between her bosoms and the world. Kathleen's calligraphied wall sign asks, "Have you done your breast self-exam yet this month? . . . How about now?" Adele presses her bad rib with two fingertips until she finds the spot that still hurts.

"Dell? Are you all right?"

"No," she says softly.

She hears Kathleen say "Shit"; she hears her sister hurrying toward her. She sees Kathleen's hand and green-clothed arm poke through the curtain, signaling something, an imperative—*stay, stop, down.*

"What?" asks Adele. "What's wrong?"

The door chimes. She splints her side and takes a deep breath. On the other side, Kathleen is checking the hem of her silk faille curtain as if it is demanding her meticulous attention, now spacing its rings, now smoothing it with the flat of her hand.

"Good," she says cheerfully. "Better." Then, hushed and barely audible, "Don't come out!"

Twenty-four

Adele holds her breath and sits as still as she can. A woman's voice, unfamiliar but not unfriendly, asks, "Was it wonderful?"

Kathleen says, "No comment."

With one finger Adele hooks the curtain back an inch. A big woman, tall, upswept black hair, a fitted suit with two vents, a smart briefcase.

"We had a great time," Kathleen says.

"Thank you! That's all I needed—that look on your face. Now I came to spend some money."

"That's completely unnecessary," says Kathleen.

Adele squints. Is this woman a threat or not? And if not, where are Kathleen's mercantile instincts?

"I meant it," says the tall woman. "I scared away your customers and I'm here to buy. I'm treating myself. The market went up two hundred and six points today."

Kathleen says, not as cordially as she is capable of, "Well, look around. Let me know if you have any questions."

"Let's start here," says the woman.

Kathleen takes a considered look at the customer's chest. Finally she asks, "What size?"

"I *think* thirty-four B. Maybe C."

Even from the dressing room, even from behind, Adele can spot a gross understatement, and can hear in Kathleen's silence prize-winning diplomacy.

"Let me check something," her sister murmurs. She comes out from behind the counter and runs her hand across the woman's broad back. "Hmmm. I'd say a thirty-six. And your cup size may have changed. When was the last time you were fitted?"

"Not that long ago. Why?"

Kathleen returns to the counter. "Each manufacturer's sizing is different. This company cuts them on the skimpy side, so I'm giving you a . . . forty double-D." She brings forth something giant and beige, and places it on the glass counter. It is a caricature of a bra, suitable for vaudeville or the Hasty Pudding Show.

"So unbeautiful," sighs the woman.

"I know. It's exactly what I said to a designer yesterday: Why in God's name—if big breasts are considered so prized, and women are paying for breast augmentation—why are your D's and double D's so matronly?"

"And what did she say?"

"*He*. He said they're trying." Kathleen puts a stretchy lace bra on the counter. Midnight blue. "This is a Goddess—about as pretty as you're going to get. Unfortunately, it comes down to the physics of the thing."

Adele doesn't understand why she has to hide. This woman appears to be safe; sympathetic even. It must be me, she thinks. I must have been acting strange, unfit for customer relations.

"Take these into the back room," says Kathleen. "Someone's in the dressing room"—she lowers her voice—"not feeling well."

Well, that does it, thinks Adele. I've got to pull myself together. She practices a firm smile, drapes the bras neatly over her left forearm, and parts the curtain. "I do like the Calvin Klein, very much," she announces as she comes out.

The customer startles and turns.

Kathleen says, "Did you want me to check you?"

"No," says Adele. "The thirty-four is perfect."

Now the customer is smiling expectantly. Adele nods and says, like the gracious professional that she is, "Hello!"

"Why, Adele Dobbin." The woman extends her hand. "I'd know you anywhere."

"And you are?"

"Cynthia John."

"Pleased to meet you," says Adele.

"I've been *dying* to meet you," this Cynthia gushes.

⟶ At first glance, it's too white and grand for Adele's taste, and ostentatious: A quick tour reveals a queen-sized bed that must have been hand-wrought by a blacksmith, its headboard depicting iron hummingbirds extracting nectar from morning glories; battery-operated window shades, the grandest of Steinway grands. Everything new: the Oriental rugs, the artwork, even the antiques. New money, Adele thinks, but immediately reproaches herself. That was Mother talking. I don't speak for Mother.

"Red or white?" asks her hostess, in her stockinged feet, her toenails shocking pink on her gleaming marble floor.

"Red," says Adele.

"Your sister said 'tea.' She said you were a little faint."

"Nonsense," says Adele. "Just a hot flash. The last thing I want is tea."

Carrying a bottle of pinot noir and two glasses, Cynthia leads Adele to the living room and a curved white leather sofa. "Cleans off like oilcloth," she says proudly. "Sometimes I take my dinner in here and watch the harbor like it was the *Nightly News.* And if I spill something—a swipe with a sponge and presto."

"It's all lovely. You've done a wonderful job."

"Not me," says Cynthia. "My decorator. I paid her a fortune, and then invested it for her." She laughs. "Put your feet up on the coffee table. Shoes and all—the glass is indestructible." She blots her forehead with a Harvard Business School cocktail napkin, and fills their glasses to the rim. "Kathleen said you're recovering from some kind of injury?"

"Minor," says Adele. "A broken rib, which they don't do anything for." She smiles a fund-raising smile. "My sister tells me we've crossed paths?"

"Well, of *course* I've seen you on television about a million times. I'm a member, of course. I give at the hundred-twenty-dollar level and tell them to keep the whaddyacallits. The umbrellas and the tote bags."

Imagine being this forthright, Adele thinks. This natural. This unconstrained. She raises her full glass carefully. "Well, here's to you, then—our grateful thanks. Is that where we've crossed paths? A 'GBH function?"

Cynthia takes a gulp of wine and shakes her head.

"No? Nothing to do with 'GBH?"

"I wish! No, nothing that clean. It's someone we know in common, an old friend of yours."

Adele knows immediately; "old friend" mentioned with this much tact can mean only one thing.

"Nash Harvey," says Cynthia, as Adele silently supplies, "Harvey Nash." She feels relief: not Marty, not Richard. Not Lorenz.

"We were together until very recently," Cynthia says.

"This year?"

"I kicked him out two days ago."

"Now it's starting to make sense," Adele says.

"What is?"

"Kathleen's behavior. When you came into the store, she signaled I should stay in the dressing room. Now I know what the potentially awkward situation was."

"Me. Cynthia M. John and her volatile emotions and her big mouth."

Adele puts her glass down. "Let me set the record straight, Cynthia: Despite my sister's view of this being a delicate matter, it's not. I have no feelings for Harvey Nash other than contempt, so I couldn't possibly be distressed over your seeing him."

" 'Seeing' doesn't quite cover it," says Cynthia. "He lived here for three weeks."

"I haven't been keeping track of him," Adele says. "I didn't know he'd been in Boston that long."

"I can tell you exactly: April twenty-fourth. I was flying back from L.A.—"

"He came to my apartment on the twenty-fourth," says Adele. "Quite late. We were all in bed."

"The plane got in around five," says Cynthia. "We came here for drinks, then dinner, then he seduced me, and I, like an old fool, let him. And then he got dressed and went to find you."

Then he seduced me, Adele imagines saying one day. *And then, immediately after intercourse . . . and then, after he fucked me . . .*

"The moment the plane touched down," Cynthia continues, "he said, 'I have to go find Adele Dobbin and make things right.' "

"And you believed him?"

"I had no reason not to! I wanted to believe he was sincere, and that he was an honorable man returning to right a wrong. I helped! I looked you up first, on the Internet—www-dot-switchboard-dot-com—over martinis."

"How clever of you," says Adele. "A modern woman who knows her way around the Internet *and* can tend bar."

Cynthia cocks her head. "I beg your pardon?"

"That may have come out wrong. I just meant that making a martini is both a skill and an art—I certainly can't—and Nash would like that kind of . . . style."

"Or maybe he likes a woman who knows how to make a martini in a million-dollar condominium." Cynthia lowers her voice. "Today, that is. I certainly didn't pay anything close to that."

"And then what happened?" asks Adele. "I mean, he left, but obviously came back here at some point."

"Only because I called your apartment looking for him."

"*My* apartment?"

"I called your number and asked for Nash—"

"Whom did you speak with?"

"You! I said something to the effect that he'd failed to show up for an appointment and I was worried, and he'd left your number. You put him on, and that's when I found out about the mugging."

"Mugging?"

"The black eye? The bruises on his face? Wallet stolen?"

"He wasn't *mugged!* One of my sisters lost her composure while holding a casserole dish, but she certainly didn't steal anything."

Cynthia says, "Well, now I'm really furious."

"He lies," says Adele. "As easily as you and I say our prayers."

"And I thought—you know what I thought? I was actually feeling guilty, like he was a runaway who stepped off the bus in the big city, and got picked up by a sugar daddy. Me! That I was taking advantage of his misfortune."

"He's charming," says Adele simply. "You'd have to be a mind reader or a former girlfriend to see through the lies."

Cynthia refills both glasses, ignores Adele's signaling *Fine. Stop.*

"Can I ask you about that?" asks Cynthia.

"About what?"

"Closure. Did he ever give you a satisfactory explanation? I mean, all those years of waiting and not knowing, like wives whose husbands are missing in action or lost at sea and they need to get them pronounced dead so they can move on."

"But I *did* know," says Adele. "He didn't want to go through with it. And it didn't take too long to realize that a marriage to him would have been a terrible mistake." She stops; wonders what she, a minor celebrity, is doing on the leather couch of a perfect stranger, opening up her private life for discussion. No more wine tonight.

"How long before you could function?" asks Cynthia. "A year? Two? Five?"

"Almost immediately. As soon as I knew he wasn't lying in a hospital bed somewhere, but had left town of his own free will, I realized it was for the best."

"*That* easily?"

"No," says Adele.

"It never is."

"It was so long ago that I barely remember the details. So to answer your question concisely, I quickly came to despise him, which allowed me to move on."

"I'm not sure it works that way," Cynthia murmurs.

"It did with me," says Adele. "Without a doubt." And then to be polite, to take a stab at being reciprocal and therapeutic, she asks, "What about you, Cynthia? Are things . . . what's the right word here?"

" 'Excruciating'?" Cynthia states calmly. " 'Raw'? 'Unfinished'?"

"But I thought you had only contempt for him?"

"And for myself! I let my guard down. Every step along the way I was violating my oath to myself, which was 'You don't need a man to be fulfilled. You make twice as much as any guy you've ever

dated.' I thought he was my reward for years of coping so beautifully with being single, for making my own way, for not dieting
or going to aerobics classes or having liposuction, but accepting
myself. And then as a cosmic joke, the gods throw a handsome,
reasonably intelligent, age-appropriate, unmarried man with an interesting career into my path to say, Only kidding, Cyn! Forget all
that crap about 'A woman without a man is like a fish without a bi-
cycle,' because now we're saying, 'A worm in a radish is happy because she's never had a taste of honey.' "

To Adele's dismay, Cynthia's face crumples. She squeezes a
clenched finger under her bottom lashes to wipe away a tear.

Adele doubts she is up to the task (her sisters don't need com-
forting; they cry in their respective rooms, if at all), so she pats
Cynthia's free hand once, twice, then hands her a cocktail napkin.
After a minute she tries, "He wasn't worthy of you. It wouldn't
have worked out. He'll probably never marry anyone or find what
he's looking for because there will always be another woman in his
peripheral vision."

"That's for sure."

"And if that's what you want—a relationship, companionship,
physical closeness—if that's the missing taste of honey, then you'll
find it. Men have a sixth sense about it. I've seen this my whole
life: the women who send out signals snag the men's attention."

"I'm too fat for that," says Cynthia. "I can send out signals from
here, here, and here, until the cows come home, and they don't
make it out the other side."

"It's not a question of fat or thin," says Adele. "I don't think I've
ever sent out those signals."

"I bet you have." Cynthia blows her nose into another napkin.
"You must have if Nash came howling at your door."

Adele says, "Nash only came to my door because he saw dollar
signs there."

Cynthia shakes her head strenuously. "That's completely illogi-
cal. If he were marrying you for your money, he'd have gone
through with it."

"Unless . . ." says Adele.

"What?"

Adele hesitates, then shakes the thought off.

"What? He met someone else? Found his scruples? Decided to follow his true love to California?"

Adele says quietly, "Sometimes I wonder if my father bought the train ticket."

"No," says Cynthia. "Absolutely not. I never met the guy but I can tell you, no way."

"Maybe not anything as blatant as a ticket. Maybe a promise of a job. He was a lawyer. He had a million contacts."

"No," says Cynthia. "No father would let it happen the night of the engagement party. Nobody would make their daughter go through that."

"I know," says Adele. "That's why I dropped it. My father loved me. He may have been a snob, but he wasn't cruel. I think I would have known. I think there would have been a word or a hint over the years."

"Did you ever confront him?"

"I asked my mother."

"And?"

"She said it was nonsense, and she'd do me the favor of not re-laying such an insulting question to my father. And really, if you'd known him, you'd know how outlandish a theory it is." She forces a smile. "That's all it was, Henry James—a protective father who doesn't want his beloved eldest daughter to marry beneath her station. Or leave. Too many episodes of *Masterpiece Theatre* under my belt." She touches the face of her watch. "Is Kathleen meeting me up here or was I supposed to go back downstairs?"

"Did you ever sleep with Harvey?" asks Cynthia.

"No!" says Adele. Then: "Not quite."

"Even though you were engaged?"

"Never formally, don't forget. It hadn't been announced."

"And what year was this?"

"Nineteen sixty-seven."

"Not exactly the dark ages," says Cynthia. She stands, and goes to the kitchen; returns after a few minutes balancing a half-eaten chicken carcass in a plastic boat on top of two plates, a roll of paper towels under her arm, no cutlery, and a single, gorgeous, two-toned martini glass, brimming. Adele stands to help, and Cynthia hands her the martini. "*Skol.* Sit. Mesquite barbecue. I live off these. I cooked real food when Nash was here, which was another thing in the plus column."

"When did he leave?"

"Sunday morning."

"And where do we think he went?"

"I don't know. Maybe he got on a plane and went back to his California girlfriend. His equipment's there. He was hamstrung without it, grand piano or no grand piano. No one writes jingles with a keyboard and a pencil anymore. He called a bunch of Boston jingle houses and said, essentially, 'I'm your fellow composer from L.A. and I have a deadline. Could I use your studio for a few hours? I'll return the favor when you're on the West Coast.' Balls, huh?"

"I should say so."

"But no bites, not the whole time, which makes me think he went home." Cynthia rips a drumstick off the carcass and offers it to Adele.

"No, thanks. How did you leave it with him?"

"Horribly. He spent the last night in the guest room. We had people over and he flirted with this long-legged car saleswoman— who lives one floor below me, no less—and I threw him out the minute he came back."

"Came back from where?"

"Escorting her home."

"A floor below!"

"Exactly!"

"It's so interesting," Adele murmurs. She takes a sip from her martini and offers the glass to her hostess.

"No, thanks. *What* is?"

"People. Their ability to . . . act. To take action. To seduce and be seduced. Obviously they're made of different stuff than I am."

Cynthia wipes her hands on a paper towel, closes her eyes, and massages her temples. "Am I getting a message here? That there's something else you need to tell me, someone out there you'd like to reach, but the Ghosts of Boyfriends Past, or more likely, the Ghosts of Parents Past won't let you."

"I don't know what you're talking about."

"A man. Not Harvey Nash. Someone in *your* peripheral vision."

Adele doesn't answer.

"Someone who's not perfect, is my guess," says Cynthia. "Someone who's waiting for a signal from you. And either you're afraid to come clean with him, or you're afraid you'll wake up some morning and read about yourself in 'Names and Faces' in the *Globe.*"

"It's not that," says Adele.

Cynthia opens her eyes again, and tears a wing off the chicken. "Is it a woman? Because you're allowed. I have dozens of lesbians as clients. I *love* lesbians."

"No, sorry."

"Married?"

"No."

"Is it something really weird and complicated—like your brother?"

Adele actually laughs. "You can rest assured it's not my brother."

"Then you have to come clean. And let me tell you why: because of what I do for a living. I'm like one of those Internet safe servers—'Why you can purchase on-line with us using your credit card without fear.' Clients trust me with their financial histories. I'm a professional secret keeper, as good as a therapist."

Adele looks across to the picture window. "It's been such a peculiar day," she says. "At work, then at The Other Woman, now here: confiding things I never told anyone. Drinking a martini with a colossal green olive in it. It makes me wonder, looking out your window, why I live miles from the ocean, with no view. Well, I know why I do—because my parents did. I sleep in their bed and eat on their dining room table, surrounded by their children."

"Who's the *guy?*" asks Cynthia.

Adele helps herself to the remaining wing. "I shouldn't. I haven't even told Kathleen."

"I have two sisters, and I tell them *nothing*. They'd pass it on to their husbands, which would fuel their grudge against me—essentially, that I make four times as much money as either one of them. Besides, Kathleen's going to be less and less available as roommate-confidante. If I need to talk, I call a friend."

Adele repeats, "A friend. That's good advice. I have friends at work."

"I'm a *fabulous* friend," says Cynthia.

"What if you know him? He might be a client."

"Don't be such a prig," says Cynthia. "It's tiresome. And I can only think it must be just as tiresome for you."

No one speaks to me like that, Adele marvels. "Marty Glazer," she says.

Twenty-five

Call it a moral and medical imperative: thirteen close friends lost to AIDS and, by Byron Sprock's assiduous count, forty-four acquaintances (neighbors, actors, understudies, collaborators, costume and lighting designers, favorite waiters, ushers, dog walkers, sublessees, house sitters, and bank tellers) dead or dying. Accordingly, he will not, under any circumstances, have anything but unerringly safe sex. Dina goes along with his scrupulous practices for the first dozen acts of intercourse, but now that she is ovulating she has to pop the question: Wouldn't he enjoy *not* using a condom? Just this once, and maybe again in the morning?

"Sorry," says Byron. "I don't do that."

"Ever?" asks Dina.

Byron shoots to a sitting position in bed. "I can't believe what you're asking! What do you think all those little red ribbons are telling you: Wear a condom! Don't take a chance! And what about that tomcat you used to live with? Can you vouch for him?"

"I had to," she says. "You can't use a condom when you're trying to make a baby."

And thus Dina confides the plan: I selected you—your height, your brains, your supposed easygoing nature, your jokes, your pale blue eyes, your rosy toenails, your high arches, your silky heels.

Byron finds his eyeglasses on the night table and puts them on.

"You thought—let me understand this—after some magic number of safe sexual acts, I'd let down my guard and impregnate you?"

"Jeez," says Dina. "You'd think I was asking for marriage and child support. What's the big deal?"

"It's a huge deal—'making a baby' as you so coyly put it. A child of mine raised in a single-family home as if his father's a deadbeat dad who wasn't smart enough to use protection. What kind of example is *that*?"

Dina touches his freckled back, and he shrinks from her hand.

"So the donation route is out, too?" she asks.

"I'm not your man," he says.

"Even with no responsibilities attached?"

"Except after my child finds me through some birth-father network support group, and we go into therapy so I can explain that I was recruited for the job while on a business trip, and left him in the care of a woman I hardly knew?"

"Now you're hysterical," says Dina.

"Only in California," he rants. "Only in the land of perpetual sun and, and, cult suicides—"

"No one impregnates women on the East Coast? No one makes donations to sperm banks?"

"That's different," he says. "That's science. People sign papers. I can't believe what you're asking. I can't believe the risks you took with that philanderer." He flops down, rises again. "A philanderer who could return at any moment and become my child's in loco parentis."

"You pompous ass," says Dina. "I want a baby. Nash and I were practically married. My doctor didn't throw up his hands in horror and say, 'What kind of idiot are you? You can't try! You'll get AIDS!' "

"In that case? Seriously? I'd change doctors. He has no business pushing you into unprotected sex in the name of procreation."

Dina gets out of bed, and for the first time ever in his presence, in the bedroom, puts on a robe. She opens a bureau drawer and sticks a digital thermometer in her mouth, then sits on the edge of the bed, her back to him. She doesn't speak until the instrument bleeps. "Some men would be flattered," she says.

"Stupid macho men!"

"Is it that you're gay?" she asks. "Bisexual?"

"Is that your call to arms? 'Prove you're a real man. Prove you weren't a flight attendant before you became a playwright'?"

Dina yanks a tissue from a pop-up box. "What a terrible person I am. I want a baby and I picked you to inseminate me."

After a moment, Byron touches her back. "It's one thing if we had a relationship, and you were tested, and we waited the proper interval—"

"I'm perimenopausal," she says, elbowing him away. "I don't *have* a proper interval in me."

"If you couldn't get pregnant by him," he asks, "what makes you think it would be different with my sperm?"

"Honestly? A feeling. It seemed to me that you were sent by forces in the universe. You said as much yourself: I backed into your car, and there you were—tall and nice and wanting to romance me, and with the right number of letters in your name, according to my numerologist. I'm a very spiritual person. I don't believe in accidents."

This is what Byron likes least about Dina, her belief in everything. Tonight it seems less charming and more vapid than usual. He doesn't want her raising a daughter to believe in angels and aromatherapy, and he doesn't want a son's science to turn on the theory that all bodily functions begin and end in his feet.

Thus, after three weeks of highly satisfying safe sex, he is willing to have none. By the next day, he misses New York acutely—its speeding taxis and its public transportation, its libraries and magazine stands, its maître d's and its homeless. His newfound love for palm, lemon, avocado, and olive trees has given way to sardonic jokes about Dina's home state's starlets, its mud slides, its earthquakes, its smog, its automobile brassieres. Suddenly he can't live without some stupid sausage or gyro or French fry sold only on the streets of New York, with its famous creative and intellectual energy—like that's a reason to pick a place to live.

The people who flew Byron Sprock to Hollywood for one month are now sending him home. There is no movie in his play, no appetite in Hollywood for making fun of Renaissance Weekend or the Clintons. He is going back to theater—Broadway, off-Broadway, off-off-Broadway, regional, big, small, whatever will have him. Though he and Dina have stopped having sex altogether, and exchange no pledges to call or write, she drives him to John Wayne Airport and kisses him good-bye, on the cheek, at curbside.

She tells him that a soul chooses its parents, and she shouldn't have tried to play God.

"Good luck," he says. "I'll call you."

He will type "Act One, Scene One" on his laptop while still waiting at the gate: "Southern California. The exterior of a modest beachfront rental belonging to a pretty, slightly faded, wistful, tanned ex-model who has embraced New Age malarkey. Enter, on in-line skates, a bespectacled New York intellectual." They collide. They share enough common ground and chemistry to date for the duration of his business trip. The man thinks he may be falling in love against type, while the woman feigns affection as she measures him for the job of biological father. He declines out of epidemiological prudence and moral indignation. A third character, a spectral presence achieved through lighting, a disembodied, ex-live-in, cheating common-law husband hovers over the set, as does a giant ticking clock. For added poignancy, he gives the leading man a fatal, time-bomb genetic disease and a conscience. The man and woman part.

Twenty-six

She has the number, and uses it. Mrs. Chabot says, "He's on the third floor. I'm gonna have to walk up there. It might take a coupla minutes."

"Fine," says Dina.

He doesn't answer the bellow from the second-floor landing, which obligates Mrs. Chabot to climb another half flight to his door, and reinforces her house rule: No phone calls after nine P.M. She knocks. No answer. "Mister . . ." What the hell is his name. "You in there?"

She descends the stairs slowly, hand sliding down the banister. Lighting's bad. Maybe a brighter bulb will be enough. She's learned not to rush back to girls calling boarders who prove not to be in. "Not here," she barks into the phone. "Don't call back later, 'cause I'll be asleep."

"Can you give me his address with zip code?"

"This one?"

"Is he still registered there?"

"Fifty-five Grove Street, Boston, Mass., oh two one one four."

"Room number?"

"He'll get it. It all comes to me."

"Thank you," says Dina. "That's all I need."

He takes the Commonwealth Avenue trolley to Brighton and walks down the hill. His thirty-year-old key fits into the gummy lock and, with some twisting and finessing, opens the door. The kitchen is exactly the same, just dustier and stickier: faux red-brick linoleum, yellowed appliances that look old-fashioned and bulbous. If he were a sentimental man, his childhood would flood back to him. He'd notice the stain on the ceiling where the pressure cooker blew, the ivy-tendriled wallpaper, the curtains sewn from percale sheets, adorned with three colors of rickrack, and, if he opened the oven, carbon stalagmites from his mother's Comstock-filled pies. No one wants to buy it—three rooms down, two up. One bath, with no half-bath potential—along with lead paint and high radon levels— are said to be the problem. No one wants to rent it or call it their starter home. He could live rent-free here, utilities and taxes only. Say it's his studio; tell clients and lady friends that he pulls all-nighters here, hence the bedroom and the kitchen; hence the lived-in look. When his musical ship comes back in, he could remodel.

He shows up at the station in a suit, bolo tie, and cowboy boots, and asks for Adele.

"You could have called first," she says when she fetches him in the lobby. "Some people make appointments."

"Two minutes," he says.

He follows her; notes her brisk walk, her low heels clicking, her ankles trim, her rear end firm. "Pretty dress," he says. "Brown is your color."

Adele says affably, "You are so full of shit. Does anyone believe anything you say?"

"Some. The less penetrating. Where are you taking me?"

"Third floor, Development."

She introduces him all around: Nash Harvey or Harvey Nash— Michael and Scott, the coworkers.

"Nice boots," says Michael.

"From Santa Fe," says Nash. "Great city. Wall-to-wall souvenir shops—cowboy and Indian stuff. You'd love it."

"Time's up," says Adele.

Her office is no bigger than a tool shed. The furniture is laminated white, the carpet is cool gray. Plants line the windowsill, and a Tanglewood poster adorns the wall behind her desk. "I've got lots of work to do today," she begins.

"One question: Who does your station IDs?"

"IDs? I have no idea. Why?"

"Why do you think? I'm in town, and I'd like a shot at it. What-ever they're charging you, I can do it cheaper."

"I have nothing to say about that."

"Then who does?"

"Sorry," says Adele.

"What's his name? The head guy?"

Adele coughs delicately into her fist. "Mr. Glazer."

"First name?"

"Marty. Martin."

"Can I meet him?"

Adele says, "No," then reconsiders, if only to report to Cynthia that she did something socially adventurous. She hits four numbers on her phone. "Carmen? It's Adele. Is he in? No, don't interrupt him. I'll just come by."

"One tip," says Nash. "You could say—and I know this doesn't come as naturally to you as it does to me—'It's my great pleasure to introduce Mr. Harvey, the composer, visiting from the coast,' and if you deliver it with a certain expression and in a certain tone of voice, it would send a very strong signal, i.e., 'Give this guy any-thing he wants. His money's got money, and I'm reeling him in.' "

Adele laughs. "As a friend of mine recently taught me to say without blanching, 'You've got balls.' "

"Is that a no? Because it's not a lie. Let's just say you character-ize me with a few words—'composer,' 'Los Angeles'; even hum a few notes of my Legacy jingle under your breath—*Legacy . . . it sets you free.* . . . He won't know I make nothing from it. Then, if *he* fills in the blanks, it's not a lie."

"I'm doing this for my own reasons," she says, "not because I want to do you a favor. I'll ask about the promos, period. He'll say, 'Sorry,' then you'll leave. You'll go straight to the airport—"

"Not today, kiddo. First of all, my ticket isn't open-ended. It's for Friday. And what about my luggage? Also, in case I haven't mentioned it, I'm looking at a little house-cum-studio in Brighton. So, no way. Too many loose ends to tie up."

"Since when," Adele asks, "did you care about tying up loose ends?"

He rubs his face with his open palms, then announces, his eyes bleary, "It wasn't all my fault, you know."

Adele is rooting around in her top drawer for something, but she stops. "What wasn't?"

"Running out on you before the party."

"Then whose fault was it?"

"I meant, I was a product of my environment—the little prince, their one and only with perfect pitch. I could do no wrong. That, and what I've already apologized for—my immaturity, my bad manners, my Hollywood dreams."

Adele asks, unexpectedly and lightly, "Did my father have anything to do with your leaving Boston?"

"No, he did *not*," says Nash.

"I think it's possible," she says. "In fact I think it's likely."

Nash takes a moment to study the pointed toes of his boots. When he looks up he says, "What kind of thing is that to carry around with you? Wondering if you should hate your old man retroactively? It's better if you hate me."

"Why?"

"Because he's your old man! It'll make you bitter and suspicious of everyone, and it'll hang you up for life."

"Or liberate me," she says.

⟍⟶ "Nash Harvey," says Nash, pumping the hand that isn't offered. "I know you're way too busy for this. In fact, I'm disgusted with myself for taking up the time of a man running this distinguished operation. *How* many Emmys last year?"

Marty looks to Adele, who offers nothing.

"Miss Dobbin has graciously agreed to advance my request to the next level," Nash continues.

"Concerning?"

"Business. How mine intersects with yours."

"He writes advertising jingles," says Adele, "and has some notion that you'd give him a crack at our station promos."

Marty says, "We're not thinking of changing at this time."

"Hey! Last thing I want to do is take advantage of my friendship with Adele. She didn't jump at the idea, either, but I can promise you this much—"

"How do you know Adele?"

Nash says, "We go way back."

"To what?"

"We were children together," says Adele.

"An item," says Nash.

"When?" asks Marty.

"After college," says Adele.

"In my case," says Nash, "after the conservatory, but before film."

"Things didn't work out," says Adele.

"But now I'm back," says Nash, who notices that the more personal he gets, the more forlorn this Martin Glazer looks.

"*For?*" asks Marty.

"*For?*" Nash repeats. He looks around the office. "Mind if I sit? It's a long story."

"I'm late for a meeting," says Marty.

Nash takes a visitor's chair, but Adele retreats to a couch against the wall. "I'll be quick," he says. "A thirty-second jingle out of my life's reel: I never settled down, never had kids, never went to a P.T.A. meeting, never owned a lawn mower. So I finally asked myself the hard question: Why the hell not? What's the hang-up? And you know what I came up with? All roads led home. Which is the same thing as saying, All signs pointed to Adele. I mean, why the pull? Why do I keep writing songs about her? Why have I kept her picture in my wallet for thirty-odd years?"

Adele looks up.

Marty asks, "You have an old picture of Adele?"

Nash says, "I *hope* I have it. I might've put it in a photo album with another bunch I have of her."

"Of our engagement party, no doubt," says Adele.

Nash brings forth his wallet and its gatefold of expired credit cards.

"Don't bother," says Adele. "I'm sure it's hideous."

Nash searches one compartment, then another. Finally he slides two fingers behind his driver's license. After some shuffling of what appears to be his lady-friend photo archive he says, "Here. A little moth-eaten around the edges, but that's our girl."

Marty takes the photo, studies it, measures it against Adele, puts it down on his blotter, but doesn't give it back.

"Always a looker," Nash says happily.

Marty's already high color deepens.

Adele murmurs, "I had no idea."

"I'm a sentimentalist," says Nash. "I thought you knew that about me."

"I must have forgotten," she says.

Marty looks at his watch.

"One more question," says Nash.

"Which is?"

"Studio space: nothing elaborate. A piano and a pencil. Any old empty corner."

"What's he talking about?" Marty asks Adele.

"I'm never quite sure," she says.

"A place to work," says Nash. "To show you what I can do."

Marty asks, "Do you mean right now? For a couple of hours? Or something permanent?"

Nash swivels around to face Adele, cinches his bolo, and with as true and as unflirtatious a stare as he's ever dispensed, says, "That's up to you, darlin'."

She takes a magazine from the coffee table in front of her, flips through half of it without reading a word, puts it back, then says, "I don't mean to be cruel, Harvey, but if it were up to me, you'd be on the next plane."

"Out of the question," says Nash. "I'm not going stand-by."

Adele looks toward Marty. His head and upper lip are damp. He rises to announce in a slightly deeper voice than usual, "We have no recording studios. And if we did, we wouldn't lend them out like study carrels in a library." He presses a buzzer. "Carmen? Can you escort Adele's guest to the reception area?"

"What's there?" Nash asks.

"The door," says Adele.

Carmen appears, eager, helpful. Mr. Glazer has seemed depressed all week.

"Will I see you tonight?" Nash asks Adele.

"I need her for a project we've been working on," says Marty.

"Later, then? What time will you get home?"

"It doesn't matter," says Adele. "We have an answering machine now."

"Welcome to the world," says Nash. He walks to the couch, takes her hand, caresses it, presses his lips to her knuckles. "I must be losing my touch," he says.

"Or not," says Adele.

"I need to speak to Adele in private," says Marty.

"Carmen, this is Mr. Harvey," says Adele. "He's an award-winning arranger."

"Wow," says Carmen.

"Nash," corrects Nash.

"Shut the door on your way out," instructs Marty.

Twenty-seven

Lois reads the perplexing note, scribbled in Kathleen's hand and stuck to the refrigerator: "I'll be staying chez Lorenz tonight." Well, that explains half of the ghost town she has found at Stearns Road—no chains latched, no bottles set. But where's Adele? She hears no TV, no music, no water running. The usual hallway lamp is lit, next to—what's this?—a new phone, white, buttons, functions, a small red dot of light . . . a built-in answering machine! Because of me, she reasons: If I wanted to get in touch with them, they wouldn't miss my call. The digital readout says "01." She hits the "play" button. "Adele?" says a woman's voice. "This is Sin. Any progress today? I want a report."

Her own room is unusually neat and inviting, and she takes credit for its perfectly made bed and uncluttered surfaces. Too uncluttered, she realizes: The magazines piled high and slipping off her maple nightstand are gone, and the precise order of her knick-knacks and mementos has been upset by someone dusting with no sentimental blueprint. She lifts and flops her suitcase onto the bed. She's been gone almost four weeks: April 26 is still on her Word-a-Day calendar, "Mendacious."

Next door, Kathleen's room is dark, and at the end of the hall, so is Adele's. Slightly annoying, this lack of any reception. Well, of course no one expected her. If I were the one missing, she reasons, they'd know *Movie. Date. Drink with a coworker.* Silly of me to be concerned, Lois thinks. Old maidish. Parental.

It's lovely to have the place to herself, though. She unpacks her terry-cloth robe, her boiled-wool slippers, her creams and her toners, and goes to the bathroom. No place like a single-sex home—rug on the floor, toilet seat down, no mildew in the grout. A real showerhead instead of a rubber hose and a sprinkler. Her mother's monogrammed hand towels, usually saved for company, are hanging next to the sink. And it is in the long, hot shower (uninterrupted by any boarders rapping on the door or Mrs. Chabot reminding her of the hot water heater's capacity) that she feels a stab of grief for her dead parents, the one that returns at odd moments, after unexpected encounters with cross-stitching on a towel, or hairpins in a drawer. No one is home, she reminds herself. Acoustics be damned. Perfectly understandable—a touch of homesickness she didn't know she felt.

She puts on her good bathrobe, the satin quilted one, emerald green, that she wears only on holidays. She finds sliced whole wheat in the bread box and a new pineapple marmalade in the refrigerator. Obviously, with her away, Kathleen and Adele have been indulging their orange-yellow jam preferences; she likes the purples and reds. But how nice to be in her own kitchen, eating on a china plate, drinking milk from a refrigerator instead of warm soda from a windowsill.

She returns to her room and sits in her rocker. She gets up again to rearrange the five things on her vanity. The top drawer of the vanity yields the missing heart-shaped frame, faceup. Didn't I look fabulous that day, she thinks. Weren't we a lovely couple?

Where did she hide that book he sent? She's never read it, never wanted to be caught reading it. Never opened it until now. "If you're willing," says the card inside, "there are other titles I can recommend."

⌒⌐ Like all mornings when he's in the office, Richard eats a Boston Kreme Donut and rifles through the papers in the Hold box, annoying his secretary, but only slightly.

"Anything good?" she asks.

"This asshole again," he says. "I testified twice already. Now they're saying they don't have an address for him."

"Lieutenant Diaz got engaged last night," she says.

Richard stops midpile, paper in hand. "Well, I'll be damned . . ."

"They've been going out for at least two years. Have you seen her, in person, I mean?"

"Look at this," says Richard.

Stephie reads the first few lines. "So?"

"I know him."

" 'State of California,' " reads Stephie.

"I'll take this one," says Richard.

⟶ Mrs. Chabot wonders what good word of mouth has brought so many nice-looking gents to her establishment of late. "Do I know you?" she asks.

"Lois Dobbin's brother?"

"Lois," she breathes. "One of my favorites."

"I've visited her here," he says. "I'm Richard."

"The cop!"

"Suffolk County Sheriff's Department."

"She's not here anymore."

"I know. I'm looking for a Mr. Nash Harvey."

She shakes her head. "Out."

"Can I wait?"

"Where?"

"Your parlor?"

"Can you come back?"

He reaches into his breast pocket. "I'm on official business for the Commonwealth."

"About what?"

"I'm sorry. I can't say."

"You have to say. I live here, too. I don't want any dangerous criminals under my roof."

"Not dangerous." He hesitates. "Spousal support. A civil matter."

"You mean money?"

Richard folds the papers lengthwise and returns them to his pocket. "I could wait inside or I could wait outside. Your choice."

"Is your cruiser parked in front?"

"Not right in front. Did he say when he'll return?"

"They don't tell me. I bake, and then I go back to bed."

Richard smiles. "What do you bake?"

"Scones one day, muffins the next."

"And today?"

"Muffins. Oatmeal peach."

"Mmmm."

"Maybe there's one left. Sit. You want coffee?"

"You're a doll," he says. "And a pat of butter?"

"I got oleo," she says.

⁓ He rises from the parlor love seat when he hears footsteps. Nash looks happy to see him, not surprised, not perplexed. Does a goofy two-step.

"Harvey," says Richard. "I'm afraid it's not social. These are for you, from Orange County. Served through us."

Nash takes the papers, scans them. "Hey! This isn't right. We're not married. How can she be asking for spousal support?"

"Sometimes it's not what it seems," says Richard. "Sometimes it's to establish a husband-wife contract and for the judge to determine if she was your common-law wife."

"No way," he says. "Not interested."

"Have an attorney look at them, Harv."

"What attorney would that be?" he snaps.

He leaves them on the arm of the sofa and starts for the stairs.

Richard says, "You don't want them? You want to leave them here? They can rot here, but if you don't take any action, the court will find against you and that'll be only the beginning."

Nash walks back, sits down. "Why now?" he asks. "She knows what I have. She knows, musically, I'm on the back end of not being wanted anymore." He lowers his voice. "Eight hundred dollars a month from the A.F.M. from when I worked as a sideman. Why would she be going after me?"

"It's not the money," says Richard. "I've seen this. Papers get served sometimes when a man leaves. She doesn't want spousal support, Harv. It's not about that. She wants you back."

⁓ Someone has to pay Mrs. Chabot's bill. Richard, willing to drive him to the airport, says, "I'd cover it, trust me, but I can't do it on the heels of in-hand service. It's too weird."

"You don't suppose . . . ?"

"Adele? Never. You'd have a better chance of sweet-talking Mrs. Chabot out of the debt."

"I could still write the thing. All it would do is bounce. By then I'll be home—"

"Larceny by check," says Richard. "Over two hundred and fifty dollars is a felony in this state."

"Can I borrow a quarter?" he asks.

—◦ Cynthia says, "Believe it or not, I'm almost glad. In some strange and perverse way, I think this is a perfect ending to our little affair—your asking me to cover a bill for the only nights you weren't under my roof."

"A loan. Just until I get home, open my mail, and get to the bank."

"How much?" she asks wearily.

"Three hundred and thirty. Made out to The Lucky Duck."

He thinks he hears a pen scratching on paper. "Are you still there?" he asks.

"You know why I'm doing this? Because there's a lesson here for me. An entry in my check register that screams, 'See what you let yourself in for? Even though you knew better? Well here's the tariff: three hundred and thirty bucks. Probably a bargain. You're a little devastated, but maybe you're also a little wiser.' "

Nash waits a polite interval. "Is that a *yes?*" he asks.

Twenty-eight

*R*ichard gives him two twenties at the gate and says, "Don't come back, Harv. Stay out there. Try to work it out with what's her name, the plaintiff."

They are approaching the line of ticket holders waiting to have their bags X-rayed. "I'm understandably ambivalent," says Nash.

"You can't afford to be."

Nash looks down at his load—one carry-on bag and one empty hand. "I didn't even get her anything. After a month away, I should be bringing her a little something. Do they still pack up lobsters for shipping?"

"Don't bring her lobsters, Harv. First of all, I'm not paying for them, and secondly, it's not the right tone. She served you papers. You're gonna have to repair the damage, bring her your guts on a plate. You're gonna have to go the distance here, you know."

"I know."

"Spell it out for me, Harv. What do I mean by that?"

"Marry her," says Nash.

"Not that I'm an authority on marriage. I see the irony in my being the one who—"

Simultaneously, they notice the woman—midforties, blue jeans, high heels, gold hair that has retained the shape of her hot rollers, designer garment bag. She is talking on a cell phone ahead of Nash in line, and her face gleams with bronze and silver accents. "I've got to go," she is saying. "They make you shut these things off. It interferes with their radar or something. I'll call you from Los Angeles."

Richard puts a guiding hand on Nash's arm. "I can't go through the metal detector with a badge and a gun, Harv, so I'm leaving you here. You're on your own."

Nash nods, but is already wearing a new expression.

"Ticket?" asks Richard.

Nash pats his jacket pocket.

"Subpoena?"

"Ditto."

"And what are you going to do first thing tomorrow morning?"

"Call a lawyer."

"It's serious, Harv. Listen to me. No wiggle room."

The woman is making the metal detector squeal. She gives up her belt of foreign coins and chains, sets off the alarm again, rolls her eyes as she comes back through the frame.

"Call me after you talk to the lawyer," says Richard.

But Nash has already said his good-byes. He is smiling in solidarity with the inconvenienced fellow passenger. "Miss? Could it be the brass studs on your jeans?"

The woman looks back over her own shoulder and down at her rear end. "Oh, brother—the stupid studs. You'd think they'd tell you."

"Or maybe not . . ." and his voice implies, We're not dealing with helpful, intelligent, sophisticated people, are we? Not people like us.

"I hate this," she says, as the man in blue waves his metal-detecting wand up and around her legs.

"I get stopped for studs, too—those and my spurs get me every time." He laughs a wry and playful laugh, and waits as Security finishes the job.

Now she is free to go, free to collect her belt, her bracelets, her cellular phone. Nash is next. The old pro, he passes through without a bleep.

Richard watches and listens from behind the line. As they separate their bags from the pile they have made, Nash is announcing

his West Coast name and his line of work, which makes the
woman look up. They shake hands. Now there is a disagreement, a
tug-of-war. But it is short-lived. Whatever argument he is mount-
ing, whatever words he is whispering, they work. Her garment bag
is transferred to his shoulder, and the privilege of accompanying
her to the gate—*their* gate, amazingly enough—is proclaimed.

All is settled. The weight of their bags is evenly distributed
across his shoulders. Nash voices one last grievance about airport
security, about the overzealous measures that we law-abiding citi-
zens have to endure. The woman can't agree more. It's her own
fault—all those metal accessories today. Stupid.

Although, she points out, one meets the nicest people when
those buzzers buzz.

Nash blushes beautifully and says she beat him to the punch.
That was what he was really trying to say. Petty of him to complain
about a little inconvenience when you consider the alternative—a
bomb on your plane. A small price to pay, isn't it, for peace of
mind? It's the world we live in. It makes us cautious, and—if she'll
permit him a moment of personal reflection and possible imperti-
nence—it makes us brave.

Acknowledgments

My thanks to composer Steve Karmen for graciously allowing me to put his words into my character's mouth and to quote from *Through the Jingle Jungle: The Art and Business of Making Music for Commercials* (Billboard). Thanks, too, to Ned Ginsburg, for that fruitful tip and for his musical insights.

I am grateful to Senior Deputy Sheriff Lincoln S. Flagg of the Commonwealth of Massachusetts' Hampden County Sheriff's Department, who gave of his time generously and cheerfully so that Richard Dobbin could do his job; and to Judith Fine, Amy Dickinson, and Emma Dostal of The Gazebo for the foundation on which I built The Other Woman.

I enjoyed every conversation, every task, every word shared with Deb Futter and Lee Boudreaux at Random House. As usual, I relied on the friendship and wisdom of Mameve Medwed and Stacy Schiff every day in the writing of this book. Special thanks for all things big and small to Ginger Barber, Jennifer Rudolph Walsh, Jay Mandel, and Claire Tisne, and to Martin Asher at Vintage for his votes of faith.

ALSO BY ELINOR LIPMAN

THE INN AT LAKE DEVINE

It's 1962 and all across America barriers are collapsing. But when Natalie Marx's mother inquires about summer accommodations in Vermont, she gets the following reply: *The Inn at Lake Devine is a family-owned resort, which has been in continuous operation since 1922. Our guests who feel most comfortable here, and return year after year, are Gentiles.* For twelve-year-old Natalie, who has a stubborn sense of justice, the words are not a rebuff but an infuriating, irresistible challenge.

In this beguiling novel, Elinor Lipman charts her heroine's fixation with a small bastion of genteel anti-Semitism, a fixation that will have wildly unexpected consequences on her romantic life. As Natalie tries to enter the world that has excluded her—and succeeds through the sheerest of accidents—*The Inn at Lake Devine* becomes a delightful and provocative romantic comedy full of sparkling social mischief.

"Light, warm and modest, like a glass of tea steeped in the summer sun."
                                                                —*San Francisco Chronicle*

Fiction / Literature/0-375-70485-X